A SEAL'S RESOLVE

By Cora Seton

Author's Note

A SEAL's Purpose is the fifth volume in the SEALs of Chance Creek series, set in the fictional town of Chance Creek, Montana. To find out more about Kai, Addison, Boone, Clay, Jericho and Walker, look for the rest of the books in the series, including:

A SEAL's Oath
A SEAL's Vow
A SEAL's Pledge
A SEAL's Consent
A SEAL's Purpose
A SEAL's Devotion
A SEAL's Desire
A SEAL's Struggle
A SEAL's Triumph

Also, don't miss Cora Seton's other Chance Creek series, the Cowboys of Chance Creek, the Heroes of Chance Creek, and the Brides of Chance Creek

The Cowboys of Chance Creek Series:

The Cowboy Inherits a Bride (Volume 0)
The Cowboy's E-Mail Order Bride (Volume 1)
The Cowboy Wins a Bride (Volume 2)
The Cowboy Imports a Bride (Volume 3)
The Cowgirl Ropes a Billionaire (Volume 4)
The Sheriff Catches a Bride (Volume 5)
The Cowboy Lassos a Bride (Volume 6)
The Cowboy Rescues a Bride (Volume 7)

The Cowboy Earns a Bride (Volume 8)
The Cowboy's Christmas Bride (Volume 9)

The Heroes of Chance Creek Series:

The Navy SEAL's E-Mail Order Bride (Volume 1)
The Soldier's E-Mail Order Bride (Volume 2)
The Marine's E-Mail Order Bride (Volume 3)
The Navy SEAL's Christmas Bride (Volume 4)
The Airman's E-Mail Order Bride (Volume 5)

The Brides of Chance Creek Series:

Issued to the Bride One Navy SEAL
Issued to the Bride One Airman
Issued to the Bride One Sniper
Issued to the Bride One Marine
Issued to the Bride One Soldier

The Turners v. Coopers Series:

The Cowboy's Secret Bride (Volume 1)
The Cowboy's Outlaw Bride (Volume 2)
The Cowboy's Hidden Bride (Volume 3)
The Cowboy's Stolen Bride (Volume 4)
The Cowboy's Forbidden Bride (Volume 5)

Visit Cora's website at www.coraseton.com
Find Cora on Facebook at facebook.com/CoraSeton
Sign up for my newsletter HERE.
www.coraseton.com/sign-up-for-my-newsletter

CHAPTER ONE

"**C**URTIS, ARE YOU sure about this?" Anders Olsen asked.

Curtis looked in the mirror one last time, adjusted the collar of his blue Revolutionary Era uniform and nodded. At his feet, Daisy, the yellow dog who'd become his constant companion these past few months, whined. "It's too late to change my mind. The guests are here. The officiant's ready. It's time to do this thing. You got the wedding band?"

"I've got it." Anders patted his pocket. He was wearing an old-fashioned uniform, too; it had become tradition for the men of Base Camp to wear the historical outfits when one of them got married. His face was grave, his hair sticking up wildly where he kept running his hand through it. "But Michele doesn't even like you."

"Keep your voice down." Curtis looked over his shoulder to make sure the door to the room where they were preparing for his wedding was still closed. For once, a cameraman wasn't hovering nearby, a miracle since he'd been filmed just about every waking hour since he'd gotten here. He and nine other men who'd served with the Navy SEALs were participating in a reality television show named for the model sustainable community they were helping to build. Having no privacy had seemed a small price to pay for the opportunity, but Curtis had learned in the last six months or so the cost was steeper than he'd expected.

For one thing, *Base Camp's* producer, Renata Ludlow, had managed to lay bare all his secrets. This wasn't the first time he was attempting to make it to the altar. Martin Fulsom, the eccentric billionaire funding this project, wanted the show to garner a lot of attention, so he'd tasked the participants with a number of challenges to meet within a year's time frame. They needed to build ten tiny houses that consumed one-tenth of the energy a normal dwelling consumed. They needed to grow or raise all their own food. They needed to create a green energy supply to power their homes and machinery.

That wasn't all, however. In order to prove that their community was truly sustainable—that it would continue on into the future, after the show was over—all ten men at Base Camp needed to marry before the year was up. Three of the couples needed children on the way.

So far five men had married, and two of their wives were pregnant. Each time they held a wedding, the remaining single men drew straws to see who was next. Today it was Curtis's turn.

Curtis swallowed, adjusting the collar of his uniform

again. He'd drawn the short straw once before, but he'd blown that big time. Boone Rudman, the leader of Base Camp, had found him a bride—a pretty damn good one. Too bad he'd panicked, drunk too much the night before he was supposed to pick her up at the airport, and Harris Wentworth had gone instead—and married her that very morning.

Embarrassing.

Not nearly as embarrassing as being left at the altar, though. Renata had made sure everyone learned about that debacle, too, forcing him to recount on camera the whole sorry story about trying to marry his high school sweetheart at nineteen. Angela Minetta had been all for it—right up until the day of the wedding. She was the one who'd spooked that time, driving off in her parents' SUV and ending up in California before anyone heard from her again. That day he'd stood at the altar for a full half hour before Angela's father walked down the aisle and broke the news she wasn't coming.

Curtis had thought he'd die of the humiliation. Then he'd joined the Navy thinking he might as well do something for his country while letting someone else pick him off and put him out of his misery.

And then he'd learned that he loved the Navy, loved the adventure of it all, and was a damn good SEAL. He'd grown up enough to realize Angela had done them both a favor. Neither of them had been ready to marry and settle down.

Still.

"I can't back out now," he told Anders. "Besides,

it's only for a year and a half or so. I'll get through it."

"You realize that makes no sense." Anders joined him in front of the mirror. "If Michele thinks she needs a husband to win the election, why won't she need a husband to keep hold of the seat?"

"I don't know, but our agreement says eighteen months."

"This isn't going to end well."

Daisy barked, as if in agreement. Curtis bent to scratch her behind her ears.

"What do you want me to do? Walk out on the wedding? Ruin this for everyone?" He wasn't entering into a sham marriage for kicks. When he'd pulled the short straw—on purpose—thirty-five days ago, he'd wanted to take charge of his life and stop letting Fate jerk him around. He'd spurned Boone's offer to find him another bride and had gone out to the local bars every night and spent hours on online dating sites every day.

That's where Michele Case had found him. An up-and-coming political hopeful based in Billings, she contacted him, they chatted back and forth, and then met for drinks at restaurant in the city. Renata had sent a single cameraman with him on that date, and when a disturbance across the restaurant distracted him, Michele had leaned forward and slipped an envelope into his hand.

"Burn it after you've read it," she'd whispered.

He'd pocketed it quickly and they'd picked up their conversation right where they'd left off before the cameraman focused on them again.

When he'd gotten back to Base Camp late that night and read the letter, he'd understood why Michele wanted him to destroy it. She was aiming for the House of Representatives. There was one year to go to the next election. She knew her conservative constituency in Montana wasn't going to vote in a single woman.

"I need a husband, and you need a wife. Let's strike a deal."

Curtis had admired her forthright, thoughtful style of writing. Liked her politics and her emphasis on the environment. Understood why she thought they'd make a good team.

"I will make sure you get your sustainable community if you make sure I get a seat in the House," she'd finished up.

Problem solved.

Or so he'd thought.

The truth was, he was regretting this decision bitterly.

"I've been on the show's website." Anders broke into his thoughts. "People don't like Michele. They think she doesn't love you. She's coming across as forced. Phony."

"I know." When Curtis had first met her, she'd been attractive and intelligent enough he'd thought maybe they could transcend their business deal and grow to care for each other—maybe even fall in love. It didn't sit well with him to enter into a fake marriage, as much as he needed one. He wanted a real marriage, for God's sake. He'd wanted that for—

Years.

Curtis sighed. Maybe it wasn't the most macho thing to admit, but he'd always known he was the marrying kind. He'd looked forward to it. His parents had a fantastic marriage, and they'd made it seem so simple and normal.

He wanted that, too.

He wasn't going to get it with Michele. He'd figured out that much on their second date. They'd talked about everything—their pasts, their future plans, their interests—

Thirty minutes in, Curtis realized he was bored. Not nervous, not awkwardly trying to figure out how to get to know her. Just—

Bored.

Michele had seemed equally uninspired. They'd done their best—he could tell she was trying as hard as he was. At the end of the date, when he'd given her a peck on the cheek, it was about as sexy as kissing his aunt Mary.

"She's trying too hard. You're trying too hard." Anders echoed his thoughts. "There's no spark at all. I think it would be better if you two hated each other. She won't even wear your ring—"

Curtis straightened up again. Took another look in the mirror. "It's not the right size, and there's not enough time before the wedding to send it to be fixed." That's what Michele had said, anyway. He'd tried to put it on her finger when he'd fake proposed for the cameras. When it didn't fit, Michele had taken off a chain she wore around her neck, threaded it through the ring and had worn it that way ever since. "We'll send it off the moment we're married, and then I'll wear it always," she'd said, not quite convincingly.

"It's a bad sign," Anders said.

"I know." What could he do, though? A storm was barreling their way across the plains, with forecasts for several feet of snow over the weekend. A real Montana blizzard. They'd hastily moved up the wedding in order to get it done so guests could fly home again. His family couldn't make it, unfortunately. Curtis found he was relieved. The seats on his side of the aisle would be full of friends from Base Camp and town. Michele's side would be full of business associates and political allies.

Daisy went on alert as someone knocked on the door.

Latisha Finnerty, Michele's ever-present assistant, opened it and stuck her head into the room. Her normally regal features were pinched, and her eyes were red, like she'd been crying. Curtis's stomach tightened. If Latisha, who never betrayed an emotion, was rattled by this fake wedding, maybe he should be panicking. "It's time, gentlemen." She withdrew just as quickly as she'd arrived.

"Okay. Let's do this," Curtis said. He needed to get it over with before the doubts crowding his mind got the better of him. With one last look to make sure all was right with his uniform, he turned to leave. Daisy kept close to him.

"Curtis, I think—" Anders began.

"Curtis?" Byron, the youngest of the cameramen working on the show, barged into the room and closed the door behind him, blocking Curtis's way, video camera in hand. "I need a minute."

"I've got to get downstairs." The wedding was being held at Westfield Manor, the regency style B&B up the hill from where they were building their sustainable community. It was a beautiful old three-story stone mansion. On any other day, Curtis would have appreciated the venue.

"But there's something you need to know—"

"Byron, I've got to go." He didn't want to be filmed. He didn't want to think about what he was about to do. He wanted to get through the ceremony and the next year and a half—somehow—

"But you can't—"

"Out of my way!" Curtis shoved him aside and gripped the handle of the door.

"It's about Michele. She's not—"

Curtis yanked the door open and stormed through it, Daisy at his heels. He couldn't listen to whatever Byron was going to say. He had to do this—now—before he lost his nerve and he ended up being the one to leave someone at the altar.

He strode across the hall, down the stairs and into the ballroom, where rows of folding chairs had been set up to accommodate their guests. Daisy kept pace, and murmured exclamations followed him as he marched down the aisle and took his place near the officiant, a skeletal older man who kept casting glances at the gathering clouds outside the windows.

A few moments later, Anders joined him, and Daisy settled at their feet. "I told Byron to keep the hell away from you," he murmured.

"Thanks."

He spotted Latisha in the doorway he'd just entered through, checking to make sure all was ready and waving toward the aide who was in charge of playing the recording of the processional. Her rose-colored bridesmaid gown set off her mocha skin. As always, she wore scarlet pumps. Her trademark, she'd once told Curtis. "Red is bold. It reminds me to be bold, too."

She wasn't looking bold right now, though. She looked like she was due at the guillotine any minute.

Hell, she looked exactly like he felt, Curtis thought wildly.

He didn't want to marry Michele.

He wanted a wife—someone to love—

"Curtis, you sure you want to do this?" Anders whispered. "It's not too late to get the hell out of here."

It was too late, though, because the music was swelling, Latisha had started down the aisle in her capacity as bridesmaid, and here came Michele, dressed in a dove-gray sheath, every hair in place, her chin held high.

Cameramen around the room documented her progress, some from Base Camp, some from her political campaign and some from the local and regional press.

Time slowed down as the women made their way toward him.

No, Curtis thought.

No, he couldn't do this—

Daisy whined from her position at his feet.

This was all wrong. This wasn't how his life was supposed to go. He wasn't meant for a sham marriage. He wanted the real thing. He had to do something—

"No!" Latisha exclaimed, coming to a halt two-thirds of the way down the aisle. Behind her, Michele stopped, too. Daisy stood up, as if sensing danger.

"What are you doing?" Michele shoed her assistant forward. "Start walking."

"No." Latisha turned around. "I won't be a part of this." She stalked back to Michele, grabbed the engagement ring that still hung on a chain from Michele's neck, yanked it hard enough to break the necklace's clasp and hurled it across the room.

Everyone gasped. Daisy quivered, on full alert.

Curtis couldn't seem to move his feet. When he leaned forward, Anders grabbed his arm, but Curtis didn't need his restraining hand; he couldn't have intervened if he tried. It was as if he was frozen, watching the events unfolding from somewhere far away—above himself.

It was as if he'd known this would happen all along, even though he hadn't had the slightest premonition of it.

He was about to get left at the altar—again.

God, he hoped he was about to get left at the altar.

When Latisha dropped to one knee, he nearly laughed out loud, surprised and not surprised all at once. Daisy whined again, an almost questioning sound.

"I love you," Latisha began, "and I know I promised I would wait until you'd established yourself, but I can't wait. I can't watch you marry someone else. It's not right."

"Latisha!" Michele's shocked cry carried over the murmurs of the guests, and she turned as if she'd flee, but Latisha reached up and clasped her hand, keeping her there.

"Please. Marry me." With her free hand, she plucked a tiny box out of the neckline of her elaborate gown and held it up. "I've been carrying this for four years, Michele. I've been waiting and hoping. Don't break my heart."

"But the House—"

"You can't hide who you are. Who we are. You have to win that election as yourself. You have to do that for you—for me—for all of us—"

Michele was facing her now, and Latisha opened the box. Curtis couldn't see the ring clearly, but light glinted off its facets, and Michele's expression softened.

Curtis held his breath. *Say yes*, he willed at her.

After a long moment, Michele sank down to her knees, too, and a tear spilled over her cheek. "It's beautiful," she whispered to Latisha.

The room was silent except for the clicking of the cameras. Curtis thought everyone was holding their breath.

He sure was.

"I want forever with you," Latisha told Michele. "I

want to fight this fight together. And if we can't make it here, we'll go somewhere else and try again. I believe in you, and I love you way too much to let you live a lie."

Michele looked up then, caught Curtis's gaze. Her eyes went wide, and he knew she was realizing what this meant. If she seized her own joy, she was going to ruin everything for him. The rules of the reality television show were clear: one wedding every forty days or the inhabitants of Base Camp lost everything.

Curtis didn't care—not at this moment. This was an example of the true love he'd hoped to find for himself—and he still had five days until his deadline was up on Monday.

"Say yes." Curtis cleared his throat. "Say yes," he said again, making sure his words carried. "Goddamn it, Michele, tell her yes."

Daisy barked her agreement.

Michele smiled tremulously, the first genuine smile he'd ever seen on her face, and his heart squeezed at the transformation to her features. He'd nearly ruined this woman's life—ruined his own. If it wasn't for Latisha's braveness—

All around the room, the film crews pressed forward, angling for a better view. The murmurs of the guests in their seats were growing louder.

Michele turned back to Latisha and held out her hand. Latisha slid the ring onto her finger.

"Yes," Michele said, her chin trembling, another tear sliding down her cheek. "Yes, I'll marry you."

Latisha threw herself forward to embrace Michele,

and the women rocked together, still on their knees, crying in each other's arms.

"I nearly lost you," Curtis heard Latisha say.

"You could never lose me," Michele told her.

Curtis let out the breath he'd been holding and nearly laughed in relief. Daisy pressed against his legs, and he bent to reassure her.

"You okay?" Anders asked.

"Hell, that was close."

"Too close," Anders agreed.

"What do we do now?" someone asked. Was it Michele?

Curtis straightened, clapped his hands together to quiet the room. "We've got an officiant right here," he pointed out. "We've got guests, food, music—you two ladies want to put it all to a good use?"

Michele exchanged a look with Latisha. "Is it too soon?"

"After dating for over a decade? It's nearly too late," Latisha countered. She stood up, took Michele's hand and pulled her to her feet. "Let's do this!"

Michele nodded. Anders and Curtis hurried out of the way, Daisy trotting after them happily. Byron joined them in the corner of the ballroom as the women walked down the aisle together and stood in front of the officiant, holding hands.

"I tried to warn you," Byron said in a low tone. "Renata's known for weeks about Michele and Latisha. She was making plans to out them in the next episode and expose your wedding as a fake. She said it would make great television."

"Why didn't you tell me sooner?"

"I didn't know until this morning."

"Now what are you going to do?" Anders asked as the officiant began to speak.

"Hell if I know," Curtis said.

"HOPE? I'M LEAVING," Raina Harrison said as she struggled to pull her suitcase over the broken sidewalk to her car.

"I know you're leaving. I'm coming with you to Bozeman, remember?" Hope Martin took the bag from her, folded away its handle and hefted it into the trunk of Raina's Chevy Cruze. She didn't bother to chide Raina for how heavy it was, or for bringing three other equally large suitcases along on this trip. Or for the other boxes and bins that filled the trunk and back seat of her friend's car. Raina was getting married on Sunday. Brides got to pack as much luggage as they wanted. "Are you ready to spend twenty hours in a car with your best friend?" she asked brightly. She was thrilled that Raina was marrying Ben, but privately she couldn't help feeling nothing would ever be the same. She'd have to share Raina now. Thank goodness they'd still live in the same city, even if they wouldn't be roommates anymore. Skokie wasn't that big, and she'd see Raina all the time.

"I mean, I'm leaving Illinois." Raina bit her lip, gripping her purse as if it were a lifeline. "Ben's project got extended for another three years, and it looks like it could go on longer than that. We're thinking about buying a house near Bozeman…" She trailed off, and Hope realized the expression she was seeing on Raina's face wasn't new. She'd thought it was nerves. Raina loved Ben Willis with all her might—had since they met in college, when she'd been a sophomore and he'd been finishing his master's degree in Anthropology. Now he was working in Montana.

"His project is supposed to be over. He's coming back here, right?"

Raina looked guiltier than ever, and Hope's heart sank. Raina, who couldn't keep a secret to save her life, had kept this from her? For how long?

"I've only known a couple of weeks," Raina burst out. "I wanted to be sure before I told you. I knew you'd be upset."

"I—" She was upset, but she couldn't admit it. How pathetic was it to be her age and crushed by the news your best friend was moving over a thousand miles away? She was twenty-five, for heaven's sake. Much too old to expect that the people she loved would all stay in one place. None of their other college friends had stuck around, after all. Deena White had split for Europe the day after they graduated three years ago. Sarah Ellsmere and Ward Clark had gotten married and returned to Texas. All her college pals had headed off for one adventure or another. Why should Raina be any different?

Her heart beat hard in her chest when she thought of life in Skokie without Raina, though. Raina wasn't like all the others, coming into Hope's life freshman year and disappearing after graduation. Hope had known her since kindergarten. They'd lived four blocks away from each other their entire childhoods. They'd gone to school together. Rented an apartment together afterward while Ben headed to Montana.

He'd appreciated that Hope was there to keep an eye on Raina when he embarked on the year-long project. When he was in town visiting, he used their apartment as a crash pad.

Hope cleared her throat. She'd always known the situation had to come to an end. "I thought you were going to buy a house here." She'd depended on it. She wasn't going to marry for at least another ten years and still had several more semesters of night school classes to finish before she could change careers. Meanwhile, her plan was to work hard and save money, letting her social life make up for the monotony of her day job as a receptionist in a physical therapist's office. She'd picked the work for its steady hours and decent paycheck. Hanging out with Raina when work let out was what kept her sane.

"We were, but Ben can't pass up this opportunity. You understand, don't you?"

"Sure." She hated the waver in her voice.

"You don't have to stay in Skokie, you know. You want to work at Yellowstone—that's less than two hours away from Bozeman. Why don't you apply right now?"

"I'm not due to apply for another two years!" Hope pulled out her planner, which sported a spring-green cloth cover with a jaunty bison print Raina had made for her. She flipped to her life plan section. "I have four more semesters of night classes to take before I'll be qualified as a ranger—"

"Ben knows someone who works there. He can help you get a job."

Hope pointed to the date in her planner. "It's not time—"

"Hope, I'm *leaving*," Raina said again. "I'm not coming back after the wedding. Here, you need to talk to Ben." She pulled her phone out of her pocket and tapped the screen, then lifted it to her ear. "Ben? I told Hope. She's freaking out. Make this right." She held the phone out.

"I'm not freaking out." Hope took it reluctantly. "Hi, Ben."

"Don't freak out," he said. "Look, I want you to meet a friend."

"Marriage is *not* in my plan for—"

"Not like that," Ben cut in. "Scott Leahy is a head ranger at Yellowstone. If he likes you, he can find you a position. Hope?" he added after a moment. "You still there?"

A position at Yellowstone—now? Hope tried to take it in. A rush of wanting twisted in her chest so hard it left her breathless. She was being stifled by her current job. Hated it, if she was honest. Couldn't wait until—

"I don't have the qualifications—"

"You've got something better. Connections," Ben argued.

Hope looked down at her planner, at the neat boxes in a vertical line, all ready to be checked off one after another. "But—"

"I know this wasn't in your plans, but sometimes plans change, right?"

Hope hugged her planner to her chest. Bad things happened when you changed your plans. But— Yellowstone. She'd wanted to work there all her life.

"Just get Raina to the wedding on time like you promised," Ben said. "There's a storm heading your way. It's supposed to miss Bozeman, but eastern Montana is going to get hit hard. You've got to get here by tomorrow night, okay?"

"Of course." She flipped to another page where she'd listed drive times, distances, directions and rest stops. "We'll be there by bedtime. I promise."

"Then I promise Scott will get you that job. Raina needs you nearby, you know."

Her heart squeezed. "Really?"

Ben sighed. "Of course, really. Hope, I'm not taking her away. You know that, right? You two will always be friends. I knew when I got hooked on Raina you were part of the deal."

"O-okay."

"Get her here on time for once in her life. That's all I ask."

"Got it. We're leaving right now." Hope shut the trunk and shooed Raina toward the passenger side door. "I'll drive," she mouthed.

"You be careful. I want both of you here in one

piece."

Hope looked up at the sun shining in a bright blue sky. "We'll be there before you know it." She handed the phone back to Raina, got into the driver's seat, shut the door and checked the time on her dashboard clock against a notation in her planner. "Time to go," she told Raina, who had ended her call and was buckling her seat belt.

"Let's get this party started." Raina rolled down her window and shouted, "Bye, Skokie! Hello, Montana!"

"READY TO FACE the music?" Anders asked late that night when he and Curtis pulled into the access road that led to the bunkhouse, Base Camp's official headquarters. They'd slipped out of the manor hours ago, as soon as the ceremony had ended, not wanting to make things awkward for Michele and Latisha. Curtis had needed time to process what had happened before facing his friends again. After dropping Daisy back at the bunkhouse, they'd headed to town.

"I guess so." When they'd passed the manor, lights had still been on, but the line of vehicles parked outside when they'd left were all gone. He hoped Michele and Latisha were well on their way to some sort of honeymoon. He and Michele hadn't planned one because of the show.

Anders led the way into the bunkhouse, and Curtis followed, his heart sinking when he took in the scene, even as Daisy loped over to greet him. Boone was seated at the wooden desk where he handled the small community's paperwork. Renata stood nearby, her arms crossed over her chest. A few of the cameramen ranged around the room. Walker Norton, Greg Devon and Angus McBride, all single members of Base Camp who still bunked down here while they were waiting their turn to marry, were present, as was Avery Lightfoot, the only single woman in the community.

"Well, well. The prodigal returns," Renata said dryly. "Lost another bride, huh?"

Ouch.

"Which leaves all of you about to lose everything you worked so hard to gain," Renata went on. "So how about it? Did you find another wife yet?"

Boone turned around in his seat and Curtis wasn't surprised to see lines of strain etched on his face. More than any of them, Boone needed this venture to pan out. The ranch on which they were building their community used to belong to the family of his wife. Losing it would devastate her.

"Not yet, but I will."

"Of course you will," Anders said. "Rose Johnson said you would, remember? When you bought your engagement ring?"

Curtis's stomach lurched, and he wondered where that ring was. He'd forgotten all about what had happened when he bought it. "She said whoever wore that ring would lead me on a merry chase. I thought she meant it would be hard to get her to the altar."

"Michele never wore it," Anders pointed.

"Guess Michele was part of the merry chase," Avery

said. "Now you need to find the woman who's really supposed to wear it."

"Tomorrow," Curtis said firmly. He didn't think he could take any more tonight. "Time for bed."

"Not quite yet." Boone got up. "Greg, Anders, get some chairs out. Avery, can you call the others and tell them to gather here?"

"What's up?" Anders asked.

"Fulsom's coming," Renata said. "He'll be in and out of here fast. He's got another appointment in New York first thing tomorrow."

Anders got busy pulling folding chairs out of the closet where they were stored. Greg joined him. They were all used to the eccentric billionaire's whirlwind visits. He came and went when he pleased, and they did what they needed to accommodate him.

The door opened, and Harris and Samantha Wentworth came in. A moment later Boone's wife, Riley, came in, too.

Boone joined Curtis as the room filled with people. "You said you didn't want me to find you a bride. You said you'd do it yourself, so I backed off—"

"I know. I get it, I screwed up."

"You have five days—"

"Go ahead and find me a backup bride." Curtis lifted his hands. "If I don't find a bride on my own, I'll marry her Monday."

"The whole point of marrying Michele today was that a blizzard is coming. What if it doesn't let up in time?"

Curtis didn't have an answer for that.

"Look," Jericho Cook said, joining them. "The one thing we've found is that there's always someone desperate enough to step in and marry one of us."

"Thanks a lot," Samantha said, passing by on her way to grab a seat near her husband, Harris. "Sorry things didn't work out, by the way," she said to Curtis.

"I'm not sorry," Jericho said. "I knew right from the get-go you two weren't right for each other, but you still need someone to marry."

"If the roads are blocked, you won't be able to get out, and no one will be able to get in," Boone said.

"Then maybe I should get out right now." Curtis moved to leave again, Daisy following him. He felt bad enough already. He didn't need this scolding.

"Sit down," Boone ordered and pointed to a folding chair. "You can't leave until Fulsom's had his say."

Curtis dropped into a seat with a sigh. Daisy followed more slowly and settled at his feet. "I'll get it done, I swear."

"Fine," Boone said reluctantly. "I'll do what I can to line up a backup bride. Hell, I'll line up a backup bride for the backup bride, too. We've got a lot riding on this."

"I know." Could this evening get any worse?

"Here." Byron sidled up to Curtis's chair when the others finally left him alone. "I found this for you." He dropped the engagement ring Latisha had thrown across the ballroom into Curtis's hand. "Figured you'll need it."

"Thanks." Curtis pulled the little box out of his

pocket that held the wedding band he should have given Michele tonight. Anders had passed it back to him earlier, and he'd briefly considered throwing it out, but hadn't. He wondered what the women had used for the ceremony, but it wasn't his problem.

He needed to find a new bride. In five days.

Almost four now, he corrected himself.

He stored the engagement ring with the wedding band in the box and shoved it back into his pocket. He'd give himself one night to sleep off this debacle—

Then start all over again.

Fifteen minutes later, Fulsom burst into the bunk-house, followed by several members of his entourage. The camera crew members hurried to focus on him. Everything that happened at Base Camp was recorded for the show, especially Fulsom's visits.

He handed his jacket and gloves to an assistant and marched to the head of the room, where he shook hands with Boone and surveyed the rest of them, already in their seats. His hair was silver, but his face unlined. He wore black jeans and a black turtleneck, topped with a blazer.

"No wedding today, huh?" he said cheerfully. "That's fantastic. Ups the ante for the show. We'll have everyone on the edge of their seats."

"It's not fantastic for us," Boone reminded him.

"Ah, well, you'll figure it out. You always do, right? But just in case you don't, let me update you on what's going to happen here at Base Camp." He nodded at one of his entourage, who opened the door. A gust of cold air brought in another middle-aged man Curtis recognized. He was short and stocky, built like a bulldog.

"Hell," he muttered under his breath. Did Fulsom really think they needed scaring? They knew the penalty for not hitting the show's goals.

"It's been a long time since Montague, here, has gotten to visit Base Camp," Fulsom said.

"That's right!" Montague had nowhere near the star power that Fulsom had, but he had a voice as loud as the billionaire's. He, too, strode to the front of the room and faced them. "It's been months since I've spoken to any of you. I'm delighted to inform you that my plans have changed."

Curtis exchanged a look with Anders. Had the developer grown a conscience in the last few months? Montague was their mortal enemy, made so by the way Fulsom had set up the show. If they failed to meet all of Fulsom's dictates by the end of May, Fulsom would kick them out and hand the whole ranch, including Base Camp and the manor, to Montague to develop.

Montague had shown them his plans before. He intended to raze every structure on the ranch and build seventy identical houses in a subdivision. Just the thought of it made Curtis's blood boil.

"I was thinking too small, but all that's changed," Montague said smugly. "Fire up the presentation, Fulsom."

To Curtis's surprise, Fulsom did just that, as if he was working for the odious little man. He got busy typing on a laptop he'd set up and, with Boone's help, projected the first slide in a presentation onto the screen on the wall.

Base Camp—the Theme Park, bold letters proclaimed.

"What the—"

"Theme park?"

The room erupted into noise and confusion, and Daisy jumped up, barking, until Fulsom raised his hands to calm them down. "Hear him out!" He tapped on the keyboard to advance to the next slide. Curtis soothed Daisy back into a sitting position.

Montague beamed at them, hands on hips. "You are going to lose," he proclaimed happily. "Which is a damn good thing because you all know nothing about business and making money. In fact, if I tried, I couldn't make less money off this ranch than you all are managing to do. It's like you're deliberately trying to fail."

Curtis's fingers balled into fists. Beside him, Anders leaned forward as if he might explode from his seat to confront the man.

"Luckily for you, you've got me! When you're done making a colossal mess here at Base Camp—which, at the rate you're going, will be in about five days," Montague added, pointing a finger at Curtis, "I'll swoop in and turn this place into a gold mine. How am I going to do that? I'll tell you." He slapped the screen. "Base Camp, the theme park! See, I was just a lowly housing developer when you first met me. When I took a look at this property, I saw its potential. Houses. Lots and lots of houses. Big ones! On teeny, tiny lots! What a dream, right?"

"He's got to be kidding," Anders said.

"You're right—I was a fool! Because meanwhile, you all were taking this ranch and making it famous! With a little help from Fulsom, here." He patted the billionaire's shoulder. "Next slide."

Fulsom tapped a key. The next slide appeared, showing an artist's mockup of an amusement park, complete with roller coasters, a Ferris wheel and other rides.

"People all over the world are watching *Base Camp*, and what's more, they want to be a part of it. Five million hits to your website this month alone!" He let that sink in. "It occurred to me—all those idiots would be glad to fly in and see where the show is made. Once they're here, it won't be hard to part them from their hard-earned dollars. Rides, food, lodging—I'll have it all right here!"

"Our audience doesn't want amusement parks, they want to learn about sustainability," Kai Green protested.

"Like hell they do. They want cotton candy and roller coasters, and I'm going to give them to them."

"Are you going to make a sustainable theme park? Like… run everything on solar or wind energy?" Avery asked.

"Hell, no. Solar!" He waved the idea away. "You can't run a decent ride off solar. But you'll like this— there's going to be a wax museum. Each of you will have a statue in it so people can see who started it all. Not to mention the dude ranch experience. We'll keep a handful of bison and let tourists herd them around.

They love that kind of shit. Paired with an endangered species safari, we'll be turning people away!"

"You can't make an endangered species safari," Boone sputtered.

"You're having us on," Curtis said. "There's not going to be a safari or a dude ranch or an amusement park. Montana is too damn cold half the time for that. It would be a waste of space."

"Ah, but we haven't even begun to talk about the ice rink complex, and the luge and giant slalom training complex we're going to build. Athletes will fly in from around the world during winter months to hone their skills—"

"If you put thousands of people on planes flying to Chance Creek, you'll burn so much carbon everything we've done will be for nothing," Boone exploded.

Montague grinned. "I know. Good times, right? You self-righteous idiots sitting here week after week making people feel bad about spending their money. I can't wait to destroy what you've built."

Curtis pulled back, surprised by his venom. That went a little far, didn't it? "We know all you care about is business," he started, but Montague stepped forward and cut him off.

"No, you don't know that. You think you do, but you don't get it at all. I don't want to win because I want this piece of property. There's property everywhere, and I could set up twenty subdivisions tomorrow if I cared to. I want to win because I want to stick it to you and everyone like you. I worked my whole life to get where

I'm at, and it's time for me to develop big properties. I'm not building tiny houses, or green houses, or sustainable houses, or any of that crap. I'm building honking big McMansions, because it's my turn to build them! To put my mark on this planet. I didn't work this hard to *consume less*. I did everything so that I'd have more. More houses, more cars, more vacations, more steak, so I don't need you people to tell me to think about the future of the earth. I don't care about the future. I don't care about climate change. I don't care about the stupid glaciers, or the polar bears, or the wetlands, or the goddamn tree frogs in Venezuela!"

"Do you care about having enough to eat?" Boone interjected. "Do you care about millions of people having to move because of rising oceans or scorching summer heat? Do you care about the spread of disease and—"

"Shut the fuck up!" Montague roared.

Daisy whined. Curtis put a restraining hand on her collar. You could have heard a pin drop in the bunkhouse.

"You don't get to tell me that me doing my job has anything to do with any of that." Montague shook his finger at Boone.

Boone opened his mouth but then shut it again and shook his head. Curtis knew what he was thinking. You couldn't change someone's mind once they began to take the earth's natural processes personally. Climate change wasn't some kind of divine retribution the planet was wreaking on people because they'd sinned; it was more like a well-executed science experiment. If you add chemical A, you get result B—every time—no matter how much you wished things might go differently. Curtis had seen scientific articles from the 1800s that forecasted everything that was happening today. None of it was a surprise.

That didn't change the fact that people wanted the lifestyle they wanted.

"We were all taught to want big, beautiful houses," Curtis tried to explain to Montague. "Now we need to learn something new. That doesn't mean your work isn't valuable—"

Montague reared up to his full height. "Of course my work is valuable. My work represents all that's great about this country, which is why I'm going to win. Why everyone on my side is going to win!" He looked around. "I'm done here." He stalked across the room, grabbed his coat from one of Fulsom's aides, pulled the door open and slammed it shut behind him as he left. The bunkhouse was silent until Fulsom spoke again.

"What do you say?" he asked. "Think we should let the show rest on its laurels and just ride out the rest of the season?"

"No," Boone said shortly.

"You got the motivation you need now to find yourself a wife?" Fulsom looked at Curtis.

"You're the one making it hard for us to succeed," Curtis pointed out. Fulsom was the one who'd come up with all the rules for Base Camp, after all.

"I came up with a way to make people interested in

something they're not interested in at all," Fulsom countered. "As evidenced by Exhibit A." He pointed to the door through which Montague had stormed out. "So find a wife. Then find a way to make people understand what's at stake." He made a chopping motion, and the camera crews shut down and began to pack up.

Renata crossed over to talk to Boone. Curtis couldn't help overhearing them. He gave Daisy a pat, needing the reassurance as much as she did.

"We're all pulling out of here tonight before the storm hits," Renata said, "but we'll leave Byron with you. You give him full access, you hear me? Remember what we talked about."

"We'll give him access," Boone assured her tiredly.

Curtis eyed him uneasily, and he wasn't the only one. Boone usually handled these kinds of confrontations with more equability.

"Fulsom's been unhappy," she went on in a lower voice, glancing back at where the man in question was speaking to his aides. "He thinks the show is getting boring. I'm not sure what he'd have done if Curtis hadn't canceled the wedding last minute. He said it was the first interesting thing to happen in weeks."

"We'll do our best to make things interesting, although with this blizzard coming, we're going to be stuck inside—" Boone trailed off.

"You'll think of something."

"You going to be able to get back to town? The snow is starting to come down hard," Clay said to

Renata.

"The 4x4s will make it. We're taking two and leaving the other one with Byron. Don't let him drive it unless it's a real emergency, though. That kid couldn't find his way out of a paper bag, and the insurance on the thing is through the roof." She turned away, and it wasn't long before the bunkhouse cleared out.

WHEN RAINA'S PHONE blipped again, Hope bit back a sigh and kept driving. She could have understood her friend's obsession with the gadget if it was Ben texting her, or even if it was Raina's mother, who'd been in Bozeman all week. Since Raina had worked right up until the last minute, unwilling to leave her little charges at the daycare center before she had to, her mother had been helping make sure all the last-minute wedding details got done.

It wasn't either Ben or Diana getting in touch, however. Hope had grown to recognize all the alerts Raina got on her phone. Sometimes she got actual calls or texts, but more often it was a message from one of the dozens of television shows and celebrities Raina followed. Over the last two days, a steady succession of pings had punctuated their every conversation until she'd almost given up.

"It's a *Base Camp* Bulletin!" Raina cried, proving Hope right.

"What's a *Base Camp* Bulletin?" Hope knew she'd regret the question, but she asked it anyway.

"You know *Base Camp*. I've told you about it a dozen times!"

"The one where the naked people are performing on the street?"

"That's *Stripped and Busking*."

"The one where toddlers commit crimes?"

"That's *Baby Breaking Bad*."

"The one where dogs go out on first dates?"

"That's *Dogs Swipe Right*."

"Really?" She'd made that one up.

"Stop putting down my shows. *Base Camp* is the one with the Navy SEALs who are building a sustainable community."

That sounded better than *Dogs Swipe Right*. "What does the bulletin say?" Raina would only marry once, she hoped, and she was going to make this trip a good one if it killed her.

"Oh my god. Oh my god, it happened again! He got left at the altar!" Raina grabbed her arm and shook it. Hope tried to stay on the road. "OMG, his fiancée married her assistant!"

"Who married her assistant?"

Raina stared at her for a long minute, then let go and tapped furiously at her phone. "Now he's single again. And he's not the only one. There's Walker, Angus, Anders and Greg—" She cut off and snapped her mouth shut.

"What are you talking about?" Hope demanded.

"What? Oh, nothing. Forget it." Raina turned to stare out the window at the scenery passing by.

Was she serious? "It wasn't a nothing a minute ago

when you were shaking me!"

"Okay, it's something. Maybe something big, but you don't care. You don't even watch the show. Pull over at the next rest stop, would you? I need to pee."

A half hour later, refreshed from their break and back on the highway, Raina was her chatty self again. In the driver's seat now, focused on the road, she couldn't get distracted by her phone anymore. Hope soon wished she could. She was happy for Raina that she'd found her soul mate and was getting married, but Raina was in that impending-marital state that made brides want to fix up all of their single friends.

"It's too bad Scott's got a serious girlfriend. Wouldn't it be great if you fell for him and we had a double wedding?" Raina said.

"Given that I'm not going to meet him until the day before your wedding, I doubt there'd be a double ceremony even if he was single."

"But I want you to get married, too," Raina complained. "I hate it when we're not in sync."

Hope bit back a smile. Good ol' Raina. Best friend a girl could want. "You know I'm not getting married for a decade." It was in her planner. She simply didn't have time right now for that kind of connection.

"In a decade my kids will be going to high school."

Hope shot her a look. "Your math skills suck."

"They don't suck. I'm going to have really smart kids." She was quiet for a moment, but Hope knew it wouldn't last. She was right. "What kind of guy are you going to marry—in a decade?" Raina pressed.

"I don't know."

"Describe him."

"Are we back in seventh grade now?"

"Dark hair or redhead?" Raina demanded.

Hope sighed. Raina was only going to keep going until she gave in. "What about blond?"

"Not available."

"What do you mean not available?"

"There aren't any blonds left on—there aren't any blonds available."

"In the whole world?" Hope asked.

Raina ignored the question. "Well?"

"Dark hair." She'd never dated a redhead.

"Skinny or burly? Like… not super skinny, but rides a bike skinny."

"Burly." Raina liked the skinny guys. Soccer players, long distance runners, cyclists who wore those stretchy little bike shorts. Ben was like that. Hope liked guys with a little more meat on their bones.

"Accent or no accent?"

That stumped her for a minute. An accent was always interesting, she had to admit, but in her experience guys with accents didn't get serious about women like her. They were into flings and moving on, and despite the fact she wasn't getting married for a decade, she didn't find flings attractive.

"No accent."

"Okay. That's one down for sure. And Walker really should end up with Avery."

"Who's Walker?"

"No one. You sure you don't like wiry guys?"

"Nope. No offense."

"None taken. My husband-to-be is impervious to your criticisms."

"He's perfect for you."

"And I know who's perfect for you."

Hope refused to give her the satisfaction of asking who.

Raina kept her eyes forward. "I think Ben's right; it's definitely going to snow."

When Hope turned her way, Raina was smiling.

"CAN SOMEONE GIVE me a hand?" Anders asked, opening the bunkhouse door and leaning in rather than tracking snow into the entryway. "Snow's starting to come down hard; we'd better get the plow on one of the trucks and clear the lane to the road. Probably have to do it several times tonight."

"Take Curtis and get it done," Boone said with a sigh. "He'll need a way off this ranch if he's going to find a wife."

"I'll find a bride, Chief, no matter how much it snows," Curtis promised, but he got up gladly. He'd spent last night and all day on the dating sites without much luck, and it was probably time for him to try the local bars again tonight. He'd help Anders with the plowing and then head into town. He couldn't say he was much in the mood, though.

How did you go from buying a woman a drink to proposing in a just a few days? Michele had been the one to get things going last time.

"Come on, Daisy." He followed Anders outside, Daisy trotting happily at his heels. She didn't care what the weather was like as long as she was in on the action. She'd been far happier since Michele had gone than she'd been in weeks.

"It's a good thing you guys finished the next few tiny houses," Anders said as they waded through the snow to one of community's trucks.

"I think so, too." Curtis was glad to change the subject. They had rushed during the past few weeks to frame in and roof four of the five remaining tiny houses they needed. They'd make it through the winter and build the last one come spring.

Daisy snuffed when a flake of snow landed on her nose and tried to shake it off.

"I hear you, girl." Curtis looked around and whistled. The snow was piling up. "Guess I'd better get going if I'm getting to town tonight."

"Not sure you're going anywhere," Anders said, his tone even.

"I can't stay here."

"Not sure the bars will be open much longer, the way this is coming down."

He hadn't considered that. "I really blew it, didn't I?" For the first time he allowed himself to think about what might happen if he didn't marry before the end of Monday night. He'd never let himself consider that possibility as if it could be a real outcome. "Anders, what am I going to do?"

"You're going to plow the lane. You're going to take a look at the roads and see if it's worth it to drive to town. If not, you're going to go back inside and try your luck online. That's all you can do." They climbed into the truck, Anders at the wheel, Daisy curled up at Curtis's feet.

"What if I blow this for everyone?" It was the question he'd never dared ask aloud. "You guys—you're like my family." He searched for the words to describe how he felt. This was uncharted territory. He was a doer, not a talker.

"We're going to figure this out," Anders said. "Together. You're not alone in this. You know that, right?"

Curtis turned toward his friend, who was hunched over the steering wheel, peering through the driving snow that had cut visibility down to nearly nothing.

Anders shot a glance his way. "I'm serious. That's what Base Camp is all about."

"I guess." But he couldn't help feel that the fate of the whole community was resting on his shoulders. "This snow is ridiculous," he added. It was coming down in sheets, making it impossible to see more than a few feet in front of the truck.

None of them would be going anywhere tonight.

Which meant no chance of finding his bride.

"SLOW DOWN." HOPE gripped the armrest as Raina's foot pressed down harder on the gas, sending her car lurching forward on the slippery highway as the snow pelted down around them. "You can barely see ten feet ahead of you—this isn't the time to drive like you're in the Indy 500."

"If we don't make it to Bozeman tonight, we're not going to make it at all. You heard what the weatherman said. Two feet of snow, and more coming tomorrow. We've got to push through now." Raina had been distracted since yesterday afternoon, and at the hotel last night, she'd spent hours on her phone, doing research, as she'd put it, barely watching the funny wedding movie Hope had found for the occasion.

In the last couple of hours, Raina had grown antsy, and she refused to let Hope drive, even when was her turn. They'd crossed the border into Montana just past dinnertime. Hope couldn't wait to get to Bozeman and be done with the long trip.

"If we go off the road, we might not make it at all. Ben told me specifically I was to get you to your wedding in one piece." Hope reached down into the large purse at her feet, drew out her planner, flipped it open to the correct page and looked at the items left unchecked on her list. She pulled out her phone and tried to bring up a map, but she'd lost reception. A sign flashed by outside her window. Chance Creek—10 miles.

"Stop worrying so much. New topic: I've decided to find you a man."

"You're already helping me find a job. I don't need a man. Can you see at all?" she asked Raina, leaning forward to polish the windshield with her sleeve. It was dark, and the snow was coming down so hard their headlights reflected back off the swirling flakes. "Watch out—you're not even on the road!"

"Yes, I am." Raina bent forward to peer through the windshield, too. "How many miles to Bozeman did that sign back there say?"

"It didn't say anything about Bozeman." They were going so slowly she couldn't remember when she'd seen a sign that did. They hadn't passed a vehicle in miles, either. There was no one else dumb enough to be driving in this storm.

"Crap." Raina banged the heel of her palm on the steering wheel rather dramatically, Hope thought.

"What?"

"We need gas. We're under an eighth of a tank."

Hope leaned over to see. "There's at least a quarter of a tank—"

"I always fill my car when there's under a quarter tank left. We're not going to make it to Bozeman."

Hope swore. "Are you sure?" Where would they find gas in a storm like this?

"Positive. My car has a very small gas tank. Wasn't that Chance Creek back there? We've still got hundreds of miles to go to Bozeman."

That didn't sound right, and Hope checked her planner. Chance Creek wasn't on her list of towns, but surely—

"Chance Creek will have gas," Raina said confidently. Hope wished she shared that confidence.

Hope watched the gas gauge as the minutes ticked by, glad to see that Raina had finally slowed down. It was getting difficult to see where the highway ended and the shoulder began.

"Chance Creek. Gas, food, lodging," she read aloud in relief when she caught sight of another sign.

"I told you. It's bigger than it looks."

Hope turned to her. "You've been here before?"

"Uh… no. Of course not. I saw a population sign back there," Raina said quickly.

Hope hadn't noticed a population sign. She gripped the armrest more tightly when Raina turned off the highway and the car skidded in the deeper snow on the ramp. It seemed like no one had driven here in a good long while, and even their snow tires were no match for accumulation.

"What were we supposed to do tonight? Read off your list," Raina said.

Hope turned a page in her planner. "Unpack, steam your clothes, check with your mom about the details about the rehearsal and the dinner." She kept reading through her list, flagging items they still might be able to do when they arrived tonight and putting tiny arrows by the items they'd have to shift to tomorrow.

She wasn't sure how much time had passed when she looked up again.

"Where's the town?" As far as she could tell in the darkness, all they were passing were pastures. She hoped any cattle living out here had a place to shelter tonight. "Did we go the wrong way?"

"I followed the signs," Raina said.

They kept going. Ten minutes later, however, there

was no pretending they were on track.

"We're lost," Hope declared.

"Not lost, exactly," Raina said. "Just not where you think we should be. Maybe I did take a wrong turn." But she kept on going.

"We'd better stop and go back toward the highway."

"That's not going to be easy. This road is so narrow—and it looks like the shoulders slope away. Are those drainage ditches? What if we slide into one?"

She had a point. "Keep going until we get to an intersection. You can turn around there."

"Sure thing."

Why was Raina so damn cheerful? Hope's heart was in her mouth. What if they ran out of gas before—

She looked at the gauge. Still nearly a quarter tank left.

Raina seemed determined to pass by every turnout in the county before she finally called out, "There!" She spun the wheel suddenly and swerved in an awkward arc across the road toward a lane that intersected it. Hope caught sight of a sign: *Base Camp*. She wrinkled her nose. Where had she heard that recently?

She didn't have time to think it through. "Watch out!" she cried. Raina wasn't turning fast enough—they were going to miss—

Both women shrieked as the sedan hit an icy spot, spun round and slid backward into a ditch. They landed with a dull thud that boded ill for the car's back bumper, but Hope was just grateful it had all happened so slowly neither of them had been hurt.

"You okay?" she asked Raina, just to be sure.

"I'm fine, but the car isn't," Raina said in a little voice. "I didn't mean to—" She broke off and buried her head in her hands. "Ben is going to kill me if I'm late!"

"He's not going to kill you."

"I'm supposed to meet his grandparents tomorrow night."

"We'll get there in plenty of time for that." Hope understood her reaction, though. Ben—affable, loving, wonderful Ben—had put his foot down about the wedding. He expected Raina to be on time—not just to the wedding itself, but to all the events that preceded it. "He'll understand about the snowstorm." Hope didn't have to explain what she meant; both women had been obsessed with getting this right since Ben had first stressed how important it was. That's what happened when your husband-to-be was a saint, Hope thought wildly. If she married—and the emphasis was on the if—she wouldn't pick someone quite so wonderful.

It was a lot to live up to.

"That's not the point. The point is he wants me to be there—on time. And I want to be there, even if I want to find you a—I mean... I don't want to miss anything!"

Raina wasn't making much sense, and Hope leaned over to see if she'd hit her head. She didn't see any bumps or bruises, though.

"You won't miss anything. I promise." Hope needed Raina to calm down before she got too wound up.

They were sitting in a car in a ditch in the middle of nowhere, and it was dark and getting colder by the minute. They needed to figure out a game plan.

"Should we stay with the car or look for help?" Raina asked, echoing her thoughts.

"I don't see any houses—"

"The bunkhouse is at the end of the lane." Raina slid a guilty look her way. "I mean—this is a ranch, right? There's bound to be a bunkhouse—or a regular house—or something."

Hope peered at her friend again. Raina didn't usually babble like this. She decided to be practical. "Let's try to get the car out of this ditch first."

"I don't think it's going to work."

The car was tilted at a strange angle, as if they were in an amusement park ride, heading up the first hill of a roller coaster before they rushed down the other side.

"Maybe we should call Triple A," Hope decided. She pulled out her phone. Raina grabbed it out of her hand. "What are you doing?" Hope demanded.

"No bars. I'm not getting any reception either. We need to go find the people who live here."

Hope took her phone back, wondering why Raina sounded relieved, when her own anxiety surged with the news. "I'm supposed to have coverage everywhere."

"This is the country," Raina reminded her, as if she needed reminding. "It's getting cold. We can't just stay here."

"What if there isn't a house for miles? Some ranches are huge, right? Maybe we should stay with the car. It's warmer in here than we'd be out there, right?"

"Won't the heater blow cold air if we sit here too long?"

"Maybe you're right." Hope was getting nervous. "I don't suppose you have a bag of sand in the back of the car."

"I did," Raina said in a tiny voice, "but I took it out to make more room for my things." She looked so guilty Hope couldn't stand it anymore.

"I promise you this is going to work out, no matter what," she said. "I swear to you on… on my future as a Yellowstone park ranger."

Raina tried to smile, but Hope knew it was time to stop talking and start acting. "Come on, let's start walking."

"Wait—did you see that?" Raina pointed toward the lane they'd slid past.

"See what?"

"A light!"

"IT'S REALLY GETTING slick out here," Anders said the third time they drove the truck down the lane to plow it.

"Glad we didn't wait for the snow to pile up." Curtis knew it was better to stay on top of this kind of thing. They'd plowed the lane up to the manor, too, and from there out to the road along the main driveway. They'd be glad they'd done so tomorrow once the highway was clear and they were able to come and go at will. Just like he'd thought, he wasn't getting into town tonight, and all the time he'd wasted this month trying to make it work with Michele was killing him.

"We'd better call it a night after this." Anders was quiet a moment. "You're not going to make it to town in this weather. You're going to have to work the internet again."

"Yep." He wasn't looking forward to it. "Tomorrow I guess I'll—"

"Hey—what's that?" Anders interrupted and pointed at a glow at the end of the lane. "Are we expecting company? Looks like someone's coming."

"Or maybe someone's stuck," Curtis said as they got closer. The light didn't move as they approached.

"You're right." Anders stepped on the gas, although he kept his speed down. Curtis knew he didn't want to lose control of the vehicle.

"They're in the ditch—hey, watch out!"

Anders spun the wheel, sending the truck sliding across the icy surface of the road as two women had appeared around the end of the car, leaving little room for him to maneuver past them.

Anders brought the truck under control and stopped it, then edged it forward to park at the side of the road. "Jesus, that was close."

Curtis was already halfway out of the truck, Daisy bounding out ahead of him, barking at the new faces.

"What the hell are you two doing? Are you trying to get killed?" Curtis shouted when he'd rounded the truck.

He took in two sets of frightened, female eyes and got his temper under control, blowing out a breath that plumed white in the freezing air. "Sit, Daisy," he commanded. Daisy sat in front of the women, her tail swishing eagerly. She loved visitors to the ranch.

"You scared us," Anders called out as he caught up. "Pretty icy out here. Thought I might hit you."

"You shouldn't have been driving so fast," the taller woman said. Serious, with dark hair and thin, dark brows that framed her blue eyes like wings, she stepped forward to meet them.

"Sorry," the other woman said, pushing in front of the first. She was petite, with thick, dark curls. "We were just so excited to see you. We thought there might not be anyone around for miles. I got us in the ditch. Do you think you could pull us out? I'm Raina, by the way." She was smiling, looking from one to the other of the men in a way Curtis recognized.

A fan of the show, if he wasn't mistaken. Weekly episodes of *Base Camp* garnered record audiences around North America and beyond. This wasn't his first brush with an excited fan.

Anders took her hand when she offered it and shook. "I'm Anders, and this is—"

"Curtis," Raina said, confirming Curtis's suspicion. "Good, you're here." She bent down to let Daisy sniff her hand. "You're Daisy, aren't you? I recognize all of you."

"Recognize them? How?" her friend demanded. Curtis exchanged a look with Anders. It wasn't often they went unrecognized these days. When he went to town, everyone asked about the show. One of the hardest parts about trying to meet women online was that most of the ones who solicited him already knew who he was. He was never sure if they liked him—or wanted to be on the show, too. At least Michele had been open about wanting to make use of his notoriety.

"Hope's never watched a single episode of *Base Camp*," Raina said with a shake of her head. "Can you believe that?"

Curtis perked up. "Not any of them?"

"I don't watch TV. I don't have time," Hope said.

He liked her clear-eyed gaze and her self-deprecating smile. Curtis had immediately pegged her as the strong one. The determined one. She looked like a woman who pursued her goals steadily—and relentlessly. Raina didn't seem that way at all.

Behind Hope, Anders waggled his eyebrows at Curtis in a "this is an interesting turn of events" type way.

It was an interesting turn of events. He needed a woman, and lo and behold—here one was. Even cocooned in a winter jacket, he could tell Hope had an athletic figure, and her practical outdoor clothes labeled her as a woman with a good head on her shoulders. No fur and bows for her—just a quality jacket and gloves that would hold up in rough conditions. She moved nearer to pet Daisy, too, crouching down, pulling off her gloves and rubbing Daisy's ears like she couldn't help herself. Curtis's heart lifted.

A woman who liked dogs.

"Can you get us back on the road?" Hope asked. "We've got a lot of miles to cover tonight."

Curtis exchanged another glance with Anders. "I don't think you're covering any more miles tonight. We'll get you out of that ditch, but then you'd better come with us up to the bunkhouse—"

"I'd love to see the bunkhouse!" Raina squealed.

Hope sent her a bewildered look. "The bunkhouse?" she repeated. "What about Ben?"

"Who's Ben?" Curtis asked.

"Raina's fiancé. He'll be wondering where we are."

"We'll make sure you get in contact with him. He won't want you driving in conditions like this. Come on, let's get you warm and dry and get your car out of that ditch. Do you have a fiancé, too?" he added. Might as well find out right away.

"No, she doesn't," Raina said. "She doesn't even have a boyfriend. She prefers men with dark hair over redheads. Guys with a little meat on their bones. Ones without accents."

"Raina!" Hope looked scandalized.

Curtis tried to control the smile tugging at his mouth and wondered if he'd succeeded. "That's all good information," he told Raina.

"Ask and ye shall receive, right?" She shrugged innocently. "I got a *Base Camp* Bulletin yesterday. Heard all about the way Michele married her assistant instead of—" She broke off. "Anyway, enough of all that. Let's just say I'm up to date on all the Base Camp news."

Jesus. "You know about Michele—?"

"I know everything. You're still looking, right?" she asked innocently.

She didn't beat around the bush, did she? "I'm still looking," Curtis confirmed.

Hope, obviously baffled by their banter, cleared her throat. "We really need to be on our way *tonight*," she said firmly, but she slid a glance his way. Was she checking him out?

She was.

For the first time since the show began, Curtis thanked the social media department. He and most of the others on the show avoided the *Base Camp* website and marketing efforts as much as they could. He hadn't known why anyone would want to get updates on their phones.

Now it seemed kind of brilliant.

"How'd you happen to be near Base Camp, anyway?"

Raina's eyes went wide, and Curtis realized he'd stepped in it.

"We needed gas," Hope said.

"Gas is the other way—ouch!" Anders rubbed his shoulder when Curtis punched him. "What did you do that for?"

Curtis shot him what he hoped was a significant look, and Anders said, "Oh... right. Anyone could have made that mistake in a snowstorm."

Not exactly true. The signs for the gas station and the center of town would have been hard to miss. How had Raina managed it?

Had she come here and crashed her car on purpose? That was gutsy—or crazy. Curtis wondered if he ought to be worried.

"It was an honest mistake," Raina said, but when Hope turned to look at the car, she winked at Curtis. "Thought you could use a hand."

"We're the ones who need a hand." Hope pointed to the car's back bumper. It was crumpled, pressing into the left back tire.

"Come to the bunkhouse, and we'll get this sorted out," Curtis said again. "We'll pull out your car in the morning." He figured two women—even if they were unhinged—couldn't do much damage with a passel of Navy SEALs around. Besides, Raina might be little weird, but Hope seemed pretty normal to him.

"I don't think we should go anywhere with strangers," Hope said to Raina.

"They're not strangers. I've watched every episode of *Base Camp*. I know these guys better than they know themselves. Come on, Hope, please? How often do you get to see where a television show is filmed? There'll be film crews everywhere, so we'll be perfectly safe, right?" She turned back to Curtis.

"Unfortunately, almost the whole crew already packed it in and headed to town about an hour ago, before the roads got too bad, but you'll still be safe with us. There are plenty of other women in camp."

Hope shivered, and Curtis resisted the urge to unzip his jacket, pull her in close and wrap the sides of the garment around her. They could warm each other up—

Heck, he was getting ahead of himself. Although maybe he should, given his looming deadline.

"What do you think, Hope?" he asked. Raina might talk a lot, but he knew Hope was the head of this operation. She was the one who'd make the decision.

"Fine, we'll come with you. But the minute the snow stops, we get back on the road."

She didn't sound too pleased, but Curtis was already counting his lucky stars. So far he liked Hope, and he didn't have any other prospects. Luckily, according to the weather report, the snow wasn't going to stop for several days.

Maybe that would be enough time to convince her to like him back.

"WHY ARE YOU being such a stick-in-the-mud?" Raina hissed ten minutes later when she and Hope climbed out of the truck and Curtis and Anders ushered them toward a long, low building they referred to as the bunkhouse. The men had transferred their luggage from their car into the truck bed and were lugging some of it along now. Hope had snatched her planner from the front seat and hugged it to her chest, trying to keep it dry.

"Because I don't know who these people are," Hope hissed back. Trust Raina to get them into another crazy situation. She did it all the time, and she never worried for a moment about the consequences of her actions. Hope was the one who had to do that.

Daisy bounded ahead of them, waiting impatiently at the front door until Curtis caught up and opened it. She slipped inside, and when Hope followed the others, she found herself in a large room filled with several men in jeans, boots and sweaters, and a woman unaccountably dressed in what looked like a Regency ballgown.

Hope was still trying to get her bearings. She dimly remembered Raina nattering on about a reality television show she'd become obsessed with several months ago. *Base Camp* focused on sustainable practices, right? That's what Raina had said. But whenever she talked about it, it seemed to Hope the show focused far more on the participants' love lives than their desire to save the world.

"I've been watching the show for months; I know all about these people," Raina said. "That's Greg." She pointed to a no-nonsense-looking man with a shock of black hair coming to greet them. "He helps Jericho and the others with the solar system and things like that. That's Walker Norton and Avery Lightfoot over there." She pointed to a tall Native American man and the petite, strangely dressed woman. "They're in charge of the bison herd. Anders works with them. You already know Curtis." She and Hope had already attracted everyone's attention, and people were gathering around them.

Hope was still stuck on *bison herd*. There were bison here?

"Watching people on TV isn't the same as knowing them," Hope muttered, refusing to betray her curiosity to Raina. "They're actors playing parts. Don't expect them to act like their characters."

"It's a reality TV show." Raina rolled her eyes. "I

swear, you never listen to me. Look—we're being filmed right now."

Sure enough, a young man was scrambling to lift a video camera to his shoulder. Hope resisted the urge to turn around and head back out of the building.

"Found these two in a ditch at the end of our lane," Anders announced cheerfully to the others in the bunkhouse. "Thought we'd better take them in for the night."

"You poor things!" Avery bustled over. "Are you cold? Hungry?" Her dark blue gown was striking with its high waist and low neckline. Avery was a redhead with an engaging smile, and Hope bet she was one of Raina's favorite characters.

"I'm hungry," Raina said, at the same time Hope said, "We're fine."

"We're not fine," Raina corrected her. "We just went off the road in a snowstorm. We're going to be late to my wedding. We're thoroughly devastated," she told Avery cheerfully. "We'll definitely need some hot chocolate to restore us."

"Hot chocolate sounds like a great idea. Get your wet things off and come with me to the kitchen." Avery led the way, her dress swishing behind her, and Raina followed, stripping off her coat. With a glance at Curtis and Anders, Hope tagged along, shrugging out of her coat, too. She didn't know what else to do. Curtis took their outer garments, hung them up near the door and came after them.

To her consternation, everyone else filed into the

kitchen, too, including the young cameraman, leaving the relatively small space crowded. Hope tried to keep out of the way, but Curtis leaned against the counter next to her. His large frame was hard to ignore, as was the smile that curved his mouth when she glanced in his direction. He had short, light brown hair, hazel eyes and well-formed features. She had to admit he was handsome. He seemed inclined to be friendly, too. If they'd met at a bar or through a mutual friend, Hope would have been tempted to get to know him—

Even if she'd promised herself no distractions until after she got her job at Yellowstone.

Besides, she and Raina would be back on the road tonight—tomorrow at the latest. No sense being attracted to a man she'd never see again.

That didn't mean she couldn't be polite.

"Why is Avery wearing such a fancy dress?" Hope asked Curtis as Raina peppered Avery with questions, getting in the woman's way at every turn as Avery tried to make the hot chocolate.

"You've really never seen the show?" Curtis cocked his head, studying her.

"No. Sorry," she added. "Not much of a TV person."

"I'm not either. Believe me, none of us came here to be on television. It just sort of happened. Avery and the other women here dress like that because… well, it's a long story. Maybe you'd better ask her."

Hope stifled a sigh. That was cryptic. Raina looked like she was having a fabulous time, and Avery was chatting with her like they'd known each other forever, but Raina made friends with everyone she met. Hope wasn't nearly as good at it.

Questions. That's what Raina always said when Hope asked how she did it. "Ask people questions. They love to talk about themselves."

She slid a glance Curtis's way and found him watching her. Feeling herself flushing, she tried again. "What is this place—a ranch of some kind?"

Curtis grinned. "Yes, it's a ranch. We have quite a large herd of bison here. We also grow our own food, produce our own energy, and the women run a Regency-themed bed-and-breakfast."

"Which explains the dress." That wasn't so hard. She wondered why he'd been so cagey before. She was being cagey, too, though. Everything he'd just listed interested her. Suddenly she had a million questions. Bison? Green energy? A Regency bed-and-breakfast? How did this group manage to start such an interesting community?

"There's a lot more to it than that, but yes, that's part of it." He edged nearer, and Hope's heart gave a little squeeze. He was at ease in his skin and obviously comfortable with his surroundings—and with the crowd pressed together in the kitchen. Hope supposed that if you were being filmed for half a year, you got used to being under a microscope. She'd always been a private person herself. "My job is to build tiny houses."

She blinked. "Tiny houses?"

"That's right. Want to see one?"

She did want to see one but was worried about leaving her friend alone with the rest of these people. Raina had been listening, though.

"Go on, take a look." She turned to Curtis. "That's the one kind of show Hope will watch—the ones where people sell all their stuff and live in tiny little shacks in other people's backyards."

"They're not shacks—" Hope protested.

Raina talked over her. "I'd like to see a tiny house, too, before we go, but I'll stay and help Avery for now."

"Are you sure?" Hope asked. "We can wait."

"No, you can't. Get going." Raina waved her off.

"You need to call Ben and tell him we've been delayed," Hope reminded her.

"In a minute."

The cameraman made as if to follow them, but Raina grabbed his arm. "You need to stay here and film my call to Ben—my wedding is in less than three days!"

"Come on." Curtis took Hope's hand. "We have to go back outside, but it isn't far."

It was too late to say no, and besides, Hope's curiosity had gotten the better of her. Raina was right; she'd always been fascinated by tiny houses. She thought the craftsmanship that went into making a small home livable was amazing. She'd tried her hand at woodworking before but found she didn't have the patience for it, so she had a lot of respect for people who did.

Outside, the wind had picked up and the snow blew in flurries that made it difficult to see. Curtis stopped and peered into the sky before shaking his head. "All that plowing Anders and I did today isn't going to make a bit of difference the way this stuff is coming down."

"Raina and I really need to leave first thing in the morning."

Curtis began to walk again, his fingers still curled around hers. "We'll keep the lane clear, but you might have to wait a bit tomorrow for the plows to go by and clear the road out to the highway. They'll come past by mid-afternoon at the latest."

That wasn't good enough. Hope slipped a little, and Curtis braced her. Despite herself, she couldn't help appreciating his solid strength. "We have to leave well before that."

"What's the rush?"

"Raina is getting married on Sunday, and there's a lot to do before then. If she leaves Ben hanging at the altar, he'll kill me!"

She braced herself for Curtis's reaction. He'd probably say she was being overdramatic. He'd talk about safety. Point out that other wedding guests would have trouble reaching Bozeman, too.

Instead his pace slowed. "Where is the wedding taking place?"

"Bozeman. It's just a couple of hours from here, right?"

"Usually. Not in weather like this, though." Curtis plodded on through the deepening snow, and Hope walked with him, shivering when a gust of wind pelted her with snowflakes. He stopped in front of a wooden door leading into a house that seemed to emerge from the side of the hill.

"This is one of the tiny houses?" For a moment Hope forgot all about the wedding. The house was... magical.

Breathtaking even.

When she looked up, she found Curtis watching her again, his expression inscrutable.

"What?" she asked.

"Just when I stopped believing, here you are," he said softly.

Hope didn't know what to make of that, but she shivered again, more in awareness of the enigmatic man standing with her in the snow than from the cold.

"What... what does that mean?" she finally asked when the silence drew out too long.

"What it means is that I'll get your friend to the altar on time," he said. "I promise."

CHAPTER TWO

CURTIS OPENED THE door to the tiny house, reached inside to flick on the porch light and turned to find Hope pulling a planner out of her purse. It was a small, thick novel-size one covered in printed fabric, animals dotting a spring-green background. Curtis leaned closer. Were those... bison?

They couldn't be.

Before he could look again, Hope flipped it open to where a matching green ribbon marked a page filled top to bottom with a handwritten, but precise, to-do list. She moved into the entryway to take advantage of the light.

"Even if we get to Bozeman tomorrow, we're going to be hopelessly behind on everything. We'll have to leave well before dawn."

"We'll get there," Curtis said again—and meant it, even if Hope's bison-dotted planner had thrown him momentarily for a loop. He definitely needed to get to know this woman better. They had several days to Raina's wedding, anyway. He'd pop them in a truck and drive them there tomorrow. It would be slow going, but they'd get through.

He'd use the time it took to get them to Bozeman to his advantage. He was sure he could wrangle an invitation to the wedding from Raina, which would give him more time to chat with Hope. He'd find a local motel to stay at and make himself useful until the ceremony on Sunday. At the wedding reception, he'd dance with Hope. Weddings were romantic. Maybe she'd get carried away—

Or was that wishful thinking? He couldn't help but remember how things with Michele had turned out.

It's too late for romance, he reminded himself as they stepped inside. *Too late for anything like love. You've got to do what you've got to do.*

Under different circumstances he would have admitted he thought he could fall in love with a woman like Hope. At the very least, she was his type. As she passed him in the small space, close enough for him to catch the citrusy scent of her shampoo, Curtis's body responded with interest, and he diligently noted the hint of chemistry between them. That part would work, he had no doubt. Chemistry didn't get it done where marriage was concerned, though. He wanted more than that—

Hope let out an exclamation of pleasure when she took in the house's hardwood floors, white-washed walls and hand-carved accents.

"Curtis, it's wonderful. Whoever gets to live here is going to have a magical life."

Curtis forgot everything else when she touched his arm in her enthusiasm. Her eyes shone as she went over every little detail, and despite himself Curtis found himself moving closer.

"I sure hope so." So practical Hope wasn't all practical.

He was glad to know that. Glad to know, too, that she appreciated the work he'd done on this house. Clay had designed it, and helped to build it, too, but Curtis had put a lot of extra work into the home that was meant to be his. When Hope stroked a hand over the mantel of the fireplace, his skin tingled as if she'd touched him. Michele had eyed the place like it might be a jail cell. "It's so small" was all she'd said. At least he understood her reaction now.

Hope looked at her planner again, and the muscles at the back of his neck tightened. Who was she really? What was important to this woman?

"I need to make sure Raina calls Ben," she said apologetically. "We're supposed to be in Bozeman tonight, go over the plan for tomorrow, unpack and see if anything needs to be ironed, and—"

"Let me see that." Curtis, inspired, took the planner from her hands.

"Hey, give that back." Hope reached for it, but Curtis turned away from her. Beside each "to-do" was a time for the task to be performed and a perfectly drawn tiny square box to be filled in when she was done.

Curtis bent closer. She had an item for everything. Get up. Bathroom. Shower. Dry hair. Makeup. Some of the to-dos were in one-minute increments, for heaven's sake. Reason warred with curiosity in his mind, but curiosity won out. He had no choice but to pursue the possibility Hope represented. There simply wasn't time to find someone else.

Besides, he wanted to get to know her better. His body was responding to Hope's proximity in a way it never had to Michele.

"I said, give that back." Hope's voice slid up a notch.

"Hold on," Curtis said. Hell, this was why she was so uptight. She'd booked herself solid without a minute to spare, let alone an unexpected night-long stay at Base Camp.

"What are you doing?" she cried when he pulled the pen from its loop.

"I'm fixing your problem." He evaded her outreached hands and moved to brace the planner on the galley-style kitchen counter. Hope shrieked when he crossed out the list for the day and wrote in big block letters, "Check out bison herd with Curtis Lloyd." He checked the time on his phone and added, *eight-seventeen.* "Whoops, we're going to be late if we don't get down to the south pasture." He let her rip the book from his hands, and stifled a smile when she gazed at the page in horror.

"You crossed out my list!"

"I made a better one. Come on, let's go see those bison. If you're good, I'll let you fill in the little box when you're done."

FINE. SHE HAD a problem. A planner problem. An addiction to order that always drove less-organized humans who crossed her path to moan and tease and complain.

But no one—*no one*—had ever defaced her planner the way Curtis just had.

Hope was already plotting revenge.

No matter that Curtis was easily the most handsome man she'd ever met. Or that his mischievous smile had twisted her innards into a tangled mess of desire, the likes of which she hadn't felt since… since… well, ever.

Or that he was already leading her back out the door toward the bison herd that had consumed her with curiosity since she'd heard about its existence.

Any man—any *person*, she corrected herself; she didn't care that Curtis was a man, because she wasn't interested in men. Or she was, but not now—who didn't understand what kind of a sacrilege it was to write in another person's planner, let alone cross out her list!—was so far beyond the pale of good manners they might as well be a goat.

She was about to explain this to him when he stopped in his tracks and took her hand again before she walked right into him. "I think it's coming down harder," he said.

Distracted by the feel of his hand holding hers again, Hope had to scramble to catch up with what he'd said. She looked up. Took in the way the snow was sheeting down, realized how fast it was accumulating. "You're right."

"I'm always right," he said. "Come on. Let's go see those bison while we still can."

Hope resisted the urge to snort. *Always right.*

She knew Curtis was joking, though, and couldn't take offense, even though she was still bristling at what he'd done to her planner. All those items undone…

They'd stay undone the way things were going. This snowstorm wasn't kidding around.

All Hope could do was follow him as the realization sank in that she and Raina would be hard-pressed to go anywhere in the morning unless it stopped soon. Curtis must have heard her sigh. "Hey, I made you a promise. I said I'd get Raina to her wedding, and I meant it. Leave it to me, okay?"

"But—" Hope didn't like to leave things to chance.

"Relax. I've got this. You want to see the bison, don't you?"

"Are they out in this?"

"They're out in everything. Bison don't care about a little snow."

It took a long time to walk to the pasture, but Curtis kept hold of her, and Hope found herself relaxing a little. It wasn't like she could do anything else right now. Tomorrow they'd sort things out and get back on track. This wasn't the first Raina-induced disaster she'd negotiated.

When they reached the pasture, she couldn't see anything, and she swallowed her disappointment as Curtis scanned the area, until he put an arm around her waist, leaned close and said, "There!"

She followed the direction in which he was pointing and stared into the darkness until she made out large shapes moving toward them.

"They think I've got a treat."

Hope's throat tightened in awe as the shapes grew closer, their indistinctness coalescing into solid, shaggy beasts plowing slowly through the falling snow.

"They're so big," she whispered.

"They're really something, aren't they?"

She could only nod. She didn't mind that Curtis had put his arm around her waist, or that his hand rested on her hip. She didn't think she'd ever seen anything so beautiful as the herd crowding up to the fence. Sharing it with someone else made it more special.

"Hey," he said softly, and it wasn't until his gloved finger touched her cheek that Hope realized she was crying.

"I'm sorry. I'm being silly. It's just... I always wanted to see them again, since I was a little girl. I like to dream about what it was like here in North America before people arrived—when nature was alone."

"You're interested in history?"

"I'm interested in everything." That sounded stupid, but in the presence of the archaic beasts now clustering just feet away from them, Hope couldn't censor her words. It was the truth, after all. "If it has to do with nature, I'm in love with it."

He was going to laugh at her, she knew it. Everyone did—except Raina, which was one of the reasons she'd bonded to Raina for life. Even when they were little kids, Raina had honored her interests, bringing her birds' nests, interesting stones, dried leaves and flowers. She'd never made fun of Hope's collections. She'd followed Hope around for hours while Hope compared the items they found with photographs in identification books.

"You keep surprising me," Curtis said. He was looking at her again instead of the bison. Hope supposed he saw them every day.

"They look so soft."

"They're kind of wooly." Curtis reached in his pockets and pulled out an end of a carrot. "We're really not supposed to do this, but I can't help myself." He offered it to her.

"You mean—I can feed one?"

"Keep your hand absolutely flat and move it away as soon as the bison grabs the carrot. They aren't tame."

"Okay." Her heart beating hard, Hope stepped right up to the fence that surrounded the pasture, took off her glove, put the carrot stub in her palm and held out her hand.

Several bison eyed her nervously before one stepped forward.

It was over all too soon. The bison lipped the carrot into its mouth and crunched it up. Hope quickly pulled her hand away, then just as quickly reached out again and patted the bison's head.

"Hope!" Curtis lifted her right off the ground and whirled around before setting her down again far from the fence. "I just told you they aren't tame."

"I had to know what it feels like." She pulled her glove on again.

"I didn't figure you for being so reckless," he scolded her.

Reckless. Hope nearly laughed. No one had ever called her reckless.

She felt exhilarated, though, like her heart might leap from her chest and take wing. Like she was a child again.

"I think you've had enough excitement for one day," Curtis mock-grumbled. "Time to get you back to the bunkhouse."

"It was exciting," she admitted.

Curtis moved to face her and paused, resting his hands on her hips again, the strangest expression on his face. When he bent to kiss her, she found herself going up on tiptoe to meet him, then quickly pulling back when their mouths brushed. His kiss was whisper-soft, but that small taste of him had her pulse jumping, her body wanting more.

"I... I didn't mean to do that," she exclaimed.

"I did."

HE'D KISSED HER. He hadn't meant to do it, but he had, and now he didn't know whether to curse himself or pat himself on the back.

Hope had risen to meet him when he'd bent down, so she wasn't immune to him. Still, her instant disavowal of her intentions didn't bode well. He couldn't screw this up by going too fast. Time to change tactics.

"Let's go get that hot chocolate. You can tell Raina about the bison herd and the tiny house and check to make sure she called Ben." He congratulated himself for remembering Raina's fiancé's name. He needed to assure Hope he was paying attention and the kind of guy she could trust.

She nodded, and he led the way back, this time refraining from taking her hand. He'd let her make the next move. Any old little move would do.

Back inside the bunkhouse, they shucked off their outer clothes and found the rest of the inhabitants of Base Camp sitting on folding chairs in the main room. The cameraman focused on them instantly.

"I've got hot chocolate for you." Avery hopped up and returned moments later with two cups. "It should still be warm enough."

"What did you think of the house?" Raina asked Hope as she sat down.

"It's beautiful. So are the bison. You wouldn't believe—"

"You saw the bison?" Raina was almost as excited as Hope had been, and Curtis began to understand the relationship between these two women, who'd seemed at first to be so different. "You've always wanted to get close to bison! What were they like?"

"I got to feed one."

"You fed one?" Byron looked disappointed. "I knew I should have gone with you."

Curtis wondered what he would say if he knew about the kiss. The *Base Camp* camera people were always after them to keep the action on camera.

"You're not supposed to feed the bison," Avery admonished Curtis with an exasperated look.

"It was worth it," he said in a low voice and was rewarded with a smile. Avery knew darn well what he was up to.

"I got to pet it, too. Just for a second," Hope added.

"You pet one of the bison?" Avery shot Curtis another exasperated look.

"I told her it wasn't a good idea," he assured her.

"Curtis, did you know you just fulfilled one of Hope's bucket list items? Petting a bison. It's the first one she ever put down." She grabbed Hope's planner, flipped through a bunch of pages and held it up to show him.

She was right; on a page labeled, "Bucket List," item number one said, "Pet a bison."

When he met Hope's gaze, he found her smiling, a genuine grin that took years off her face. "I was ten when I made my first bucket list," she explained. "I've been transferring it from scraps of paper to diaries to planners ever since."

"It's tradition to keep that one in first place," Raina said. "It's the one that sums up everything Hope wants."

Curtis couldn't help smiling at Hope and Raina's excited chatter. When Hope had arrived, he'd found her attractive enough to take interest, but it was her animation about the natural world that was tugging at him in a different way.

"Drink your hot chocolate," Avery urged both of them.

"Avery's an amazing cook," Raina exclaimed.

"All I did was heat some milk." Avery laughed.

"That's more than I know how to do," Raina said seriously.

Curtis caught Hope's eye over Raina's head and raised an eyebrow. Hope shrugged but returned his smile. His heart did a funny little thump.

"Did you get a hold of Ben yet?" Hope asked Raina.

"I told him we're staying her overnight, and he was happy about it: he loves *Base Camp*, too, and he's down with all my plans. He said it's not too bad in Bozeman and the plows are running. The last of my family got in an hour ago, and planes are still landing at the airport."

"That's pretty typical," Avery said. "It can be fine there and horrible here. Something about the weather patterns."

"What do you mean, all your plans?" Hope asked.

"Oh, you know." Raina waved a hand airily. "He said go as slow as we need to tomorrow. He'll handle everything on his end. I told him I'd be there for our wedding but not to panic before then."

"He's only two hours away! Of course we'll get there before your wedding—that's not until Sunday!" Hope exclaimed.

"I know. But things can take time."

Was it Curtis's imagination, or was she scheming again?

"We'll get there tomorrow, won't we?" Hope asked

Curtis.

"Of course," Curtis said firmly.

HOPE RELAXED A little. As long as Ben knew what they were facing, maybe this was going to turn out okay. She had a hard time feeling upset about being here now that she'd had an up-close-and-personal experience with the bison. She'd pay for it with all the extra chores on her to-do list tomorrow, but it had been worth it. Like Raina said, petting a bison was a dream come true.

On the trip to Yellowstone she'd taken with her folks as a child, she'd had two magical experiences with animals. The first came as they'd driven down one of the interior roads of the park and come face to face with a bison.

The huge animal had stood its ground in the middle of the winding road, and Hope's father had kept one hand on the gear shift, the other on the steering wheel as they waited to see what would happen next. "If he comes at us, we'll have to back up. He could do a lot of damage to the car."

"He won't come at us," Hope had said from her position in the back seat. "As long as we give him space, he'll give us space, too." She couldn't say now why she'd been so sure back then, but she had been.

"You're probably right, honey."

She'd seen her parents exchange a look, but she'd kept her attention on the huge beast ahead of them. Even though twenty feet and the car's windshield separated them, she knew the bison was watching her, too. She'd felt like he had a message for her, but she'd struggled to comprehend it.

"He's looking right at you," her mother had whispered.

Hope had felt the gravity of that gaze. The bison was a wild creature, so solid and sure of itself. Its stare was implacable but not threatening at all. It was as if the creature was measuring her.

Hope had held her breath.

"What do you think he's thinking?" her mother had asked, her voice still low.

"He's thinking… I should be me, the way he's just him. I should be all the way Hope." There was more, but she hadn't been able put it into words. Something about the world being old and young and everything and only one thing. She'd wished she could get out of the car and get closer. Maybe then she'd understand.

"Sounds like a very wise bison," her father had said. Both parents had spent far more time watching her than the animal in the road ahead.

She couldn't say how long they sat there before the bison broke off eye contact with a toss of his head and ambled off the road. All she knew was that her parents were quiet for a long time after that, even after her father had started driving again.

That night they'd sat outside the tent talking after she'd gone to bed in her sleeping bag.

"She's got a big imagination," she'd heard her father say.

"She's spending too much time by herself," her

mother had countered. When they got home, her mother had enrolled her in Girl Scouts. Hope hadn't minded; her troop went on lots of camping trips.

"Has your root cellar been robbed again?" Raina asked the room at large, as if it was a normal question. Hope shook away thoughts of the past.

Greg answered without hesitation. "No, we haven't had any problems since it was robbed the first time."

"Are you still patrolling?"

"Yes. Jericho and I are about to go out—just as soon as Boone and Clay get in."

"Boone? He's coming here? He's one of my favorites on the show—" Raina broke off and blushed. "Sorry."

Right. The show. Hope had forgotten about that. She glanced up at the cameraman and looked quickly away again.

"Boone will be happy to hear he's got a fan," Greg said to Raina with a wink.

"I bet he's got a lot of fans. He's hot."

Hope turned on her friend. "Raina! Don't talk like that. What about Ben?"

Raina waved that off. "Ben says if he was a woman, he'd be hot for Boone, too."

Anders shook his head. "That's the hardest part about doing all this—knowing other people are watching—and judging."

"Anders, here, never wins the handsomest SEAL polls on the show's website," Curtis explained.

"You never do, either." Anders leaned back in his

chair and laced his hands behind his head.

"Really?" Hope clamped her mouth shut. Had she said that out loud?

Curtis grinned. "Unbelievable, huh?"

She *had* said it out loud. Hope took another sip of her hot chocolate to cover her embarrassment.

"You're cute," Raina told Curtis, giving him a once-over. "But Boone is all stern and manly. That's what gets the votes."

"Ouch." Curtis crossed his arms over his chest. "I can be stern and manly."

Laughter from several points around the room seemed to contradict that, but as far as Hope could see, Curtis was all man. He had a sense of humor, obviously, which she appreciated, but he was strong and decisive— and didn't Raina say all the men at Base Camp had been Navy SEALs?

Speaking of Raina, how could she sit there so unconcerned and banter with a bunch of men she'd never met, when she was on track to miss her own wedding rehearsal due to the blizzard of the century?

Hope took her planner back from Raina before remembering the only item left on today's page.

"Go ahead, cross it off," Curtis said. He leaned over, snagged a pen off the wooden desk that sat in the corner and handed it to her. "Or do you want me to do it?"

"I'll do it." She quickly filled in the box, feeling ridiculous.

"Don't forget to cross petting a bison off your

bucket list," Raina said. She leaned over and flipped to the right page. "There." She pointed to the little square. Hope filled that one in, too, with a sense of accomplishment even if she was squirming under everyone's attention.

"Now I'll just put that away for you until you finish your cocoa." Curtis took the little book from her hands—and sat on it.

"Hey!" Hope reached for it, then quickly pulled her hand back.

Raina laughed. "You catch on quick," she told Curtis. "That's the only way to get her to stop checking it."

The door opened, and two more men came in, stamping the snow from their boots and peeling off their jackets. Avery went to fetch more hot chocolate.

"Looks like we have guests," one of the men said, coming farther into the room.

"Boone!" Raina's shriek split the air. She scrambled to her feet.

Boone frowned. "I'm sorry, do I know—"

"Raina's a big fan of yours, Boone," Greg explained with a smile.

"Oh. Uh, nice to meet you, Raina." Boone didn't seem to know what to do with his hands, but ultimately he stuck one out to Raina and shook hers.

"Nice to meet you, too."

"Hi, Raina," the other man said.

"Hi, Clay. Glad to meet you, too."

Hope got up and shook hands, as well, still marveling at the way Raina knew all these people.

"Hope and Raina went off the road at the end of our lane. Curtis and Anders found them, luckily," Avery said, returning with two more mugs.

"I'm taking them to Bozeman tomorrow," Curtis added.

Boone laughed. "I doubt it. Have you seen it outside?"

"We'll get through," Curtis asserted.

"No, you won't," Boone contradicted. "Hope and Raina will just have to sit tight for a day or two with us—"

"No can do, Chief. I'm going to get them through."

"I need to reach my fiancé," Raina chirped.

"Fiancé?" Boone echoed.

"That's right; I'm getting married on Sunday!"

"Which is why I have to get Hope and Raina to Bozeman—tomorrow. Can't let Raina down—or Hope," Curtis said evenly. He caught Boone's gaze and held it.

"Hope doesn't have a fiancé," Raina added helpfully.

Boone's eyebrows shot up.

"She's never watched *Base Camp*. She knows nothing about any of this," Raina went on.

Hope watched the two men share a look. Without a word or even a gesture, they seemed to exchange a whole host of information. She wished she knew what the undercurrents running through the room were about. Boone nodded. "We'll talk about it again in the morning."

That seemed to pacify Curtis.

Speaking of the morning… if they were going to make an early start, they needed to rest.

Hope stood up. "Where are we going to sleep to-night?"

When the room fell silent and Curtis looked away, Hope turned to Raina. "Now what did I say wrong?"

"Anyone who isn't married sleeps right here, now that it's winter. Before the weather turned, we slept in tents outside." Avery was the one to answer.

"Here?" As far as she'd seen, this building possessed only three rooms: the kitchen, bathroom and the main room they were seated in now.

"On the floor. You don't get a tiny house until you marry one of the men," Raina said, as if that made all the sense in the world.

Why should it? Hope wondered. Nothing else had since they'd arrived at this crazy place.

To HER CREDIT, Hope hadn't complained once she understood the sleeping situation, and Curtis was impressed by how she'd gone along with the arrangement without asking questions. She and Raina had quickly got to work setting up their air mattresses and sleeping bags. Curtis gave Hope her planner back and helped them, and when things were settled, he wished them good-night.

He couldn't pretend the situation in the bunkhouse wasn't awkward. There were five unmarried men at Base Camp, all of them Navy SEALs who'd joined the project after they finished their service. There was only one unmarried woman living here currently. Avery had arrived with three friends around the same time Boone came to set up Base Camp last spring. Riley, Nora and Savannah had married already, but Avery was still waiting her turn. Per Fulsom's rules, each man was supposed to begin dating only when his 40 days came up. Curtis figured that was part of why Walker and Avery didn't act on their obvious attraction to each other.

There were rumors that something else was holding Walker back, though. Some kind of promise either he or one of his relatives had made long ago. Walker had never opened up about it to Curtis. Curtis hoped he sorted it out soon.

The men set up their bedrolls on the opposite side from the women, and soon the lights were out. All the men were used to primitive conditions from their years in the Navy and tended to fall asleep quickly. Curtis had suspected it took Avery longer to settle in most nights. He could never tell if Walker slept or not.

He'd long felt for the two. So close to each other... and yet so far.

Now he really sympathized.

It was more than distracting to know Hope was only a dozen feet away from him—and that he couldn't do anything to bridge that gap.

"Good night, Anders," Avery called out from the women's side of the room.

Curtis chuckled. He'd wondered if she'd go through her nightly ritual with two strangers here.

"Night, Avery," Anders called back.

"Good night, Greg."

"Night."

Curtis heard someone turn over in their sleeping bag. Was it Hope? It was dark in the bunkhouse, especially on this moonless night, but there weren't any curtains on the windows, and he could see the outlines of the others lying down around him.

"Good night, Angus."

"Good night, lass." Angus, who'd arrived back at the bunkhouse shortly before bedtime, always laid his Scottish accent on thick during this ritual.

"Good night, Curtis."

"Good night, John-Boy."

A woman's laugh greeted this reference to the old television show that had run long before Curtis was born. He'd only seen episodes on the internet. Was it Hope who had laughed?

He had a feeling it was Raina.

There was a long pause before Avery finished her nightly ritual by singing out, "Good night, Walker!"

Another long pause. So long Curtis swore he could tell Hope and Raina were holding their breaths.

"Night." It was one short, guttural sound, dragged out from the taciturn Native American just like always, but Curtis knew it made Avery's day.

It kind of made his, too. He didn't understand what was keeping those two apart, and he hoped like hell they figured it out soon.

Curtis didn't think he'd sleep a wink with Hope so

close by, but everyone at Base Camp worked hard, and when he opened his eyes again, it was morning, and several of the men and Avery were already up and about. A glance at the women's side of the room told him Raina was still sound asleep, but Hope, who'd slept in a T-shirt and yoga pants, was sitting up in her sleeping bag, her arms wrapped around her knees, contemplating the scene around her. Avery appeared from the bathroom, where she'd gotten dressed—with Walker's help. Avery had demanded he learn how to lace her in and out of her Regency outfit when all the rest of the women married, overriding all his protests with a temperamental, "By the time you lace me up, I'm already wearing a shift, which is more clothing than most women wear outside! Get over yourself!"

"Hope? The bathroom is free if you want to change," she said now, bending down to roll up her sleeping bag. Raina opened her eyes and sat up.

"Thanks." Hope hesitated. "Should I shower later when everyone else is done?"

"Go ahead now. Everyone else can wait."

"Morning," Hope said to Raina.

"Morning." Raina climbed out of her bag and began to root around in her suitcase. "Hurry up in the bathroom. My turn next."

The door opened again, and Kai and Addison Green walked in. Once again, Curtis made the introductions.

"Two more for breakfast," Kai noted, heading for the kitchen now that he'd stripped off his coat and gloves. "We'll have it ready in a jiffy." Addison greeted Hope and Raina and followed her husband.

"You'd better hurry up and take that shower," Avery said to Hope.

"I'll be fast," Hope said.

"I won't," Raina said cheerfully. "I'm going to see my fiancé today. Have to look my best."

IT WAS LIKE being in college again, Hope thought. If your college dorm was being filmed for a reality television show.

By the time she'd finished her shower and dressed, Byron the cameraman had his equipment ready. "We're going old-school today," he announced cheerfully, patting a video camera that rested on his shoulder. "It's just me, so let me know if you're going to do anything interesting."

As the other members of Base Camp filed in, Avery gave her a rundown of their names, jobs at the ranch and marital status. As far as Hope could tell, there were five married couples, five single men and Avery. All the women wore Regency gowns and were laughing about the difficulties of navigating through the snow in them.

The men were dressed like you'd expect men to dress on a ranch, but they mingled with the women as if they didn't even notice the stark contrast in clothing styles. They were all at ease with each other, which made sense if they'd been living in close quarters for over half a year, as Raina had explained.

The more Raina told her about the show these people were participating in, the more Hope had to admit she probably should be watching it. She was interested in many of the things they were trying to put into practice. She tagged along to the kitchen and listened with interest as Raina quizzed Kai and Addison about the way they cooked and helped to raise the food they'd be eating for breakfast, and then grilled Jericho on the various alternative energy systems they were using to power Base Camp. Raina moved on to Walker and Avery next, and Hope was treated to an expansive explanation of the care and feeding of bison from Avery, with about five additional words from Walker.

Savannah and Nora, two of the other women who lived here, finally explained to Hope about their dresses. "We came to get away from our busy lives so we could pursue artistic endeavors we'd put aside after college. We needed a way to guarantee we wouldn't start socializing with people in town instead of getting down to work, so we decided to get rid of our normal clothes and just have Regency things," Savannah told her.

"Of course, it didn't quite work the way we expected," Nora added. "But now we have the B&B, and it keeps us solvent while we write and paint and so on."

Next, Raina cornered Curtis. "You build tiny houses."

"That's right. Hope's already seen my handiwork."

"That was your work?" Hope was surprised into saying. Thinking back, she realized he'd mentioned it last night, but she'd been too busy looking at all the details to take that in. Her estimation of Curtis rose. "It was a beautiful house," she said truthfully. "Did you and Boone figure out how to get us to Bozeman?" she added.

Curtis had smiled at her praise, but he turned serious at her question. "We've got a plan, but I'm going to be blunt: it's going to be a slow journey. We've got a plow on our truck, but it's windy out there, and I expect there'll be drifts on the highway out of town.

Raina, who'd been flitting around like a butterfly all morning, wilted into a sad human being. "We have to make it! I promised Ben just this once I'd be on time!"

"I promised him, too." Hope didn't want to say what Ben had promised her in return. It was Raina's wedding that was important.

"It's going to take me about an hour to load up," Curtis said.

"An hour? What are you bringing?" It was only a two-hour drive to Bozeman from here, from what Hope had been able to glean from the internet. Maybe double if the snow slowed them down. They should be able to make it for a late lunch.

"I'm bringing everything," Curtis said firmly. "This is Montana, and we're in the middle of a blizzard. I'm not taking the two of you out there unless I know we can survive everything Mother Nature might decide to throw at us. Got it?"

Unease crept into her belly. She nodded but for the first time wondered if they were doing the right thing. A glance at Raina's face reminded her how important it was to her friend not to let her future husband down.

While the rehearsal dinner wasn't until Saturday, tonight they were supposed to dine with Ben's grandparents. It was the first event of the weekend.

"We'll be ready," she promised him. "Thank you," she added. He might be a desecrator of planners, but if it wasn't for Curtis, they wouldn't stand a chance of making it through.

"I'll be ready, too," Byron said.

"You're not serious." Curtis straightened up until he towered over the younger man, who was all arms and elbows, not quite grown into his lanky body.

"You know how this works," Byron said with a shrug. "Renata's orders. I go where the excitement goes."

"No. Absolutely not. If something happens out there, I'll barely be able to get the women to safety. I can't single-handedly save three of you."

"I won't need saving!" Byron put his hands on his hips. "I'll have you know I was an Eagle Scout!"

Curtis heaved a sigh. "You're not coming."

"Am, too."

"Better call Ben and tell him we'll be leaving soon," Hope told Raina quietly, urging her away from the men.

"Okay."

Hope bent to pack up her things, a quick task since she hadn't taken much out from her suitcase. Raina joined her a few minutes later.

"I can't get through." She showed Hope her phone. "I've got no signal anymore."

Hope pulled out her phone and checked. "Me, neither."

Avery, close by, checked hers, too, and shook her head. "This always happens during storms," she said.

"I texted him earlier just to check in. I hope he isn't worried," Raina said.

"We'll get service once we're out on the road," Hope assured her. Curtis and Byron were still arguing.

"I wish you two could stay longer," Avery said wistfully. "It's no fun being the only woman here who's single."

"I wish we could stay longer, too. I'm going to make Ben bring me back as soon as I can," Raina said. "We won't be too far away, living in Bozeman."

Hope's heart squeezed as Avery and Raina swapped contact information. Raina would live closer to Avery than her now. A lot closer—at least until Hope scored a job at Yellowstone.

She'd simply have to impress Scott Leahy, she told herself. She'd hardly ever see Raina if she stayed in Skokie. She frowned at all the changes she'd need to make in her planner.

"Hope? Can I get your contact information, too?" Avery asked.

"Of course." Gratitude rushed through her. Hope had to admit that when it came to making friends, Raina far outshone her. She wouldn't have been surprised if Avery hadn't asked.

"You'll have to come visit. A lot. I think you belong at a place like this," Avery said.

"Really? Why?" Hope snapped her mouth shut, realizing she'd been rude, which was exactly why people preferred Raina to her. Raina would have agreed and been making plans to move in already. Her problem was that she always held back.

"Aren't you interested in sustainable living?"

"Yes."

"There you go. You're smart. Hardworking. You were fine with sleeping on the floor last night. You'd fit right in."

Hope couldn't account for the glow Avery's words touched off inside her. To fit right in here—that sounded heavenly. Base Camp was just the kind of place she'd love to live.

But it wasn't in her plans. Curtis and Byron must have sorted things out. Curtis was leaving the bunkhouse, his jaw set, his mouth a thin, hard line. Had Byron won?

"I'll come visit," she said without really meaning it. As much as the place intrigued her, it would kill her to be on the outside of something like this looking in. Avery pursed her lips, but she didn't push.

It was past eight o'clock by the time they were loaded in one of the big, powerful trucks the inhabitants of Base Camp shared. Hope opened her planner and looked sadly at the list for the day. She wouldn't be able to tick off any of these tasks until they made it to Bozeman.

Whenever that was.

The men and women of Base Camp crowded around to tell them goodbye and to wish them well.

Hope had already given Avery a hug. "Thanks for everything; you made us feel at home. I promise I'll watch the show from now on."

"Good. You make sure to come back and see us soon. I loved having you here."

Daisy sat in the footwell next to Hope's feet. Hope scratched the yellow dog behind her ears absently, wondering if they were doing the right thing setting out in all this snow. It was falling lazily now, but it had been coming down quite quickly just a half hour ago. Maybe it would ease up and stop altogether.

Curtis seemed to know what she was thinking. He reached over, took her gloved hand in his and squeezed it before returning his to the wheel. "I'll get you there. I promised, right?"

"Right." Hope turned to smile encouragingly at Raina, who sat in the back seat of the extended cab with Byron, all the man's equipment between them. "Here we go."

"I can't wait to see Ben!" Raina bounced excitedly.

"Shoot, I forgot the hot coffee Kai made for us," Curtis said. "Byron, go grab it off the desk in the bunkhouse, would you?"

"Sure." Byron sprang out and hotfooted it toward the building.

Curtis reached back and pulled shut his door. With a roar of the engine he backed up, executed a quick three-point turn and drove down the lane.

"What about Byron?" Raina cried.

"Hey!" Byron yelled faintly, running after them.

Everyone else watched them go in shock.

"What about him?" Curtis said and kept going.

HOPE WASN'T SURE what to think about the way Curtis had left the young cameraman behind. "Won't your director be mad?" Byron had made a fuss about coming, after all.

"Renata isn't my priority. You are." He glanced in the rearview mirror. "You and Raina," he amended.

"There's plenty of room back here for Byron." Raina didn't sound pleased. She tended to get attached to anyone she met—especially strays and those less fortunate. Byron had the youthful recklessness of a puppy, so Hope wasn't surprised Raina had latched on to him.

Speaking of puppies, though... "Daisy, go see Raina," she told the dog at her feet. Maybe that would distract her.

Daisy climbed over the seat into Raina's open arms good-naturedly. Curtis sent Hope a smile. "Good idea," he said in a low voice.

She only nodded, distracted by the view through the windshield. As soon as they'd turned at the end of the lane onto the country highway, the wind had begun to drive the snow nearly sideways across the road ahead of them.

"How can you see anything?" This was going to be harder than she thought.

"I'm used to bad weather, but I'm going to take it slow. Settle in; it's going to be a long day."

Hope quickly realized Curtis was right. The falling snow made visibility nearly impossible, and when they reached the main highway what seemed like hours later, the snowdrifts became the real issue, rather than the accumulation. It looked like a plow had been by at some point, but in places Curtis had to veer into the left lane to get through.

She thanked their lucky stars Boone had helped Curtis put chains over the truck's winter tires, but still they slipped and slid as the truck pushed forward along the road. They were crawling down the highway, and more than once Curtis braked and turned the wheel quickly to get back on track. Hope gripped the armrest—she was having trouble seeing where the road ended and the shoulder began.

They didn't speak much. Hope was impressed by Curtis's concentration. Now and then he asked her or Raina a question, but even Raina seemed to understand that it was important not to distract him.

Hope pulled out her cell phone—

But she still didn't have service.

If they did go off the road, they could be in trouble.

The minutes ticked by into an hour, and she wasn't sure they'd made much progress. Curtis was right; the plows had been by here—but it must have been ages ago. While the level of snow on the road was lower than it had been on the other one, it was quickly piling up again as the blizzard continued.

They crept along, only seeing headlights of a plow going the other way once. No one else seemed to be on the road.

Curtis, who had joked around plenty last night, was dead serious now. In the back seat of the extended cab, Raina was curled into a ball, solemnly watching the snow outside her window. Their slow progress and the whirling white had almost lulled Hope to sleep when Raina lurched upright and screamed, "Stop. Stop!"

Curtis jerked. The truck hit an icy patch and skidded.

"Hold on!" Curtis yelled, spinning the wheel and trying to control their trajectory. The truck slid one way and then the other before coming to rest askew halfway off the road.

Before the truck had come to a complete halt, Raina undid her seat belt, fumbled at the door and burst out a half second later, Daisy following at a flat-out run, barking all the way.

"Raina—what are you—?"

"Daisy, get back here!" Curtis hollered.

Hope could only gape as Raina dashed back the way they'd come. Curtis swore and put the truck in reverse, but the wheels spun and the truck didn't move. Hope reached back and pulled the door mostly shut, but sat half-turned in her seat trying to see where Raina was going. Curtis threw the truck into drive, edged his foot down on the gas, and the truck rolled forward an inch or two. Hope braced herself; they were about to go right into the ditch—or where one would be if it wasn't covered in snow.

Curtis reversed again.

The wheels spun.

"Better get out and get clear," he said.

Hope did so, leaving him to extricate the truck, racing to find Raina and Daisy, who'd all but disappeared in the driving snow behind them. Her boots sank almost to the top, and she whimpered as some of the ice-cold precipitation made its way inside.

"Raina!"

Daisy barked several times, and Hope followed the sound.

"Raina!"

"Hope! Come here!"

Hope's heart squeezed in relief as she caught up to Raina and found her safe and sound, a large, bright red plastic sack in her arms. Daisy ran circles around her ankles, whining and yipping.

"What is that?"

"Help me get it open! Hurry!" Raina shrieked.

Hope lurched forward to help, her heart in her mouth when she realized the sack was writhing. A sudden fury gripped her. Something was alive in there. Something that had been discarded like trash by the side of the road in a brutal snowstorm. What if it was—?

She pulled the sack from Raina's arms, dropped to her knees and set it on the ground, scrabbled at the twine that held it shut and finally ripped off her gloves to get more leverage at the icy fastening.

Raina knelt beside her and helped her steady the shifting bag. A soft mewling from inside drove equal parts relief and anger through Hope. It wasn't a baby.

Thank God it wasn't a baby.

But it was still one of God's creatures—

Hope fought to get the bag open.

Finally, she worked one loop of the twine off, and then the slack made it easy to get the rest free. "Careful," she told Raina. "We don't want it to run away. Let's get back to the truck." They carried the bag together awkwardly, Hope realizing there was more than one creature inside, and made it to where Curtis now had the truck safely on the road.

"Hurry up," he called. "Someone could come barreling at us and hit us before they even saw we were here. What the hell is that?" he added as the two women lugged the bag into the back of the extended cab, and Hope managed to shut the doors behind them after Daisy leaped inside, too. Only when Curtis had begun to drive slowly down the road again did she open the sack and peer inside.

"Kittens!" Raina cried, looking over her shoulder. "Four—no five." Her voice broke on the last word, and Hope saw why. Four of the tiny animals were moving and mewling, climbing over each other in a pathetic search for warmth and comfort. A fifth was lying still in the bottom of the bag. "Hope," Raina's cry slid upward. "Do something!"

Hope was already in motion. She scooped the lively ones out of the sack and handed them to Raina.

"Wrap them up in your scarf, keep them warm," Hope said. Raina quickly obeyed, gathering the four little bundles of fur into her lap and twining her fuzzy wool scarf around them.

"Daisy, down. Get in the front seat," Hope commanded as she pulled out the fifth kitten. Daisy sat but continued to watch the squirming bundles in Raina's arms and the limp little shape in Hope's, refusing to jump into the front seat. Hope met Curtis's gaze in the rearview mirror and braced for his scorn that they'd wasted their time saving the animals when it was obvious they hadn't been wanted.

"Put that one inside your jacket," he said. "Close to your heart. If it's alive, that might help."

"I don't think it's alive." But she was already following his instructions.

"The others are. You never know."

Grateful for his optimism, Hope cradled the small animal against her chest and zipped up her down jacket around it. Daisy whined again, and Hope would swear she was worried about the little creatures.

Raina cooed to the kittens she held, rocking them gently in her arms. Curtis turned up the heat in the cab, and Hope gently stroked the limp kitten with a finger. "Come on, little one," she whispered. "Fight."

CHAPTER THREE

K ITTENS.

Curtis sighed and kept his eyes on the road. Kittens were his Achilles' heel. He loved dogs, especially Daisy, who'd adopted him on sight, but kittens tugged at his heartstrings in a way few animals could match.

They were so vulnerable. So… furry. So damn cute. He knew the world was full of cats, but that didn't stop him from appreciating the little bundles of mischief.

He knew he needed to pay attention as he inched forward, his vision blinded by the heavy precipitation, but he couldn't help looking back at where the two women were hunched over their furry charges.

Where the hell had they come from on a day like this? Had someone set out to deliver them to the pound and given up part of the way there, consigning them to death on the side of the road rather than taking them back home again?

He couldn't stand the thought of it.

Raina literally had her hands full trying to keep the kittens from climbing right out of her lap. Hope was whispering to the limp little bundle tucked inside her coat.

"Will Daisy hurt the kittens?" Raina asked him.

"I don't think so." He glanced back to check that Daisy was still sitting politely in the space by Hope's feet. Her interest in the goings-on was clear, but while she was watching all the activity avidly, she wasn't getting too close.

"I'm going to see if they'll drink something." Raina searched around in her backpack for a bottle of water. She poured a tiny bit into the palm of her hand and held it near to one of the kittens in her lap. It sniffed at her hand but didn't drink.

"They're too little for that," Hope told her. "Dip a piece of cloth in and see if you can get the kittens to suck it."

Curtis concentrated on the road. Silence filled the back seat. Even Daisy kept quiet. As the minutes stretched on, Curtis's heart sank.

A sudden cheer from both women made him jump.

"One of them is suckling," Hope told him excitedly. "Raina, make another piece of cloth for me. Let's see if that wakes up this guy."

"We need to find a vet," Raina said, but Curtis could tell she was fishing around for another piece of cloth.

"Where are we going to find one of those?"

"In Bozeman," Curtis said. "We can't get off the highway any sooner; we might not be able to make it back on."

"Come on, little guy," Hope crooned at the kitten

she was holding. "Come on. You can do it."

"Can't you drive any faster?" Raina asked Curtis.

"I'll try." But the snow was falling harder than ever.

HOPE DIDN'T REALIZE she was crying until a tear splashed onto the nose of the kitten she was cradling and it jerked, its tiny eyes opening in surprise. She sucked in a breath. He *was* still alive.

"Raina. Raina!" she cried.

"Oh, my goodness!" Raina passed her a handkerchief dripping with water, and Hope stuck one corner into the little creature's mouth. To her surprise, the kitten immediately began to suckle.

"It's working!"

"Curtis, he's doing it," Raina exclaimed. "Edgar's doing it!"

"Edgar?" Hope asked with an unsteady chuckle. She met Curtis's gaze in the mirror again, not ashamed he might see the tears on her cheeks. After all, he'd already seen her cry once. The kitten was alive, and that was miracle enough to celebrate.

"His name's Edgar," Raina told her firmly.

"I need more water." Of course Raina would have named the kittens already.

For a long time they passed the handkerchief back and forth, Raina taking turns to feed the other kittens while Hope concentrated on the one tucked into her shirt.

"Maybe they were just dehydrated," Hope said as Edgar wriggled around in her jacket.

"Feldspar's doing the best of mine." Raina indicated a tortoiseshell-colored kitten who was climbing over the others to get at the handkerchief she held. "Minna, Louise and Reggie can't keep up."

"I wish we had food for them. Or at least milk."

"We'll get some when we can," Curtis assured her from the front seat.

Hope was grateful he was here to drive. It took both her and Raina to wrangle the cats. She found her gaze straying to the mirror again and again, though, watching Curtis when he wasn't looking. He was concentrating so fiercely on the road he didn't even realize she was staring.

He was a good man.

They were very lucky to have found him.

It occurred to Hope as the miles passed that she didn't know what they'd do with the kittens when they reached Bozeman. Would Ben be willing to take in five felines? How long would it take before he and Raina found a house?

She couldn't take on a cat right now—not with her future up in the air the way it was. She supposed she could bring one back to Skokie, but not to Yellowstone. Who knew what her quarters would be like there.

This wasn't the right time to be forming any new attachments—to cats or men.

She glanced at Curtis again, noticing the way his eyes scanned the road constantly. He was alert for any sign of trouble. Ready to take action if a problem came up. Unlike Raina, he was an asset in an emergency.

All man.

She couldn't pretend she wasn't attracted to him—she was. Normally Hope considered herself to have a very good head on her shoulders. She judged potential dates on their intelligence, job prospects, whether they donated to good causes and were up-to-date on current events. She was a modern woman and expected any man she was with to be socially conscious and smart, too.

Hope didn't know enough about Curtis to judge his mental acuity or even his political leanings—although if he was dedicating his life to sustainable processes, she supposed that told her something about his view of the world. It wasn't any of that which attracted her though.

It was Curtis himself. His... essence.

No, that was far too *New Agey* to be the right word. It was his presence that had hooked her. His solidity. The way his hands gripped the wheel. The way he sat in his seat like nothing could shift him. The way he glanced at her in the mirror from time to time. Something in her that was purely female was reacting to the part of him that was purely male.

Pheromones? Maybe. Whatever was happening to her felt like a chemical reaction—or rather, a biological one. Something so basic it eluded thought and consciousness. She wanted to touch him. To try him out.

A flush spread through her veins, and suddenly she was far too hot in her parka. She could imagine ways to try Curtis out. Ways that left her breathless and sure her cheeks were tinged with red.

A fine time for her hormones to go haywire. It must be all the talk about weddings and forever. Raina had been a tizzy of love and matrimonial excitement for nearly a year. Hope had taken it all in, and now she was being overwhelmed by it. Her fantasies about Curtis were just that—fantasies. She knew nothing about him, and she never would.

Would there be men like him at Yellowstone when she was ready to look for love a decade from now? Or would the guys in the park be self-absorbed, the way most of the men she met seemed to be? She hadn't had much luck in the dating department.

Raina had done far better for herself.

It didn't matter, Hope told herself. In a few more hours, they'd reach their destination and she'd say goodbye to Curtis. She'd become a park ranger two years early, which meant she'd be ready to look for love in… eight years.

Glancing down, Hope's heart seized when she saw Edgar's eyes were closed again, the handkerchief slack in his mouth. Then she took in the rise and fall of his flanks; he was breathing deeply.

Asleep.

Hope leaned back, let loose the breath she'd been holding and soaked in the sweetness of his soft little weight resting on her chest. She hoped he'd grow stronger soon.

Even if she couldn't keep him.

She wouldn't worry about that now. Plenty of time for all that later, when they reached Bozeman. Along with everything else she and Raina needed to do before the wedding.

Shifting slightly, she reached for her planner, never far from her. Opening it to the correct page, she sighed to see how off-schedule they were.

Curtis met her gaze in the mirror. "Something wrong?" he asked softly.

Hope realized Raina's kittens were sleeping, too.

"We're late, we haven't gone to the dress fitting, or stopped at the florists, or—"

"Relax," Raina said. "We've met Curtis and saved five kittens. That's what really matters."

Hope opened her mouth to disagree...

And realized she was right. Despite all the reasons it wasn't a good time to allow romance into her life, meeting Curtis had already changed her. Already got her thinking about things outside her life plan.

Her gaze flicked up to Curtis's again. He smiled, and her heart flip-flopped.

No, she told herself. *No, no, no.*

Her heart didn't want to seem to listen.

CURTIS GLANCED IN the mirror again when Raina said, "You might as well put that planner away, Hope. We can't accomplish anything on this ride."

"I can reschedule all the things we missed."

Raina made a noise that made Curtis bite back a smile. "You should see her," she said to him in exasperation. "I swear she plans when to go pee."

"Raina! I do not."

"Do, too." Raina adjusted the kittens in her lap. "She plans when to get up, when to go to bed, when to eat, when to exercise, when to work, when to read. It's a good thing she doesn't have a boyfriend or she'd plan when to f—"

"Raina!"

Hope's face was crimson. Curtis decided he wouldn't mind if she scheduled when to fuck him in that book—

But no, he wanted a lot more than a quickie with Hope. He needed a bride, but it wasn't just that. He found he couldn't stop watching her, especially when she'd bent over Edgar, nursing him back to health. When she'd been worried the kitten wouldn't make it, a crease had furrowed her brow and her jaw had set in a determined line that told him she didn't give up easily when life thwarted her.

Hope was a woman who fought for what she wanted. If he had her on his side—

She wouldn't leave him standing at the altar.

He sure as hell wouldn't leave her.

He forced his gaze back to the road, the raw ache in his heart far too powerful an emotion for the short amount of time he'd been around Hope. He didn't know anything about her except that she cared for kittens. And for friends. He'd wager she'd fight a battle or two for Raina's sake any day.

She was loyal. Loving. Committed.

Those were things he wanted in a wife, Curtis admitted. When he'd first realized Fate had deposited a 'single woman in his way last night, he'd been thinking practically. He needed a wife, and here Hope was.

Now… well, now he had to admit he was curious about Hope herself. What was important to her? What did she want from life?

How would she feel in his bed?

Curtis stifled a groan. It didn't help he'd been celibate these past six months and more, even when he was planning a future with Michele. Neither of them had even brought up sex, which should have told him a lot, he supposed. Now his body, already on alert because of the need to find a wife, was going all kinds of crazy so close to Hope. He couldn't help the leap his mind made from thinking about marrying Hope to thinking about what else he could do with her.

She'd feel good in his arms; he knew that already. She'd… fit.

How would a woman who clung to her planner like a lifeline react to an unexpected wedding, though? Would she rise to the occasion, or panic?

When he let her know he was interested, would she meet him halfway, or run like hell?

He supposed he was going to find out.

Soon.

"I STILL CAN'T get reception." Raina pocketed her phone again. "I want to tell Ben what's happening. He must be worried."

"He knows we're doing our best to get there," Hope assured her, but Raina was right. Those two talked all the time. Ben would be worried about his bride.

"I want to text Avery, too. I wonder how Byron's doing."

"He's fine," Curtis said shortly. "Believe me, you don't want him here filming everything you do and say."

"You shouldn't have left him behind," Raina retorted. "It was mean."

Curtis was quiet a minute, and Hope eyed him surreptitiously, wondering what he was thinking.

"Raina—this isn't a Sunday drive. We're taking a risk heading to Bozeman in this storm. A big risk."

"We're doing fine," she said stubbornly. "And we've got all his equipment. He can't even film things back at Base Camp."

Curtis ignored that last bit. "But if something happens, I've got the means to get three of us to safety. I couldn't guarantee I could get four of us there. I didn't leave him behind to be mean. I left him behind so he'd be safe."

"Nothing's going to happen to us," Raina said. "It's my wedding on Sunday. That's not the way things work."

Curtis made a strangled sound but didn't answer, and Hope could practically see the struggle going on inside him. A muscle worked in his jaw, and she braced for an outburst. Curtis had served for years as a Navy SEAL. She'd bet he'd seen situations that didn't work out the way he'd wanted them to.

"Raina, I'm sure Curtis—"

"If he can pack for three, he can pack for four,"

Raina said.

Hope turned in her seat and looked through the back window to the bed of the truck. A tarp was tied down tightly over its contents, which she noticed for the first time were bulkier than she'd expect for a four-hour trip.

"What do you have back there?" she asked Curtis.

"Like I said before, everything we could possibly need." His voice was tight.

Raina huffed out an impatient breath. "As soon as we reach Bozeman, we need to find that vet," she said to Hope.

"After we find Ben," Hope countered. "Ben, vet, tailor, rehearsal."

"Yes, ma'am," Raina drawled.

Curtis chuckled from the front seat, and Hope was relieved that the tension in the cab had diminished somewhat. "She sounds like my old drill-master," he said to Raina.

"You have no idea," Raina told him. "There's no screwing around when Hope's nearby."

Hope appreciated the attempt Curtis was making to distract Raina. "I made Ben a promise. Raina isn't so good with time management."

"That's true; I tend to be a little late most of the time," Raina agreed, bending down to inspect a kitten that was wriggling around.

"A *little* late." Hope snorted. "More like a lot. Her fiancé knows there isn't a chance she'd make it to her wedding on time without me to make sure she's there."

"Ben bribed Hope to get me there," Raina said cheerfully.

"Oh, yeah? How'd he do that?" Curtis asked.

Hope wasn't sure why she was embarrassed all over again. After all, she did deserve some incentive for putting up with Raina's eccentricities.

Raina answered before she could. "He's setting her up with his best friend."

Hope caught Curtis's frown and wanted to throttle Raina. "Not like that," she assured Curtis, although she didn't know why she felt the need to explain herself to him. "For a job."

"What kind of job?" Curtis sounded suspicious.

"A park ranger job," Raina answered. "Hope's going to spend the rest of her days in Yellowstone, lost to all good company forever."

"Not forever." Hope got a hold of herself. Raina really could try her patience. "I've always wanted to be a park ranger," she told Curtis. "It's really hard to get a position in Yellowstone. Ben's friend might be able to help me."

"Got it."

Curtis was gruff, and Hope could have kicked Raina when she chimed in, "I think Scott will fall head over heels with Hope as soon as he sees her and ditch his current girlfriend. Wouldn't a Yellowstone park ranger wedding be sweet?"

"Raina!" She looked up to see Curtis watching her in the mirror again.

"Is that what you want? A Yellowstone park ranger

wedding?" he asked.

"No! I've never even met Scott. Besides, I don't want a man at all. I'm concentrating on my work. I want to help restore the ecology of the park."

"And find a hot ranger to share your sleeping bag. She hasn't had a date in ages," Raina informed Curtis.

Before Hope could stop herself, she pictured sharing a sleeping bag with Curtis.

The image lingered in her mind longer than it should have.

She shut her eyes. When she opened them again and met his gaze in the mirror, his interest was plain to see.

But she couldn't fall for Curtis—or for any rangers, either. No more deviating from the plan. For now, that meant getting Raina to her wedding and pleading her case to Ben's friend.

Winning the job of her dreams.

Even if it meant leaving Curtis behind.

CHAPTER FOUR

"WE MUST BE close to Bozeman now," Raina chirped from the back seat sometime later.

Curtis didn't have the heart to correct her, but he had a feeling Hope knew what he didn't say out loud. They were crawling down the highway, and he didn't think they'd gone more than eight miles since they'd stopped to rescue the kittens. He could barely stay on the road, and if conditions got any worse, they'd have to stop until a real snowplow overtook them.

If one ever did.

"I think we've still got a few hours," Hope said quietly.

Curtis glanced back. She was stroking Edgar's head, cradling the kitten under her chin. Daisy was crouched in the space between the front and back seats, her head on the cushion, watching the two women and the sleeping kittens. Curtis sent up a silent prayer of thanks she wasn't a more boisterous dog.

Raina shifted. "I'm sure—"

"Watch out!" Hope shouted.

Curtis turned forward, spun the wheel to avoid a parked car that appeared out of the swirling flakes and slammed the truck's brakes, skidding and coming to a stop some yards beyond it.

"There's someone out there," Raina cried.

Curtis caught sight of a tall figure, muffled against the driving snow, approaching the truck. He swore under his breath, wrenched the door open, climbed out and quickly shut it again to conserve the heat inside the cab.

"That's a damn fool place to stop your car," he shouted at the man. Ice cold flakes of snow feathered into his eyes, nose and mouth. A frigid wind whipped his exposed skin.

"It's stuck. I went off the road and got the right front wheel in the ditch. Can you help me out?"

Curtis followed the stranger to check out the situation. "You're in too deep. I'm not going to be able to get you out of that. You'll need a tow. Better ride with us."

The man shook his head. "Come on, man, you've got a truck. Pull me out."

"I don't think—"

"I'll make it worth your while." To Curtis's surprise, he pulled out a wallet and began counting bills. "I'm in a hurry," the man said as the wind tried to whip his words away. "My name's Barton. Blake Barton. I'm about to miss an important meeting. Besides, I'm not leaving my Jag out here."

"That Jaguar's not going—"

"You need more? Here. Take it all." Blake waved more money at him.

Curtis took it. What the hell. If this greenhorn wanted to drive a sports car in the snowstorm of the century, more power to him.

He walked back to the truck, unhooked a rope, lifted the tarp covering all the equipment in the bed, pulled a chain out of the back and got to work, stopping to inform the women what he was doing.

"We don't have time for this." Hope waved her planner at him.

"I'll make it quick," Curtis told her.

Forty-five minutes later, however, Curtis had no choice but to offer Blake a lift again. The Jaguar sat on level ground, but the front axle had been badly bent.

"Fine," Blake said caustically. "I'll take a ride."

As if he was the one doing them a favor, Curtis thought.

"Aren't you forgetting something?" Blake added, his hand out.

Curtis fished the bills he'd handed over out of his pocket and gave Blake half.

"Where the rest?"

"I'm keeping it. Pain and suffering," he added without any more explanation.

Blake shut his mouth with a snap and stalked to Curtis's truck. Pulling open the passenger side door, he bent to enter, then recoiled as quickly as Daisy bounded over the console into the front seat to check him out.

"It's like a zoo in there!"

"We've picked up some other unexpected passengers," Curtis acknowledged and climbed in on his side.

"Lunchtime," Raina greeted him cheerfully.

Curtis took in the picnic basket Kai and Addison had handed them when they'd left the bunkhouse and the food she'd spread out among the seats. The kittens, now awake again, were doing their best to escape her lap and check it out, too.

Hope sent him an apologetic look. "Raina was hungry."

"So are Minna, Louisa, Reggie and Feldspar," Raina said.

"I'm hungry," Blake said, perking up.

"Fine. Let's eat. But I'm going to keep going. I don't want to be out here after dark."

"ARE YOU MARRIED?" Raina was asking Blake when Hope managed to pack up the last of the food into the basket. She put it back among Byron's camera gear, wondering how he was getting by without it. Edgar was definitely more chipper now that she'd fed him more water mixed with a little sugar Curtis had unpacked from somewhere. The other kittens were getting downright rambunctious. Daisy seemed to have decided it was her job to herd them back into Raina's lap whenever they escaped. She accomplished this by nudging them with her nose and whining to get Raina's attention. Raina was so busy grilling Blake she seemed to have little bandwidth for anything else.

"No," Blake said. "No time for that. I'm an investment broker. I work with clients with significant wealth. Travel all over the world. Never in the same place for more than a few days."

"I'm getting married. Just as soon as we reach Bozeman."

"We're never going to reach Bozeman," Blake said gloomily, peering out of the windshield at the snow hurtling down from the heavens. Unwrapped from his coat and hat, he'd turned out to be tall and thin, with sharp features and a way of beetling his brows in concentration.

"Curtis will probably get married soon, too. He's a settling-down kind of guy," Raina went on.

Hope considered him. Was that true?

"Hell," Curtis muttered, leaning forward in his seat.

"What's wrong?" Hope couldn't keep her worry out of her voice. Were they lost?

No, they couldn't be—all they had to do was follow the highway to Bozeman.

"I know that turnoff." He pointed out the windshield, and Hope strained to make out an off-ramp leading from the highway. She hadn't even seen a sign. "It goes to Reeve's pass. Nothing up there but some hunting cabins and summer places. We're not even as far as I thought we were."

"You need to drive faster," Blake said.

"You want us to land in the ditch like you did?"

"No, but I could walk faster than you're driving."

"You can walk any time you want to—"

"Curtis, look!" Raina pointed at the faint glow of

lights ahead on the highway. Curtis slowed even further.

"Hell," he said again. Hope knew why. A cordon of orange cones and blinking lights directed traffic off the highway.

Hope read the signs. "Detour—avalanche ahead. Detour? How much time is it going to add to our trip?" She had a feeling she wouldn't like his answer.

"Looks like we're not going to make the trip." Curtis's fingers tightened on the steering wheel. "If we follow those arrows, we won't be heading to Bozeman. This detour takes us back the way we came."

The inhabitants of the truck were silent as they took this in.

"Not... going to Bozeman?" Raina looked from him to Hope. "But... we have to go. Isn't there any way around?" She pulled out her phone, but Hope could see she still wasn't getting reception.

"Like I said, they're routing us back the way we came—"

"There has to be a way! Hope—"

Hope wished she could tell Raina it was all going to be okay, but as hard as they'd tried to get through, it didn't look like they were going to make it today.

"It's too dangerous to keep going, honey. We tried. I'm sure the snow will melt tomorrow, and we'll get through then." She wasn't at all sure that was true, but she had to hold out hope.

"But I'll miss my dinner with Ben's grandparents! And what if it doesn't melt? Hope, I promised Ben—"

"Ben will understand. He's a reasonable man." It

wasn't like it snowed this way all the time, but Hope's stomach was knotting up. She should have known they were cutting it close. She should have insisted they leave several days early. Raina was the one who had wanted to work until the last minute, and now Hope knew why. She must have given notice at her preschool job when she learned Ben's project was being extended. Hope knew how much Raina loved the kids at her school and how hard it must have been to say goodbye.

"I just wanted not to let him down—just once." Raina twisted her hands together in her lap as the kittens swarmed over her.

Hope glanced at Curtis and caught him watching Raina in the rearview mirror. She couldn't decipher his expression, but suddenly he put the truck in gear and began to back up.

"What are you doing?" Hope swiveled around to make sure they weren't going to hit anyone, but the road behind them was empty.

"I'm heading back for that turnoff. We can take Reeve's Pass and reconnect with the highway past Livingston. That should be far enough it'll be beyond the avalanche.

"Is it safe?"

"I'll get us through," Curtis said.

"That's not what I asked."

"I'll get us through." He caught her gaze in the mirror. "Look, Hope, you're going to have to trust me. Can you do that?"

She couldn't look away. There it was again—that

quality she'd tried so hard to define earlier. That competence and commitment. Curtis was a man who knew what he was capable of, and he was sure he was capable of getting them over the pass.

"Okay."

"Raina? How about you? Do you want to give it a try?"

Raina nodded her head vigorously in the affirmative.

"I don't know about this," Blake said.

Curtis hit the brakes. "You can get out and walk."

"I'm not getting out," Blake growled. "Fine. Take the pass. You'd better know what you're doing."

"I know what I'm doing."

CURTIS BREATHED A little easier when he finally made it back to the turnoff and switched the truck into drive again. He didn't think he'd ever driven backward for so long, and although the highway was deserted, he'd known that someone could come barreling around a bend in the road at any moment. In fact—

Those were headlights behind them. And they were coming in fast.

He hit the gas and the truck leaped toward the off-ramp. Curtis regained control of it but took the ramp faster than he would have liked.

The off-ramp dipped down, and the headlights behind them disappeared. Poor schmuck wasn't going to be happy when he reached the detour, Curtis thought, but then he focused his attention back on the road ahead. It was plain to see there hadn't been a plow through here, and while the wooded slopes on either side sheltered it from the driving wind that had made drifts on the highway, and the overhanging boughs blocked some of the snowfall, it was still deep.

He hit the button that engaged the plow. "It's going to be slow going, and this road is deep in places. Everyone settle in and let me drive, okay?"

They all nodded. Even Blake seemed to understand this was serious.

Their progress was slow but steady. Once or twice Curtis had to stop, back up and take several passes with the plow before they got through, but each time they did in the end. He was beginning to feel like maybe this was going to work when Raina piped up.

"I've got to pee."

Curtis nearly groaned but stopped himself. It had been hours since they'd set out.

"All right, but I need to find a safe place to get off the road."

"Okay," Raina said. "Just don't take too long."

Curtis scanned the road ahead of them for somewhere he could get off onto the shoulder—without getting stuck in a snowdrift. He didn't want to be hit in the unlikely event someone else was on the road.

There. The road emerged from the trees and widened, the ground sloping away on either side. He slowed way down and moved the truck forward carefully, easing it off to the side.

"Don't be long, and don't go too far off the road. You don't know the terrain, and you don't want to get lost," he said as he navigated the shoulder.

"Blake—you'll have to hold the kittens," Raina said.

"Like hell."

"Blake!"

"I'm allergic to cats!"

"It's just for a minute."

Curtis bent to peer out of the windshield, but a gust of wind-tossed flakes blinded him. "Pipe down!" he ordered, aware the shoulder might slope away more quickly than it appeared under all that snow. He slowed to a crawl, inching forward another few feet. Should he stop here—?

Or farther on—that looked good. Up there where—

Blake turned on him. "I don't like your tone—"

"Curtis!" Hope's shriek meshed with the scrape and crash of metal on metal as something huge and heavy hit them from behind. The truck shot forward and off the side of the road. The women's screams, Daisy's howl and the shrills mews of the kittens formed a cacophony of sound that rivaled Curtis's jumbled impressions as the truck slipped and slid down the steep bank, nearly rolling over before it crashed to a halt at the bottom. Curtis gripped the wheel, breathing hard, until his thoughts caught up with him.

"Hope!" he roared, fighting to turn in his seat.

"I'm all right. Edgar!" She fumbled with her jacket, and Curtis realized her seat belt—like his—had held her in place. She still held the kitten, which fussed in her hand, blessedly unharmed.

"I'm fine, too," Raina said, but she sounded funny.

Curtis turned farther in his seat, cursed, undid his seat belt and got all the way around. He realized Raina was counting kittens. One was in her lap, as unharmed as Edgar. Another clung to the back of his seat, its tiny claws holding on tight. A third pushed its way out from under Daisy, who barked and nudged it with her nose. Raina reached down to pick it up.

"Daisy?" Curtis ruffled the dog's ears.

"She hit the back of your seat," Hope said breathlessly, "but I think she's all right. I thought for sure she'd be hurt."

The dog seemed okay, although she barked again when Curtis ran a hand along her back.

"That's where she hit," Hope told him.

"Probably bruised." He hoped that was all.

"We're missing a kitten. Where's Louise?" Raina said tearfully.

"No one asked if I'm okay," Blake said. He was splayed awkwardly in his front seat, and as they watched, he gathered himself together.

"Where's Louise?" Raina repeated.

Hope touched her hand. "She's got to be here somewhere—"

"Ouch!" Blake lifted up from his seat, put a hand beneath him and withdrew a ball of fluff. "What the hell is this?"

"Louise! Are you okay?" Raina reached forward and snatched the kitten from him, cradling it against her cheek. "I thought you were gone!"

Curtis breathed a sigh of relief. He had a feeling the

demise of one of the animals would have demoralized everyone, and he seemed to be the only one cognizant of the bind they'd gotten themselves into.

That was a hell of a slope they'd just tumbled down.

No way they'd get the truck back up it.

Hope was the first to look around. Her eyes widened, and Curtis bowed his head as it hit him things could have been a lot worse. He'd been in many tight spaces in his time with the SEALs, but back then he'd been operating with other trained men, not a truckload of civilians and animals.

Curtis knew he was lucky. Unlike many of his peers, he found for the most part he'd been able to leave his time fighting overseas behind him when he'd come home. When they'd barreled down the hill and come to a stop, he'd had one flash of the old feeling from those days—the kind of awareness you had in combat when the shit hit the fan and you needed to make a new plan, fast. Now he was firmly back in the present, evaluating the situation, taking in their new position.

"Now what?" Hope asked, obviously fighting to steady her voice.

"I'd better go see about the other guy." He hoped whoever it was had fared better than they had, although to drive so recklessly in this kind of weather… "Maybe whoever's up there can give us a hand."

"I still need to pee," Raina said in a small voice.

Curtis only nodded. Of course she did. He took the kittens from her and Hope and passed them to Blake while the women got out. He watched them pace away into the snowstorm.

"Not too far," he called out after them, but neither woman answered.

At least they were all alive.

"OVER HERE." HOPE waited for Curtis to make it up the slope before she led the way carefully through the snow, looking back over her shoulder frequently to make sure she could still see the glow of the truck's headlights. She was far more shaken than she wanted to admit, glad beyond words that no one—and no animal—had been seriously hurt, although Raina seemed to be limping. "You okay?"

"I think I kicked the back of Curtis's seat when we went over. It's nothing."

Hope wasn't fooled. Raina's usual exuberance was muted, and she knew from long experience that only happened when things were bad.

She still couldn't quite catch her breath, and her heart was beating hard, although they were walking on flat ground. The branches of the evergreens towering over them sifted out most of the snow. It was gloomy here in the woods, though.

She couldn't stop thinking about whoever had hit them and realized she was bracing herself for a shout from Curtis. What if they were hurt badly? Or worse?

"Better put that foot up when we're back in the truck," she said to Raina, although what good it would do to be in the truck, she didn't know. It wasn't like they could drive back up onto the highway.

They were stuck.

Hope closed her eyes. Swallowed. Forced herself to open them again and keep moving.

Maybe the vehicle that crashed into them was still operational. Maybe whoever was driving it wasn't hurt and had a cell phone that could get reception.

Or maybe—

A shiver traced down her spine, and tears pricked her eyes. Hope squeezed them back, eyes shut. She wouldn't give in to panic. Not now. Not until she knew what had happened.

When she was done heeding the call of nature, cleaning up with some paper napkins Raina had brought along and washing her hands with snow, Hope pulled out her phone and tamped down her rising fear when she still couldn't get reception. What good were all those satellites if she couldn't get through in a snow storm?

Back in the truck, Blake was cranky, clearly unimpressed with his temporary job as cat and dog wrangler. Curtis still wasn't anywhere in sight. Hope and Raina climbed in and waited, first shaking off the snow that had accumulated on their jackets and boots, but with every passing moment, Hope feared the worst.

"We're not getting back on the highway," Blake said, echoing her earlier thoughts. "We're stuck here. We're going to freeze to death."

A sudden spurt of anger overcame her. "We're not going to freeze to death, so quit whining. Pass over those kittens, and go help Curtis."

"Why should I—?"

"He's coming back." Raina pointed out the window. "And is that... Byron... with him?"

Hope ducked her head to see out Raina's side of the vehicle. "That is Byron. And Curtis is pissed!"

The men reached them a moment later. "Look who I found," Curtis said tightly. "He decided to come after us, and he didn't have the common sense not to speed."

"I saw you backing up—making that turnoff, but I wasn't sure it was you until I got to the detour sign. I had to catch up before you disappeared," Byron said. His shoulders were hunched against the snow, and he looked miserable. "I didn't crash into you on purpose."

"There's no excuse for driving that fast in this kind of weather!"

Hope could tell they'd been arguing this point for a while. "Is your truck still working?" she asked Byron.

Byron shook his head. "Engine won't turn over."

"So we're miles from Bozeman, and this truck is going nowhere, and your truck is going nowhere, and there's no one around, and my phone won't work, and—" Blake's voice rose.

"How are we going to get out of here?" Raina said.

"We're going to switch modes of transportation," Curtis said.

"What does that mean?" Byron asked.

"It means we walk," Hope said, defeat rounding her shoulders. "Which will take days." She imagined all the tasks in her planner sliding off the page. Raina's wedding postponed. Scott flying back to Yellowstone.

"Not quite." Curtis led the way around the truck and undid the tarp that covered the back. Hope couldn't believe her eyes.

"You brought a snowmobile?" she cried.

"I told you—you can't be too careful in Montana in winter," Curtis said grimly. "Byron, help me get this down."

"Is it still okay?" Hope asked.

He nodded. "I had it strapped in tight." When he and Byron had gotten it on solid ground some moments later, he started it up, and the engine roared to life.

Hope breathed a sigh of relief as she reached for her planner. One thing was going right.

CHAPTER FIVE

CURTIS THOUGHT HOPE would be the one to spot the problem first, but she was too busy erasing something in her planner and writing something down on another page to pay attention to what they were doing.

Raina had climbed back into the cab of the truck to oversee the kittens while they maneuvered the snowmobile down the ramp. Daisy was running in excited circles around them, barking now and then at the strange new vehicle, as if she didn't quite trust it.

Blake was staring off into space, probably wondering how any of this could have happened to someone as rich as him.

Byron was the one who finally spoke up. He considered the snowmobile—and Curtis—for a few long seconds before remarking, "How are we all going to fit on that?"

Hope looked up. Slid her planner back in her purse.

"We're not," Curtis said shortly, lifting the ramp and sliding it back into place on the bed of the truck before pulling a metal cargo sled out and setting it on the ground. It was stocked with gear for just such an emergency. Food, a first aid kit, sleeping bags and more.

"Who's going to ride in that?" Blake's eyebrows shot up. "Doesn't seem stable."

"It isn't. It's meant for gear, nothing else."

"Then how—"

"Here's what we're going to do," Curtis announced, his raised voice capturing everyone's attention. Raina climbed out of the truck again, shutting the door carefully on the kittens. "We're each going to take some of the gear, and we'll split up into two groups. We can fit three of us on this bad boy at once. I'll run two of you ahead while the other two walk in my trail. Then I'll come back and fetch the ones I left behind. I'm not going to let anyone be on their own for long in these conditions, so it'll be a lot of going back and forth."

"What about Daisy?" Hope asked.

"She'll stick with the walkers." Curtis looked grim.

"What about the kittens?" Raina demanded.

Curtis sighed. "I don't know," he said truthfully.

Raina's eyes got big. "You're not leaving th—"

"The picnic basket," Hope said quickly. "We'll line it with a sweater and put them in there. They can go on the sled, right?"

"Not without me!" Raina said.

"Then when it's your turn to walk, you'll have to carry the basket."

She nodded. "I can do that."

"We'll walk along the road?" Byron asked.

"It's the only way. It's going to be hard going. Steep in some places. This isn't a highway—it's more of a logging road."

"Are we going back or forward?" Raina demanded.

"Forward," Curtis said. "I think we're past the halfway point, so it's shorter, plus there are some cabins up ahead."

Blake straightened. "What if someone runs us over before they spot us? Or runs over the ones walking behind?" he demanded.

Curtis decided to be honest. "It'll be a miracle if we see anyone on this road. There's no reason for anyone to be up here under these conditions."

"Fine. Let's get moving. I'm getting cold," Blake complained.

"First things first. We've got to get this thing up that hill." Curtis slapped the snowmobile. "Everyone stand back, just in case I flip it."

"Wait!" Hope gripped his arm as he swung his leg over the seat. "Don't do anything dangerous!"

She was worried about him. Curtis's chest filled with warmth. Of course, she probably thought he was their only hope to get out of this mess.

And she was right.

"I'll be fine," he assured her. "Been riding these all my life." He pulled a helmet on, strapped it, revved the engine and waited until they'd all backed away to start a diagonal run up the steep bank toward the road.

It was touch and go for a couple of minutes, but the deep snow helped, and Curtis released a long breath when he got to the top and was able to ease the snow-mobile onto the road, past the mangled Chevy 4x4. He trudged down the hill again and bent to unpack some of the gear on the sled, distributing it among the group to carry. Hope and Raina had made a nest for the kittens in the picnic basket and closed the top on them. He instructed everyone to put on as much clothing as they had and could wear, and gathered up all the gloves, mittens and hats they had.

He led the way up the bank, leaving the truck behind reluctantly. They were far more exposed to the elements without it, and he couldn't fool himself into believing they'd run into anyone on this remote road in the dead of winter.

"It's snowing hard," Hope said quietly when they reached the top.

"You're right. This isn't going to be easy, but it will be possible." He caught sight of a small duffel bag Raina was carrying on top of the basket of kittens. "What's that?"

"Wedding dress." Raina began to shift the gear around to fit the basket and duffel.

"There's no room for another bag."

"It's Raina's wedding dress," Hope repeated.

"But—"

"Hope, can you help?" Raina asked.

Hope quickly skirted Curtis and bent down beside her. Together they wedged the wedding dress bag between the picnic basket of kittens and the gear in front of it. "It fits fine," Hope said.

Curtis bit back a curse, but he didn't have the heart to make Raina ditch her wedding dress, even if it was a useless item as far as their safety was concerned. "Okay. Hope, Raina, you're behind me. Blake and Byron, walk as fast as you can in our tracks. Don't leave them for any reason."

"You'd better not leave us out here," Blake warned. Daisy barked, and Curtis's heart squeezed. He didn't like leaving Daisy behind any more than she liked it. At least Byron was here; he didn't trust Blake around the dog. When he came back to pick up the men, they'd have to figure out a way to carry Daisy on the Skidoo, too.

"I won't." Not for the first time, Curtis wanted to tell Blake to buck up. In a situation like this one, attitude was everything. "Raina, you going to be warm enough?"

"Yep," she replied cheerfully. "Let's get going before I have to pee again, though."

Some of Curtis's tension eased. "All right, let's do this. Daisy, stay with Byron. Hell, Byron—what are you doing?"

Byron had pulled something out of his jacket—a video camera—and lifted it up to his face.

"Are you filming me?"

"Renata will kill me if I don't. She's going to kill me for not bringing back the rest of the gear." He gestured to the truck. "Not to mention for totaling the Chevy."

Curtis got his anger under control. "You stop looking through that thing and pay attention. Don't cause another accident."

Byron lowered the camera, his expression rueful. "I

won't."

"All right. Let's get going." He climbed on the snowmobile in front of Hope. "Hold on."

Daisy's bark was the last thing he heard as he drove away.

"CURTIS HAS BEEN gone forever," Raina said, her voice muffled under her scarf so that Hope, walking ahead of her, had to half turn to hear her words.

"It hasn't been that long." But she knew what Raina meant. Time lost all meaning out here in the utter quiet of the snowstorm. Aside from the two of them crunching through the deep snow, the only sound she'd heard since Curtis had roared away on his Ski-Doo to get Byron and Blake was the whispering of the snowflakes falling fast and thick around them. They were doing their best to follow the curve of the mountain road, staying as far to the side as possible, but the snow was so deep it was difficult to keep going, and Raina's limp was growing worse.

"We should have told Curtis you're injured," Hope said.

"I can't ride the whole time," Raina pointed out.

Hope thought she could, but it was too late now. He'd driven them for about twenty minutes on the snowmobile before unloading them and heading back for the others. They couldn't sit still and freeze while they waited for their turn to ride again; they had to keep moving.

It was cold, her exposed skin around her eyes and

nose prickling as flakes melted against it. She was carrying the basket of kittens, which made moving even more awkward. Raina carried a backpack of supplies Curtis insisted they take. Her wedding dress remained wedged in the gear on the sled.

"I don't like leaving you like this," he'd told them when he let them off the Ski-Doo at the side of the highway. "But I can't leave the guys too much longer; we'd be too far apart if anything happened."

Hope's stomach had sunk as she'd watched him disappear into the snow, but she trusted he'd be back soon, and then it would be time to ride again, which had its advantages. She'd had to snuggle in close to Curtis and wrap her arms around his broad body to keep on the seat, even though they hadn't gone that fast. She'd had an excuse to cling to him, turning her head and pressing one cheek against his back for shelter against the driving snow. Holding on to him like that had sent a rush of pleasure through her body, warming her in a most interesting way.

She missed the feel of his large, strong body now. As much as she was pretending not to be affected, it was a little frightening to be walking down this lonely road with Raina, in this storm. She didn't think they could get lost, but if anything happened to the men—

She didn't want to think about that.

"Curtis is pretty cute, huh?" Raina said.

He was, but Hope wasn't about to say it out loud.

"He's strong. And he cares about kittens. He'd make a good husband," Raina went on.

Hope made a non-committal noise. She wasn't getting sucked into this conversation. Men—and marriage—weren't on her to-dos for years, after all.

She wasn't sure why that gave her a pang; she'd put a lot of thought into her life plan. She wasn't going to deviate from it.

The sound of a motor brought her up short.

"It's them," Raina called out.

Hope shifted the kittens as the snowmobile rattled to a stop. Thank God; she wasn't sure how much longer she could walk.

"Watch it, idiot!"

"You watch it!"

"Get that dog away from me."

Byron and Blake both clambered off the machine and stumbled away from it—and each other. Byron set a wiggling Daisy down in the snow and she loped in a circle. Hope hadn't seen what had happened, but Blake's short temper seemed to have frayed even more since they'd last seen the men.

"This is ridiculous," Blake said as he approached the women. "It'll take us forever to get anywhere. I don't understand why Curtis can't run me to Bozeman, rent a truck and come back for the rest of you."

"I'm not leaving anyone out in the elements that long. Not in this storm."

Four hours later, things hadn't gotten any better. The Ski-Doo had bogged down in the powdery snow more than once, and the snow was so deep it was slipping into their boots as they walked. Hope was frozen through and through. Raina was limping notice-ably. When Curtis pulled up to them again, with Byron and Blake—and Daisy—in tow, he said, "We're stopping for the night."

"Are you insane?" Blake demanded. "We'll freeze to death!"

"No, we won't. We'll get warm and dry, and tomorrow we'll get to Bozeman. I promise."

"Where will we sleep?"

Hope turned around, took in the way Raina was drooping and went to her, shifting the kittens so she could put a hand on Raina's arm.

"You okay?"

"I don't know. I missed dinner with Ben's grandparents."

Hope wasn't sure she'd ever seen Raina so forlorn and shot a worried look at Curtis. He seemed to take in the situation. "Byron, go find us some wood—dry, if you can. Look for anything that might have been sheltered. Blake, help me pull the sled off the road. At least the ground is level here. We want to be in among the trees where it's sheltered."

Hope kept Raina company while the men began to set up camp, thrilled by how quickly Curtis managed to unpack his supplies, throw down a thick, waterproof tarp and get a small tent set up. After tossing in a couple of sleeping bags, he ordered Hope to get Raina inside.

"Strip off everything that's wet out here," he said. "Get into dry, warm gear in there, get in those sleeping bags—zipped together—and warm up."

Hope did as she was told, setting the basket of cats inside the tent, then helping Raina off with her wet gear. Curtis tramped down the snow in a large circle around them and was building a fire, but she couldn't think how he'd get it lit in this weather, even if the thick cover of trees were providing shelter from the worst of the snow.

"Leave your gear," Curtis told her when she hesitated outside the tent. "I'll do what I can to get it dry."

She slipped inside gratefully and was soon snuggled down with Raina and a number of squirming, furry shapes. Daisy joined them, content to lie down and press against the side of the sleeping bags, adding her heat to the rest.

The kittens seemed as glad of their warmth as she was. Raina had zipped the sleeping bags together, and quarters were close, but Hope supposed that was a good thing under the circumstances. Exhausted mentally and physically, heartsick at the thought of how much time they were losing on this journey, Hope must have slipped into sleep.

She woke up some time later, when Curtis slipped two cups of soup through the tent flap. "Eat up. Both of you," he commanded. "Then go back to sleep if you can."

Hope felt a little better after she'd eaten, especially since the dry socks she'd slid on had actually warmed her feet. She set her empty cup near the tent flap and shut her eyes—just to rest them.

And fell asleep once more.

"HOW MANY MILES do you think we've gone?" Byron asked in between slurping his soup.

"Thirty, maybe." Curtis braced himself.

Bryon dropped his spoon into his cup. "Thirty? That means—"

"Ninety to go."

"Jesus."

Blake looked from one to the other. "Tomorrow the plows will be out," he said.

"Maybe. Maybe not." Curtis gathered his thoughts. "This isn't just a snowstorm," he told the other men. "This is a blizzard. A true Montana blizzard can go on for days."

"Do you have enough fuel in that snowmobile to get us through?" Byron asked.

"I still say you should take me to Bozeman right now," Blake said. "One trip. Get it done. Get help for your friends. Hell, it doesn't even have to be Bozeman—just get us back to the highway and to the next little town."

"He might be right. I'd stay with the women," Byron said.

"What if I get halfway there and the snowmobile breaks down? What if I have to walk the rest of the way? What if someone gets hurt back here while you're waiting for me? We stick together," Curtis asserted.

He was probably being overcautious. Blake was right; he could make a beeline for the next town, get help and get back here—

But so many things could go wrong. The thought of

riding away from Hope, and not coming back for hours—

He couldn't do it.

"All three of us going to sleep in that tonight?" Blake nodded grumpily at the second two-man tent Curtis had set up next to the one Raina and Hope occupied.

"Going to be close quarters," Byron said.

Closer than they even knew. He only had two more sleeping bags for the three of them. They were lucky he even had that many. He'd brought an extra one just as a matter of principle, not thinking they'd need it.

"I'll stay with the women," he heard himself say. "They're smaller. There's room for me."

"How come you get to sleep with them?" Blake asked.

Curtis gave him a level look. "Because I trust me."

Blake snorted, but he didn't push it. Byron looked like he might, but he closed his mouth again when Curtis raised an eyebrow. Curtis banked the fire, made sure Byron and Blake weren't going to come to blows as they got into their tent, and undid the zip fly to the women's tent.

Both Hope and Raina seemed to be sleeping, which presented him with a problem. He couldn't even get in the tent without waking them up, let alone get under any covers.

When he cleared his throat, Hope turned over groggily.

"Who's there?"

"Me." He kept his voice low. "I need to get in there with you. I'll be a gentleman, I promise. We need to share our warmth, though."

"Oh. Okay." She rustled around and drew nearer to Raina. Curtis realized she was shifting kittens around. Daisy whined but settled in again.

When there was room, he eased into the tent—and into the sleeping bags, too, coming into contact with Hope all over, who was squished between him and Raina.

Awkward.

"Sorry," he said ruefully, although he wasn't sorry about being close to Hope.

"There's not much room," Hope said. Her face was so close to his he could easily have kissed her. Lord knew he wanted to, but this wasn't the time.

Not with Raina on the other side of her.

Curtis gently turned Hope around, tugged her against him so his bicep pillowed her head and wrapped his other arm around her waist. "Now there's room."

A stifled sound was his only reply.

"Go to sleep," Curtis told her.

"I am asleep," she asserted.

But Curtis was wide awake—and he was pretty sure Hope was wide awake, too.

THIS WAS ALL perfectly innocent, Hope told herself again. Many layers of clothing separated her from Curtis, even if his arms surrounded her—and her body was pressed up against his.

She fitted nicely in his embrace, though, and the feel of him against her woke something inside her she hadn't felt in a long time. It took her a minute to classify the fluttery ache.

Desire.

Plain and simple, she wanted the man.

She couldn't have him, though. Couldn't betray the slightest interest in him, either. She'd read the signs that he was interested in her. Curtis watched her in a way that made her feel—tingly. He was considering her. Wondering how she could fit in his life.

She didn't fit—at all, she reminded herself.

She didn't have time for men. Certainly not for large, muscular, sexy, funny men like Curtis. Men who could make you forget you even owned a planner full of things to do.

The problem was, she could get serious about a guy like Curtis. If that wasn't the case, then maybe it would be fine to flirt a little, play a little—have a little fun. She'd never thought of herself as that kind of woman, but if no one got hurt—

She'd get hurt, though. Curtis was—

Far too interesting. Far too breathtaking, if she was honest. Every move he made was so different from the moves she made. It made her want to study him, too. Find out what made him tick.

See if she could make him tick faster.

Curtis shifted behind her, and Hope stifled a moan. He was so close.

What if she turned around? What if she pressed a

kiss to the underside of his chin?

Raina.

Even if she was the kind of woman to throw herself at a strange man, she was in bed—literally—with her best friend and a jumble of kittens.

Talk about being chaperoned.

Curtis shifted again.

"Stop that," she whispered.

He did—for a moment. Then he tightened his arm around her waist. Pulled her closer. Made her thoroughly aware that her bottom was pressed against his crotch. "Go to sleep," he whispered, his voice tickling her ear.

"I'm trying."

Curtis's chuckle rumbled deep in his chest, and Hope's breath caught.

"Just relax," he whispered. "Everything's going to be okay. I'll get you to that wedding."

Hope wondered why the thought of getting to their destination and parting ways left her feeling so bereft. She was going to miss Curtis, and she was disappointed that she wasn't going to get to know such an interesting man. Then there was Base Camp, which had proved far more intriguing than she would have guessed from Raina's descriptions. Why did her plans, which seemed so crucial just days ago, suddenly make her feel...

Hope must have dozed off, but she opened her eyes again when something bright exploded in her face. Curtis swore, tried to move but was trapped by the sleeping bag, and Byron lurched back before he could get free. Byron quickly zipped up the tent again.

"Damn it, you're breaking the rules. No filming in our tents," Curtis growled after him, trying to turn over but only succeeding in getting tangled up with Hope.

"What's going on?" Raina asked sleepily.

"I wasn't filming. I was taking a photograph." Byron's voice came from outside the tent, moving farther away as he spoke.

Hope managed to push up on her elbow, took in the fact it was light enough to see clearly inside the tent—and reached out to unzip the flap again. A whoosh of cold air came in. Outside, snowflakes still sheeted down.

As one of the kittens tottered out of the sleeping bag, Raina sat up, took in Hope—and Curtis—and smiled. "This is cozy."

"Sure is," Byron called from outside. "I got a great photograph of it, too."

"Byron!" Curtis zipped up the tent flap again before the kitten could escape. "Sorry, ladies. Guess it's time to get up." He eased his way out of the bag, sat down beside it and began to pull on more layers, a difficult task in the cramped quarters.

All of Hope's longing returned full force.

She'd slept all night against the handsome man, and she wanted to do it again soon.

She had to think of her future, though. Had to focus on getting Raina to her wedding.

"Yellowstone," she said out loud.

Raina, catching her remark, rolled her eyes. "Yellowstone isn't everything," she said, sitting up.

"Yes, it is."

She caught something that sounded an awful lot like, "…lead a horse to water, but you can't…" before Raina climbed out of the bag, too, and began to pull on more clothes.

CHAPTER SIX

"**B**OSS, WE'VE GOT a problem," Byron said some minutes later when Curtis climbed out of the tent, still miffed that the young man had seen fit to cut short his time with Hope. Now Hope was stiff and huffy, put off by the idea of being photographed sleeping in close quarters with a strange man.

"You're right, we do. Stop cock-blocking me."

Byron's eyebrows shot skyward. "I think it's Raina who was cock-blocking you. She's the one who spent the night in the tent with you two. I just took a photo."

"And you aren't going to take any more."

Byron shrugged. "That's not the problem."

"What is?" Curtis growled. He wasn't ready for all this—not before he'd fully woken up, or gotten his lust for Hope under control. The snow falling in a never-ending steady hiss was getting to him, too.

"The Ski-Doo. I went to take a photograph a few minutes ago. Smelled gas."

It was Curtis's turn to shrug. "That happens."

"A strong smell of gas. I think the tank's leaking."

Curtis swore and followed Byron to the machine without another word. After examining the snowmobile thoroughly, he had to admit Byron was right. The gas tank was leaking from a small crack they must have sustained somewhere during yesterday's ride. Back at Base Camp, he could fix it in a jiffy, but not out here.

"Now what?" Byron asked.

"Now we go on foot," Curtis sighed. He'd been on enough missions to know things rarely went as you wished they would, but this particular mission had gone off the rails early and thoroughly.

No, he corrected himself. It had gone off the rails the moment he'd conceived of it. He'd convinced himself he would be a hero for getting Raina to her wedding despite the storm, and he'd hoped that his heroism would convince Hope to fall head over heels for him. That wasn't likely. Hope had her own plans— and a handful of days was too short a time to convince any woman to love him. Hell, he'd dated Angela for years and she'd left him at the altar.

He probably should have stayed back at Base Camp and kept haunting those internet dating sites. He should have let Boone or someone else take Hope and Raina to Bozeman while he found someone as desperate as he was to get married. He didn't just want anyone, though.

He wanted Hope.

Curtis gave himself a mental shake. He had to face facts. It was turning into a long shot he'd get Raina to her wedding on time. It was a much longer one that he'd get Hope to the altar.

All he could do was press on and assume that Boone would find him someone he could wed and spend the next few months with—at least until the end of the show. He wouldn't be able to help with the baby-making part—

Curtis swallowed hard, glancing at Hope again, picturing her cradling an infant, an infant they'd created together, and something shifted in him that had him reaching out and grabbing the handlebar of the snowmobile to steady himself.

"Hey, you okay?" Byron looked so alarmed, Curtis had to grin despite the turmoil inside him.

"Yeah, I'm okay. Just... life, you know?" Hell, now Byron had that silly little video camera trained on him. Turn that off."

"No can do." Byron danced away from him when Curtis reached for the camera. "Life's pretty fucked up sometimes, isn't it?"

He was right. Sometimes it was fucked up. Sometimes it was wonderful. If Hope was ever cradling his baby, it would be downright spectacular.

But her being so close—and so out of his reach at the same time—

That was definitely fucked up.

"Let's get back to the others."

"You should just tell her, you know," Byron said.

"Tell who what?"

"Tell Hope what's going on. That you need to marry by Monday. That you want her."

"She'd run like hell," Curtis said.

"Maybe. Or maybe she'd surprise you."

Curtis doubted it. That wasn't the way his love-life went.

He busied himself unstrapping the cross-country skis he'd packed for just such an eventuality, and Byron sighed. "Fine. Be a wimp. Hey, there are only three sets." He gestured to the skis.

"When I started, there were only three people going."

"You were supposed to take me along," Byron pointed out.

"Wasn't going to happen. Nothing personal," Curtis added, seeing Byron's stung look. "But I don't need someone following me around taking video of everything I do."

"You're wrong. That's exactly what you need," Byron countered and stopped filming. He tucked the little camera back into his jacket. "Remember what I said about Fulsom. He's losing interest in you guys. You aren't giving him what he asked for. Every one of you keeps secrets and hides things from us. He's talking about throwing—Shit," Byron added. "Never mind."

"Throwing what?" Curtis asked as Byron walked away. He hurried after the young man. Yanked him to a stop. "Tell me!"

"The show," Byron said. He shook his head at Curtis's incomprehension. "Who the hell do you think robbed the cold storage room?" He pulled away and kept going.

Curtis stared after him. Someone had broken into

the admittedly unlocked cold storage room they'd built for their vegetable harvest some weeks back. Had emptied it while all of them were attending an event at the manor. It had set them back considerably as far as food was concerned, and while the gardening crew had hurried to up their game as far as hydroponics and food production in the greenhouses went, it was still going to make things difficult during the rest of the winter.

Fulsom was behind it?

What else might he do to make them lose?

Curtis watched Byron meet up with Hope and Raina, who had exited their tent. If it was true, what was Fulsom's game? Did he think he'd get more publicity for flattening Base Camp and letting Montague build an amusement park over the beautiful sustainable community they'd worked so hard to create?

Maybe. Fulsom was definitely a sucker for drama. The bigger, the bolder, the more jaw-dropping the better.

He'd sacrifice all of them if it got him the attention he wanted for his pet causes.

Byron was right; Fulsom was on their side, but only to a point. Their little community was a drop of water in the bucket of his ambitions. If he could generate public outrage by letting Montague destroy everything they'd built, he'd be ahead in the long run. He could turn that outrage political—point it toward elections and real policy change.

Hell, maybe they should let him do it.

Everything within Curtis rebelled against the idea.

He wasn't giving up Base Camp for anything. He was building something—not tearing it down.

Byron was right about something else, too. He and his friends weren't giving Fulsom what he'd asked for. They were hiding. Keeping their actions—and their emotions—away from the prying eyes of the video cameras and the American public.

He'd wanted to keep his pursuit of Hope a secret. After all, he'd struck out three times on his way to the altar so far. If he was about to strike out again, he didn't want anyone to know.

Or did he?

Had every step he'd taken so far been wrong?

Blake stormed up to him, breaking into his thoughts. "Byron said the snowmobile is fucked. Now what? I told you to take me to Bozeman last night."

"If I had, we'd be stranded somewhere on our own, and Byron and the women would be back here," Curtis told him.

"Whatever."

Curtis came to a decision. "Get that video camera out," he called to Byron.

"Why?"

"Get it out. Record this. You want drama? Here's some drama." He waited until Byron had moved closer again and done what he asked. "Listen up," he called out. Hope and Raina joined them. "We've got a leak in the gas tank. That means we can't use the snowmobile anymore, and we'll proceed on foot. Hope, Raina, we'll be on skis. Byron and Blake, you'll walk. I'll pull the sled. We need to make time while we've got light, so we'll eat on the road. Let's get packed up. Oh, and Hope?"

"Yes?" She'd made a move toward the tent but stopped when he said her name.

"I'm going to marry you in a few days. Thought I'd better give you a head's up."

Byron straightened and grinned, filming everything. Hope's mouth dropped open, and she looked from Curtis to Raina to Byron and back again. "You're... what?"

"Marrying you. As soon as we get Raina taken care of. Consider yourself warned."

Curtis turned back to the snowmobile to strip it of supplies. Blake sidled up next to him.

"Does that kind of thing work?" Blake asked. "Just telling them like that?"

"We'll see."

"WHAT DID HE just say?" Hope asked Raina in a low voice. She had to be hallucinating. It was the cold. The snow. The sleepless night.

Okay, she'd slept—a lot, actually—in Curtis's arms last night, but that didn't make his statement any easier to swallow.

"He said he's marrying you. Right after my wedding. Which isn't that great, actually, because I'll be on my honeymoon. We'd better have a double wedding, don't you think?"

"Raina, quit fooling around."

"I'm not fooling around."

"Curtis is. Don't encourage him. I don't like to be made fun of."

Raina heaved a big sigh. "You never listen to me, do you? I told you to watch the show. If you had, you'd know exactly what's going on here, and you wouldn't be acting like this."

"Like I don't like people trying to make me look dumb? What is going on?" Hope followed Raina as she went to collect the kittens from the tent.

Raina ignore her, unzipped the tent, stepped inside and gathered the small, furry creatures. "Everyone is accounted for." She began to load them into the basket.

"Good." Hope followed her inside awkwardly and zipped up the tent again behind them. It wasn't exactly private, but it was better than being outside with the men.

Why would Curtis joke about marrying her? It was in pretty poor taste. She remembered Byron filming the whole thing. Was this some kind of act for the show? If it was, she was glad she hadn't watched *Base Camp*. Choosing a spouse was serious business, and it took time. She'd scheduled in a whole year for it when she was thirty-five.

"What is going on?" she asked again.

"You're going to have to ask Curtis."

Hope surveyed her friend. Normally Raina wasn't this tight-lipped, and her reticence now set warning bells ringing. "This is all a stupid gag, right?"

Raina stopped what she was doing. "You know

what, Hope? I think this is probably the most serious thing that's ever happened to you—since high school, anyway."

She bent to unzip the sleeping bags, leaving Hope stunned. That was a cheap shot, and Raina knew it. What had happened in high school—

She wasn't going to think about it. Wasn't going to let her mind go there. She was long past the time when nightmares had haunted her—

She took one of the sleeping bags and began to roll it up tightly, pushing back all thoughts of the past.

"I'm sorry," Raina said contritely when she looked up. "I shouldn't have—"

"I don't want to talk about it."

"That's the thing, isn't it? You never do."

"The past is past. I'm focusing on my future. I'm sticking to the plan."

"Right," Raina said sadly. "The plan."

Hope refused to say anymore, and fifteen minutes later they'd cleaned out the contents of the tent. Raina lugged their gear over to Curtis, and Hope began to strike the tent, needing to keep busy as her thoughts tangled in her mind.

Most serious thing—

Marry Curtis—

The past was the past—

Watch the show—

She decided the only sane way to handle the situation was to pretend everyone else she was traveling with had lost their minds. She wrestled her emotions under control, and as she stuffed the tent into its sack, Curtis approached her.

"Have you done this before?" he asked. "Breaking down a campsite? You're a natural at it."

"Of course I've been camping before. All my life. I'm an outdoorswoman. I want to be a park ranger, remember?"

Curtis passed the tent off to Byron. "Put that with the rest of the things on the sled. I'll get it packed up in a minute."

"Sure thing, boss." But he was still filming them.

"Do you mind?" Hope asked him.

"Let him take his videos. That's his job."

"Shouldn't we get going? Like you said, we need to make use of the light." Her voice wobbled, and she knew she was close to losing control.

He stopped her with a hand on her arm. "Hope, I wasn't making fun of you."

"Yes, you were."

"I'm dead serious about what I said."

Hope cocked her head and looked up at the man. This close up, he was imposing. His expression serious, his hazel eyes focused on her. He seemed to be trying to read her thoughts in her face.

"You can't be."

"Haven't you ever just known about something? Just felt it was right?" he demanded.

"Nope." Not since she'd been a child. Not since Yellowstone. On that trip she'd thought she'd known everything. Her encounter with the bison had been magical. Then there was the night she'd stood under Yellowstone's starry skies, listened to the wolves howl and thought she'd found her home.

She'd learned later that life wasn't so simple. Impulses could be dangerous. Deviating from your plans could be deadly—

And yet her impulse to return to Yellowstone had always remained strong. She couldn't forget its magic no matter how hard life got. The bubbling hot springs, the magical geysers. The bison she'd seen from the car—

The wolves howling in the dark.

That night she'd known it was her destiny to work outside, to be a steward of nature—to give her life to connecting people and the natural world.

It had been just like Curtis said—an instant knowing—and longing—that pierced her through and through. Was he saying—?

Did he feel like that—about her?

She stared back at him, unable to make her suddenly dry throat produce any coherent words.

"Yes, you have," Curtis said. "I can see it in your face. You know exactly what I mean—so you know exactly how I feel about you and our future together."

"We don't have a future together." She wasn't sure if she was denying it because she was afraid he meant it or because she was afraid he didn't, because in that moment she wanted a future with Curtis so badly she ached for it. "The man I'm going to marry is going to crave me." She surprised herself with the vehemence of her reaction. She'd never really thought about this

aspect of marriage before. It had always been hazy—
something to think about in the distant future. The
words kept spilling from her mouth now that she'd
started, though. "He's going to adore me. Worship me."
Because a man like that wouldn't do what Liam had
done in high school. "He's not going to be some
random SEAL I meet while driving across Montana."

"Walking across Montana," Blake corrected.

"Skiing, actually," Byron said cheerfully.

"Whatever!"

To her astonishment, Curtis's fierce expression
transformed into a slow grin that lit up his eyes. "Is that
all?"

All? Wasn't it enough? No man she'd dated had felt
anything like adoration for her, especially not Liam. She
wasn't sweet, petite, pretty little Raina, who transformed
perfectly intelligent men into drooling idiots wherever
she went. She was fierce, proud, Amazonian Hope, who
met many men eye to eye at five foot ten and could
chop wood, haul water and order around patients twice
her size at her receptionist job at the physical therapist's
office. She was too practical for adoration. Too capable.

"Sweetie-pie, if it's craving you want, I got it covered." Curtis winked at her. "But you'll have to wait
until later to experience it. We've got a long road ahead
of us." He walked away.

Hope gaped after him. "That man is…" She
searched for the right word.

"An ass?" Blake offered.

"A romantic?" Byron said.

"A hottie?" Raina suggested.

"Absolutely insane," Hope snapped.

"Insanely after you," Raina said and yelped when Hope swatted at her. "Hey, don't shoot the messenger."

IT TOOK LONGER than Curtis would have liked to get the women into their cross-country skis and their supplies re-packed and distributed among the group to carry. Thank goodness for the old-fashioned skis and boots that had come with the ranch. A small metal bar at the toes of their boots clicked into the mechanism on the skis, which meant they wouldn't have to change the bindings each time they switched skiers. That was the good news. The bad news was that while he had brought boots of several sizes to fit Hope and Raina, and an extra pair for himself that Blake could use, he didn't have a third set of large boots that would fit Byron. Hope offered him the largest of the pairs Curtis had brought for her. Byron was just able to squeeze into them, but it was a tight fit. Far from ideal. Hope took the next size down.

"They work," she proclaimed after lacing them up.

Curtis breathed a sigh of relief. "Wear your regular boots while you're not skiing. You don't need blisters."

Each of them had a kitten tucked into their jacket in makeshift kitten carriers Raina had devised from their extra clothes. With a small, furry face peeking out from each of their necklines, it was hard to take any of them seriously.

But this was serious.

Curtis opened his mouth to say so, but Raina beat him to the punch.

"If anything happens to Minna, I will beat you down," she told Blake.

"I told you I was allergic—"

"BEAT YOU DOWN!" Raina repeated balefully.

"Nothing's going to happen to Minna." Blake shook his head. "I should have stayed with my car."

"You would be frozen by now," Curtis told him. "Look, everyone. It's time for us to focus. We're in a precarious position, and we need to keep moving. I'm going to do what I did yesterday; get the women ahead, come back with the skis and collect you two. Walk in our tracks the best you can in the meantime. Got it?"

"Got it," Byron said.

"Yeah," Blake muttered.

It was a long morning. The powdery snow and deep accumulations made even skiing difficult, and they did more floundering than making forward progress. Walking was worse, though. Whoever wasn't on skis made barely any progress at all while waiting for their next turn. It didn't help to have a kitten sticking its pinprick claws into your chest most of the time. Curtis decided after an hour it could be a form of torture.

"Hey, you little furry beast," he said to Reggie finally. "I'm saving you; don't you know that?"

The kitten let out a little yowl and kneaded at his chest some more.

"I don't know if I can go any farther," Raina said after they'd each had two chances to ski and walk, and

Curtis had gone back and forth between the men and women. Curtis had noticed her favoring her ankle. If he wasn't mistaken, she'd injured it yesterday but had pushed through without complaint.

Judging by the rumbling in his stomach, lunch wasn't a bad idea. He didn't want anyone to cool down too much, though. That was dangerous, especially in their wet gear. Daisy had plopped herself down the minute they'd stopped, and he didn't want her getting chilled, either.

"…never get anywhere working for other people," Blake was saying to Byron as they took off their skis and boots. "I didn't get rich being someone else's lackey."

"I'm not Renata's lackey."

"Really? Sure looks like you are—"

Curtis realized he was clenching his fists. Byron and Blake had been sniping at each other all morning, and it was grating on him. They all needed their energy—

"You're the lackey," Raina said to Blake. "You're that Jaguar's lackey. You probably work half your hours just to pay for it!"

Hope and Byron both laughed. Blake turned on Raina.

"You're not even smart enough to be a lackey. The way everyone babies you—you need a sitter to get to your own wedding on time!"

"Okay, enough," Curtis said, getting between them. "Blake, go cool off. We'll eat in a minute. But first let's get a fire going. Hope, help me collect some wood." He didn't think he could take a minute more in the company of either of the men right now.

"What about Raina?" Hope asked. "I don't want to leave her here alone with these two."

"Don't worry about me. I'm not the only one who needs babysitting around here," Raina said complacently. "I'll make sure these two don't kill each other. Here, give me your kittens."

"Keep moving," Curtis told Raina and the men as he and Hope handed over their kittens. "You don't want to get cold." He held out a hand to Hope. "Let's stick close. I don't want to lose you." Snow was still falling as if it never meant to stop.

He showed Hope what to look for, and together they foraged through the trees. It was hard going, even where the trees grew close together, their boughs creating a canopy overhead. Curtis's muscles ached, and he imagined Hope's did, too. Thank goodness she was the active sort, rather than some shrinking violet. He had to let go of her hand to dig out fallen wood, and as they ranged through the trees, the distance between them increased, although he always kept an eye on her. He wasn't kidding about the possibility of getting lost in this storm.

When Hope shrieked and disappeared into a bank of snow, Curtis reached her in seconds, dropping the wood he'd gathered so far.

"Hope? What happened?"

She was up to her waist in the powder, thrashing around like she was caught in a trap.

"Water. There's water under here. My foot is

soaked."

Curtis hauled her out of the snowbank and bit back an exclamation at her sodden foot. "Hell, grab that wood." He kept a hold of her waist as she bent to pick up the pile he'd just dropped, then lifted her into his arms and staggered back to where they'd left the others, carrying both her and the firewood. He ignored their questions, put Hope down and began to rummage among the supplies in the sled.

"Get that boot off. Your sock, too." Good thing she hadn't been wearing her cross-country ski boots.

Raina helped Hope, whose teeth were chattering. When they'd managed it, he rubbed her bare foot with a sweater until it was dry and slid two new, dry socks onto it, one over the other. He pulled out another pair of snow boots from among the supplies. "See if these fit. I borrowed them from Sam back at Base Camp just in case," he said, dropping to his knees beside her.

"You always have everything we need," Hope managed through her shivers.

"That's my job," Curtis said and bent forward to kiss her. The moment she'd screamed, his heart had nearly stopped. Hope was becoming as important to him as breathing, and for one split second he'd been afraid he was going to lose her.

"What was that for?" Hope said when he pulled back.

He shrugged. "I just had to. Know what I mean?"

She nodded—and kissed him back.

SHE WAS KISSING Curtis.

He'd kissed her, and she'd leaned forward and kissed him back.

Just like that. Because she needed to feel him again. Needed that connection. She craved being close to Curtis, and that was worrisome. She refused to think about the future, however, as Curtis's hands came up to cup her face and he kissed her again. When Curtis finally broke away, his gaze raked her face, as if searching for her reaction. He was bracing himself. Ready for her anger.

Where was her anger?

Hope touched her lips with her mittened fingers, and the dusting of snow on their tips sparked cold against her skin, bringing her back to herself.

"That was just for thanks," she said, needing distance from what had just happened.

He nodded but didn't answer, still watching her.

Someone snorted behind him. Blake. "Get a room," he said derisively.

"No, do it again—I didn't get that," Byron said, scrambling toward them with his video camera.

A handful of snow down the neck of her jacket couldn't have woken her more abruptly. Hope surged to a stand, the tight boot on her left foot pinching her even before she took a step.

Curtis stood, too. "Thanks for what?" he asked as if neither of the men had even spoken.

It took her a moment to remember what she'd said. "For... for the way you handle things." She gestured inclusively. "You just take whatever happens and work with it. You don't get pissed."

It was Raina who snorted this time. "That's not entirely true."

Hope and Curtis both ignored her.

"Does no good to get pissed."

"Right." She wasn't sure she'd ever met a man who understood that. At her job, it always seemed like it was the men in the office who made consensus difficult.

"Thank *you*," Curtis said.

"Why?"

"For the same thing. No matter what happens, you just adjust, make a new plan and move on. I like that."

"Oh." Hope busied herself adjusting the new boot. Why was she misty-eyed all of a sudden?

She wasn't sure.

SHE'D KISSED HIM back again.

Curtis kept replaying it over in his mind as he got the fire going and they ate lunch. He'd leaned forward, kissed her—and she'd kissed him back.

What did it mean?

He'd done it without thinking—out of relief that she was okay. That something worse than a wet foot hadn't happened.

He'd done it because he'd wanted to.

The more he learned about Hope, the more he wanted to learn. The thought that he might not ever have met her at all made his gut tighten. He wished he had more time to woo her, but he wasn't questioning what he wanted anymore. If Fate was on his side, he'd marry Hope on Monday.

He wasn't sure he could face the alternative.

"All right; we need to get moving again," he announced less than an hour after they'd stopped. "Hope, Raina, get your skis on."

As he set about dousing the fire and repacking the few items he'd taken from the sled, Raina passed out the kittens again, and everyone tucked theirs in their jackets. They'd spent lunchtime in the basket Curtis had lashed to the top of the pile of supplies on the sled, but Raina had decided that for the travel stretches, they were better riding in people's jackets.

"Are you going to take them on your honeymoon?" Curtis teased her.

"No. You and Hope are going to take them back to Base Camp."

He opened his mouth to answer that, but couldn't come up with anything. Was she giving him a hint? Did she think he might succeed with Hope?

"Go get ready," he finally managed.

She grinned at him and gave a cocky little salute. "Yes, sir."

The snow had lightened a little, and Curtis's spirits were high when he set out with the women, leaving the men to follow in their tracks. Surely they'd reach the highway again soon where the plows must be out by now.

He almost wished they wouldn't be. It gave him a pang to think of reaching Bozeman. Despite what Raina had said, he didn't see Hope giving up all her plans to stay in Montana with a man she'd only known a day or so.

"Haven't seen you check your planner recently," Curtis said. "What if we're off-track?"

"We're so off-track we won't catch up for years," Hope said glumly.

"Do you really have every day lined up in there?" Mostly he was talking for the sake of talking. He liked the sound of Hope's voice. Strong, but feminine. Serious, but able to laugh, too.

"Her day, her week, her year, her life," Raina said. She'd fallen behind a bit, and Curtis slowed to let her catch up.

"Your life? Where does this Yellowstone gig fit in?" He tried to sound casual.

"I'll make contact with Scott at Raina's wedding. After that it depends on him, but I'll do my best to make the transition quickly," she said without hesitation.

"Huh." The woman definitely had a plan. He tried to think of other milestones. "When will you buy your first home?"

"Two years from now."

"When will you upgrade to a bigger one?"

She shot him a look. "Eight years later."

"Why eight years?"

She shrugged and increased her pace. Curtis realized Raina was lagging again.

"Because that's when she's getting married," Raina supplied, out of breath, trying to catch up.

"Hey, slow down a little," Curtis told Hope. "That's when you're getting married, huh? In ten years?" Inconvenient for him.

"We'll see. I have to redo my plans if I get the job in Yellowstone." Hope kept her gaze forward, but she did slow a little.

So she was able to change her plans if pressed. That was encouraging. "What about kids?"

"Two years later."

"No kids for twelve years? You'll be what? Forty? You sure you want to wait that long?"

"Thirty-seven. And it's none of your business, is it?"

"It is if I'm supposed to marry you on Monday."

"I'm not marrying you on Monday!" Hope snapped at him and redoubled her pace.

Hell, now he'd pissed her off. He went after her, realized Raina had really fallen behind, and slowed up again.

"You all right?" he asked her.

"I'm fine. I'm just no athlete," she said. "Hope! Hold up, you're going too fast."

Hope slowed down again, too, but she didn't look at Curtis, and she didn't seem in the mood for conversation anymore. When he glanced at Raina, she shrugged.

He'd have to change Hope's mind, Curtis decided.

He just didn't know how.

THIRTY-SEVEN, NOT FORTY.

She'd be thirty-seven when she had her first child. If she stuck to her plan—which she would, she hastily reassured herself.

She had a lot to do in the next twelve years. She was determined not just to be a ranger at Yellowstone, but a ranger at the top of the food chain, where she could influence what happened at the park. After all, there was no use doing something unless you were doing it right.

She wanted to work to maintain the pristine beauty of the park. To keep its ecological systems in balance. To help the magnificent animals that lived there. To teach people about the wonders of nature.

She couldn't think of a better place in the world to do so than Yellowstone. It had captured her imagination since the first time she'd traveled there as a child.

But if she had her first baby at thirty-seven, she'd be in her forties before her child was old enough to learn about nature from her. Somehow she'd never realized that before. What would she be like in her forties?

She simply couldn't picture it.

A glance at Curtis showed him to be lost in his own thoughts. He moved with the controlled energy of a mountain lion. She knew he could do this all day, and while she was in good shape, too, she had to admit she was tiring already.

And Raina kept falling behind.

They weren't making as much progress as they should be, and Hope was beginning to wonder if it was a sign. Was her plan all wrong? Is that why they'd been stopped in their tracks?

Could she possibly be on the wrong road?

No. Hope found her strides lengthening, and she

shot ahead of Curtis and Raina on her skis before getting under control again.

She'd spent so many hours toiling over that planner. Days and days poring over books about life and careers and retirement—even old age and dying. She'd thought it all out meticulously. Brilliantly.

There were reasons for putting off marriage and children.

Why were they so hard to remember when she looked at Curtis?

He'd be a good father.

The thought popped into her head without warning, and the heat of a blush stole up her cheeks. Thank goodness for the falling snow—which, now that she thought about it, was falling much harder again. A few minutes ago, she'd thought it was tapering off.

Hope sighed. As if they weren't going slowly enough, already.

"Hope's going to have two children. A boy and a girl," Raina announced.

"Raina—"

"How are you going to manage that?" Curtis asked curiously.

"Of course I can't predict that," Hope began.

"In twelve years, things will have progressed far enough so that we'll be able to choose the sex of our children. That's what Hope thinks."

"Raina!"

Curtis stopped abruptly. "You'd do that? Choose the sex of your child?"

"It's not wrong to want one of each," Hope sputtered, thoroughly embarrassed. Why was Raina telling Curtis all this?

"Don't you think Mother Nature knows what she's doing?" he asked.

Hope lifted her hands to the sky. "Right now Mother Nature's doing everything she can to stop me from getting the job of my dreams!"

"Don't you mean she's stopping me from marrying the man of my dreams?" Raina asked softly. "I'm missing my wedding rehearsal right now."

Hope stiffened, the wind sucked from her lungs. "Oh, Raina—you know I didn't mean it that way. You know I'm trying to get you to your wedding."

"So you can get your interview." Raina skied away, and Hope watched her go, regret making her throat ache.

"I didn't—" she tried again, but Curtis skied off after Raina.

"I didn't mean anything by it," she said softly to the falling snow, but it wasn't regret for what she'd said to Raina that kept her rooted there. It was the flash of a vision that filled her mind suddenly, a feeling so strong she felt she must have lived it before. She sat in a rocking chair, a newborn baby in her arms, and the love she felt for her child—because it was *her* child—

She shook the thought from her mind. Banishing the baby, and the sense of Curtis close behind her, loving both of them—

There'd be no children with Curtis.

There'd be no children, period. Not for twelve years.

Which suddenly seemed like a long, long time.

THE SNOW WAS falling faster and faster, but Raina was skiing more and more slowly. The last time Curtis had gone back to get the men, they hadn't been very far behind. Halfway through the afternoon, when the dim light began to fail, he made a decision. They'd keep moving but stick together.

Raina was moving so slowly on her skis she might as well have been walking. Byron plodded along, only filming every now and then, conserving the backup batteries he'd stuffed in his pockets when he'd collected his gear from the truck. Hope had been quiet since her argument with Raina. Only Blake talked—incessantly. A series of whining, griping complaints that had them all on edge.

"You know, for someone who's so rich and wonderful, you're pretty miserable, aren't you?" Hope snapped at him mid-afternoon.

"I've got everything a man could dream of. I'm not miserable," he said scornfully.

"Really? Everything? You've talked about your job, your condo, your cars, your summer houses and a couple of your clients, but you haven't mentioned parents, or siblings, or friends, or any kind of partner. Do you ever spend time with people? Or are your social skills so bad because you're on your own all the time?"

Maybe it was time to take a break, Curtis thought.

"I've got... family," Blake said.

"When's the last time you called your mom?"

Everyone waited for Blake's answer. He shrugged. "I don't know. We talk once in a while."

"What about your dad?"

"I talk to him every few months. He's CEO at Barton, Finch and Wheatley. Still works seventy hours a week."

"Do you play softball in your spare time?"

"No."

"Build houses for the homeless?"

"Not my thing."

"Go hiking? Surfing? Snorkeling? Bowling?"

"I have a boat."

"Ah. Sailing," Raina said. "That's something. Do you know how to do all the rigging?"

"It's a yacht. I have a driver and a personal chef on board."

"Does your girlfriend like your boat?" Raina pressed.

Blake didn't answer that. "Don't have one," he said finally.

"Boyfriend?" Byron ventured.

"Don't have one of those, either," Blake snapped. "My life is fine. It's a hell of a lot better than any of yours," he said. "Look at you Base Camp people—working for nothing."

"They're changing the world," Hope said. "What are you doing for the world?"

"I'll tell you what—I'm not—"

"My dress," Raina exclaimed, stopping as suddenly as she could while still on her skis. "Where's my dress?" She pointed to the sled, and Curtis's heart sank. She was right; the duffel bag wasn't visible anymore.

Raina hurried to the sled and went over its contents, as if the oversized bag could be hiding among the other items. "Curtis, where is it?"

She was edging on hysteria, and Curtis knew what happened next could affect them all. They were cold, tired, unsure of their location or how far they had to go to reach the highway. Blake was furious at the women. Hope and Raina were estranged. He wasn't dealing with a highly trained group of professionals, like he would have been in the service—this was a group of civilians who'd probably never done a trek like this before.

He spun out possibilities in his mind, a tactic he'd learned early on in his military training. He could force them forward, and Raina's morale, already low, would bottom out and bring them all down.

He could go back, fetch the dress—

And raise all their spirits.

"I'll go get it," he said quickly.

"That's crazy," Blake said. "We don't know how long it's been gone."

"Yes, we do—it was there the last time we stopped. I saw it," Raina insisted.

That was good. They'd been moving so slowly they hadn't gone that far. Skiing alone, he could cover the ground easily.

"All right. Byron, take the sled. Blake, you trade off

pulling it with him. Keep going until I get back. Don't go off the road. Got it?"

"Got it," Byron said.

"Got it," Raina echoed. She held out her hand. "Better give me Reggie."

He handed over the kitten and watched as Raina went to collect the basket and gather the rest of the critters from everyone else. "They can stick together for a while," she said.

Hope took the basket from her. Blake muttered grimly and trudged off.

"Stay together," Curtis shouted after him.

"Whatever."

At least he slowed down. Curtis handed the sled's lines to Byron and turned around. "Be back as soon as I can." He'd already struck off and gone a few paces before a feminine voice carried after him.

"Be careful!"

It was Hope. Curtis waved and kept going, but his spirits strengthened. Another sign that she cared what happened to him.

As he walked, he thought about Blake's answers to the women's questions. Although the man had protested that he was happy, he hadn't done a very good job at defending his quality of life. He wondered if Blake had spent more time with normal people in the past day than he did most months. Maybe it was good for him.

Exercise—even forced exercise—could lift people's spirits, too. Being out in nature and fresh air was good for all of them—as long as they didn't freeze to death.

He nearly passed right by the place where they'd edged off the road the last time they stopped. Their tracks were barely visible under the blanket of new fallen snow. He scouted around a bit until he found the green duffel bag protruding from the white powder. It must have fallen when he began to pull the sled again.

Funny he hadn't noticed.

Too busy ogling Hope, he figured as he picked it up, turned around and headed back toward the others as fast as he could.

Too busy wondering if he could persuade her to marry him in the little time he had left.

"WE'RE NOT GOING to make it to Bozeman tonight, are we?" Raina asked.

Not at this pace, Hope wanted to say but didn't. They'd switched off again, and now Byron and Blake wore the skis. Raina was limping. Badly. She wasn't doing much better. Her tight boots pinched so much every step was excruciating. "I don't think so. Unless someone comes along with a vehicle."

"I can't believe no one has passed us on the road yet," Raina said dispiritedly.

Hope eyed her with concern. "Maybe you should ride on the sled."

"There isn't room for me on the sled."

She was right about the lack of traffic, Hope thought. It was downright eerie up here in the woods. So was the lack of houses. Hadn't Curtis said this road led to hunting cabins and summer cottages? She hadn't seen anything like that so far.

"We probably should have turned back and headed home when we got to that detour," Blake said.

"I know." Raina sounded remorseful. "If anything bad happens to us, it'll all be my fault."

To Hope's surprise, Blake reached for the basket of kittens. "It looks heavy," he explained when Raina looked like she'd stop him. "I'll take it for a while. And I'll be careful," he added before Raina could say anything.

"It's no one's fault things haven't gone according to plan," Byron said. Hope hadn't realized the young man had caught up to them. He was filming again. Of course.

"Are you kidding?" Hope couldn't let that slide. "We shouldn't even have set out in a snowstorm. You shouldn't have been driving like a maniac and run us off the road. Curtis should have brought more than one snowmobile—or at least more skis. And he should be back by now. Where is he?" She slowed down. Her feet were really killing her. Blake kept going.

Raina's expression softened. "You're worried about him."

"I'm worried about you. About your wedding."

About getting her job at Yellowstone.

Although she hadn't thought about that once since Curtis had gone to fetch Raina's dress. Raina was right; all she'd thought about was Curtis. Where he was. If he'd found it.

If he was coming back.

She felt safer when he was nearby, but it wasn't just that; she felt—enlivened. Was that a word?

She was pretty sure it was, and it encompassed the feelings in her body perfectly. When Curtis was around, she found herself checking for him, looking to see how he reacted to something someone had said, seeing if he was still nearby.

She liked him nearby.

Which was a big problem.

"There he is!" Raina exclaimed, and Hope's heart jumped.

"Where?" But she could already make out his shape in the dimming light through the driving snow. Thank goodness he was back.

"I got it!" Curtis waved the duffel bag triumphantly over his head as he joined them. "Where's Blake?"

Hope looked around. "He was here a second ago."

"Blake!" Raina called out. "Blake, get back here with those kittens right now!"

Hope held her breath. He wouldn't have done something to the kittens, would he?

When another shape approached them from the opposite direction that Curtis had come from, she relaxed.

"What's the problem now?" Blake demanded. "You all are so damn slow!" He was still carrying the basket of kittens.

"Time to stop for the night," Curtis said. "It's getting dark. Let's head off the road and find a place to camp."

"Or we could just break into that cabin up there." Blake pointed farther down the road.

Curtis straightened. "Cabin?"

"A couple of hundred yards ahead," Blake said with satisfaction. "See? If we'd stuck together we'd have spent another night outside unnecessarily."

Hope smothered a laugh as Curtis's hands flexed and was impressed when he managed to hold his tongue. Blake would try a saint.

They all picked up their pace, even Raina. When Curtis managed to force open the door to the little log cabin Blake had spotted through the trees, they spilled inside.

"It's colder in here than it is outside," Raina said, clapping her hands against her arms.

"I'll take care of that in a jiffy." Curtis gestured to a pile of dry wood stored against one wall. "People up here stock their cabins carefully because you can get freak storms in early autumn or late spring. We could stay warm here for a month with all that fuel."

"Do they have a land line?" Hope asked, searching the small space but coming up empty.

"Up here? Not likely," Curtis confirmed.

"They don't have cell phone reception either," Raina said a moment later.

Curtis didn't seem surprised. Moments later he had a blaze going in the old cast-iron woodstove that stood in one corner, and they'd all stripped out of their wet things and hung them to dry. Once the fire was taken care of, Curtis moved into the kitchen, bringing the backpack full of food items he'd carried along.

"A nice hot dinner will cure all our woes," he said as he began to rummage through it, putting cans of food on the counter.

"Not all our woes," Hope said softly, coming to join him while the rest of the party kept close to the fire. "Raina's going to miss her wedding tomorrow."

Curtis's movements slowed. "Not if I can help it."

"Face facts. We're not going to make it." She was tired of pretending this was all going to work out.

"We'll be up first thing. Dry, fed—we'll make it. Somehow," he added grimly.

His answer irritated her. He was a Navy SEAL, after all. He should be practical.

Truthful.

When you messed with the schedule, things didn't work out. He had to know that.

Hope struggled to get her rising emotions under control. She was tired. In pain.

"You don't understand how important this is," she burst out. Hope wasn't sure why her anger was flaring now. Curtis was right; they were safe and dry—surely that was all that mattered. But Raina's words from earlier were haunting her. This wasn't about her job; this was about Raina. Her best friend. The woman who'd cheered her on for years no matter what goals she set.

She'd made Raina and Ben a promise. And they hadn't stuck to the plan. And now everything had gone wrong. She didn't know if Raina's injury was serious— didn't know what else might happen—

"I understand how important—"

"Do you? Really? When was the last time you waited and waited for someone you cared for, and they simply didn't show up?"

Hope was surprised to find herself shaking with anger, memories she'd pushed into the recesses of her mind for so long shattering free and cascading into her mind one after another. Her beautiful gown. Her hair and nails done just so. Her mother waiting with her camera.

The prom date who never came.

She blinked back the tears that pricked her eyes. She was just tired. She'd put what happened with Liam behind her a long time ago.

"You don't know as much about me as you think you do," Curtis growled.

"I know you have no idea how Ben is going to feel waiting at the altar tomorrow when Raina doesn't show up!"

A thump, followed by a chorus of meows, alerted her that everyone—including Raina—had heard her.

"Don't say that." Raina stood across the room with her hands on her hips. The basket at her feet spilled out curious kittens, delighted to finally be set free. "Don't you dare say I'm not going to show up. Curtis is going to get me there. He promised he would, and he will."

"He can't get you there. Don't you see that?" Hope contradicted. "This is my fault. I should have built contingency days in. I should have known not to trust someone who crosses out pages and writes over my—"

"Raina's right. I promised her I'd get her to her wedding, and I damn well will," Curtis said, cutting her off. "Because you're wrong—I know exactly what it feels like—"

He didn't finish. Instead, he grabbed his jacket from where he'd hung it in the entryway, flung open the front door, stalked outside and slammed it behind him.

"Jesus, Hope. Don't you watch *Base Camp*?" Blake asked, joining Hope in the kitchen, picking up a can, fumbling around in the drawers until he found an opener, and beginning to open it. "Everyone knows Curtis's first love left him at the altar fifteen years ago." He opened a few more cans and bent to search for a pot in the cupboards.

"His first love?" Hope's heart sank as she replayed in her mind the words she'd just said to him. Curtis had been left at the altar?

Raina was watching her. "That's right. His high-school sweetheart. Then earlier this year Samantha married Harris instead of him."

"He wanted to marry Sam?" She remembered the woman from their short time at Base Camp. She and her husband had been there at breakfast and had come to wave them off.

"Boone set her up with Curtis, but she preferred Harris instead," Byron explained. "It's not that he wanted to marry her, but it was a blow to his ego."

Raina nodded. "From what I've seen on *Base Camp*, Curtis is the kind of guy who wants to find a wife and settle down, Hope. It just hasn't happened for him yet."

Liam's face flashed through Hope's mind again. The giant crush she'd had on him. The way her mother had waited so eagerly to capture photos of them on prom night, like Byron when he filmed everything.

She shoved the memories down. She wouldn't think of them. Couldn't.

But she could apologize to Curtis.

"Excuse me," she said.

CHAPTER SEVEN

HOPE HADN'T WATCHED the show. At all. She didn't know what kind of a loser he was. Dumped—twice—by women he was supposed to marry. Skunked a third time when he tried to make a go of it with Michele. Everyone else here knew about his past, but Hope had no idea. He'd kind of hoped to win her over before she learned about it.

Curtis checked over their skis and the other equipment they'd left on the front porch. He didn't know what he was doing out here—he needed to get warm, dry and fed like everyone else, but he couldn't stand the look of pity he knew he'd see in Hope's eyes when she realized his track record with love and marriage sucked.

The door opened behind him, and Curtis sighed. Couldn't a man nurse his pride in private?

"Hey," Hope said, and he stiffened. He'd expected Byron, or maybe Raina.

Not Hope.

"I'm sorry." She shut the door behind her and joined him in the cold.

This was stupid, Curtis thought again. They shouldn't be out here in this weather.

"I didn't know you'd been left at the altar," Hope added.

"I didn't want you to know." Was that all Raina had told her? Did she know any of the circumstances? Maybe not. Maybe Raina had left him a way to keep a little of his pride intact.

"Want to tell me about it?"

"Not really." She didn't look like she was going anywhere, though. Curtis sighed again. Time for a bit of truth, he supposed. "I was a teenager, and I'd dated Angela all through high school. I was absolutely smitten. She... decided at the last minute she wasn't. I can see now we both got carried away and tried to grow up much too fast. I should thank her for making the right choice for both of us. Somehow it still left a scar."

"Of course it did. You'd planned to spend your life with her. It doesn't matter that you were kids. What happened with Samantha? I'm not sure I understand that. Were you in love with her, too?"

"With Sam? Hell, no." He snapped his mouth shut, realizing that sounded harsh. "I mean—Harris is a good friend of mine, and I don't hold anything against them. It's just—she was coming to Base Camp to meet me, and she met Harris instead and fell for him right away. I just... panicked... afterward. Thought maybe I'd never find the right woman."

"I'm sure you will."

"Did Raina tell you I tried to get married again just

before you arrived?"

"No!" Hope drew back, stuffing her hands in her jacket pockets, her eyes wide. "Oh my goodness, Curtis. What happened? You must be devastated—" She winced, and he knew she had to be thinking of the kisses they'd shared because her expression darkened. "Is that why—?"

"No, it's not why I kissed you. I'm relieved it didn't work out. Michele and I didn't love each other at all. I think we both gave up on love altogether for a minute there and tried to make marriage a kind of business arrangement. We thought we could help each other, but we were wrong. She was in love with someone else, and I decided I wanted to hold out for the real thing."

"Why... why are you trying so hard to get married?"

Curtis could tell he'd lost all the ground he'd gained with her. Now she thought he was careless about marriage and love, when she couldn't be further from the truth. Something held him back from telling her about his deadline, though. Hope wouldn't like it. She would think he was trying to use her. "Why are you trying so hard to avoid marriage?" he countered.

"Because of my plan—"

"Baloney. What's the real reason?"

She was quiet for a long time before she turned to survey the woods at the edge of the lot, as if she'd only just noticed she was outside. "I actually do have plans— lots of them. Dreams that are important to me."

Curtis nodded, knowing there was more and hoping she trusted him enough to tell him. "I get that. I don't want to stop you from pursuing your dreams, Hope."

"It's more than that, though."

He waited to hear an explanation. She was still gazing out into the falling snow. Whatever had happened in the past was alive and well in her mind right now. He hoped she'd share it with him, but in the end she just shook her head.

"You live in Montana, and from what I understand you're pretty set on staying in Chance Creek."

"That's right." He was, and she needed to know that.

"Yellowstone Park is in Wyoming. That's too far—"

"We'd make it work. I know we could figure out something—"

"You know what? It's cold." She turned away, reaching for the door handle, but she stopped before touching it. "Curtis, I wish—"

She didn't finish. She didn't have to. He knew everything she was trying to say. She wished the timing was different. That she was different—or that he was.

He didn't realize he was moving until he'd crossed the porch and taken her into his arms. "If you aren't going to give me a chance, at least kiss me one last time so I can remember what I'm missing." He pulled her tight against him, cupped the nape of her neck and met her mouth with his own, savoring every sensation.

She was sweet and soft, yielding to the heat of his desire. Once he started, Curtis found he couldn't stop. He pressed her up against the wall, boxing her in, kissing her—sliding his tongue between her lips.

When Hope sighed against him, Curtis was lost. He wanted more. So much more.

Finally, he drew back, keeping his gaze on her face.

Hope stared back at him, a look that contained so much emotion he thought he could drown in it. She opened her mouth to say something, and he knew instinctively she'd package up this experience in a box to put on a shelf—to leave behind.

He pressed his mouth to hers again to stop her. Kissed her thoroughly, knowing it was probably the last time. She'd stated her case. Told him she wouldn't change her life to fit his.

When he couldn't bear it anymore, he pulled back and led her inside without another word.

A flurry at a nearby window alerted him that Byron had been filming them. He didn't think Hope had noticed, though. Inside, the small cabin was full of the aroma of cooking food. His stomach gave a ravenous grumble, despite the ache in his heart.

"Something smells good." Hope sounded as dazed as he felt, even as she tried to act like nothing had happened. Maybe he should let her go so she could follow her plans and reach her dreams, but he was having a hard time thinking that was a good idea.

"Blake's made chili," Raina called out cheerfully. She was sitting on the floor surrounded by kittens, Daisy curled up a few feet away. "Turns out he's a man of many talents. He should find a woman to cook for."

The stack of bowls hit the counter with a crash, and Blake swore as he saved them from sliding to the floor.

"Hell, that was close."

"Raina hit a nerve, huh?" Byron asked, filming him.

"I don't need a woman," Blake said. "My money keeps me company."

Curtis shucked off his coat and helped Hope out of hers. Every brush of his fingers against her was agony. He wanted to lead her into one of the other rooms and use every means at his disposal to give him a chance to change her mind.

"All right, folks. Let's eat," Blake said.

Curtis led Hope to the counter where he'd begun to dish the chili into bowls. He had no idea how he'd get through the rest of this trip.

"I'M STAYING RIGHT here," Raina said when dinner was over. She was stretched out on the couch, her left foot resting on a pillow. Hope had taken a closer look, pronounced her ankle sprained and wrapped it tightly in an elastic bandage. "Keep it elevated." Hope placed a decorative pillow under her, then passed her a pile of blankets and another pillow for her head. They were all sleepy after their rigorous day and heavy meal. There were two bedrooms off the main living space, one large one with a queen-size sway-backed bed and one small one that struck her as an afterthought—a closet made into a bedroom or something along those lines. That one had a twin mattress on a homemade wooden frame.

"I can sleep out here on the floor near Raina," she suggested. The couch wasn't the fold-out type, and she didn't think curling up in the moth-eaten easy chair would be too comfortable, but even the hard floor would be better than sleeping in a tent in the snow.

"You take the small bedroom. Blake and Byron can take the other one. I'll sleep out here on the floor and keep the woodstove going," Curtis said.

Disappointment surged through her. She couldn't say why. She hadn't been hoping to share a room with Curtis, of course.

But now that she'd thought about it, somehow she couldn't get the image of it out of her mind. What would it be like to share a bed—alone—with a man like Curtis? To touch him intimately?

To sleep with him—in both senses of the phrase?

She had a feeling it would be wonderful, and she began to wonder how she could ever have been cold today, because right now she was feeling pretty darn warm.

She couldn't sleep with Curtis, though. Couldn't think about a future with him, either. Opening her heart to a man was dangerous—especially one with such a checkered past.

She and Curtis took charge of cleaning up the meal, while Byron and Blake began a kind of awkward dance of maneuvering around the bedroom they were to share, spreading out their things, making up two separate sleeping arrangements on the bed and generally behaving like teenagers afraid their manhood was about to be questioned.

"We get it; you're both straight!" Raina called out finally. "Get over yourselves. None of us would care if you weren't."

Blake grunted his displeasure. Byron kept rummaging through his bag, as if he'd lost something.

Finally, they settled in, and Hope prepared to do the same.

"You have everything you need?" she asked Raina for the fifth time as Raina snuggled under her covers on the couch.

"Yes. Go to bed. All of you. You're driving me insane. I have to sleep so I look pretty for my wedding tomorrow."

Hope stifled her warning that there might not be a wedding tomorrow. Raina didn't need to hear that again. Instead, she kissed the top of Raina's head and made her way to the smaller bedroom.

"Good night," she said to Curtis. "And—thanks. For everything."

"You're welcome." He came closer, and for a moment she thought he'd kiss her again.

She wanted him to.

So badly.

He didn't. He simply nodded and turned to the pallet of blankets and comforters he was using to make a bed on the floor.

Come sleep with me, she wanted to say but didn't.

Alone in her room, she wished for once she'd tossed her plans to the wind and followed her heart.

HE HAD TO let her go, Curtis thought. It was the right thing to do. The only thing to do. Hope deserved to live the life she wanted without his interference. She'd made contacts that would help her secure a job. She'd undertaken to get Raina to her wedding—mostly because she loved her friend but also to do a favor for a man who could help her along that road.

And something had happened in her past to make her shy away from long-term commitments. If she was clear that she wasn't able to have a relationship with him, he should thank her for her honesty.

Not sit here scheming about how to change her mind.

What he was feeling was just an infatuation, he told himself. It was an impulse honed by evolution to make sure the species survived. He hadn't known Hope long enough to know he wanted to marry her for real. It had been nice to think so, given his circumstances, but chances were time would tell them they weren't any more compatible than he and Michele had been.

So why did it feel like they might be? Every time he saw the little things Hope did to make sure Raina was safe, happy, comfortable, he knew she was the kind of person he valued in the world. The kind of person who saw the web of interconnectedness shared by everything on earth. The kind of woman who tended that web.

That was why she wanted to go to Yellowstone so badly, and he couldn't blame her. Where else could someone work among the most beautiful scenery of the world and possibly influence the thinking of so many people?

Visitors came to the park to be awed by the geysers

and the grandeur of the scenery, but once there they were taught about food chains, the importance of predators, the way fire interacted with the landscape and the ways humans should—and shouldn't—mess with that system. And so much more.

Of course, she wanted to keep that dream. If he hadn't committed to Base Camp, she easily could have persuaded him to come with her. He *had* committed to Base Camp, though, and he wasn't a man to walk out on commitments.

Which meant he had to let her go.

Pain squeezed his heart, and something more— something too close to panic for comfort. He had to marry someone the day after tomorrow. Boone had promised him a backup bride, but he was still stuck out here in the snow. Still miles from where he was supposed to be.

What if he didn't make it?

What if he didn't marry?

What if he ruined everything for everyone?

He couldn't stand it if that happened, but he wasn't sure he could stand losing Hope, either. He wanted to hold her close. To be with her. Spend his days—and nights—with her. He'd tried to keep himself from envisioning the latter but had failed miserably, and his discomfort grew with every tantalizing imagined moment.

"Oh my god, would you stop snoring?" Raina cried.

"I'm not snoring." Curtis propped himself up on his elbow, the better to see across the dimly lit room. He didn't snore. And he hadn't even been sleeping.

"Yes, you are. You're going to shake the whole house down. It's my wedding tomorrow, Curtis. I need sleep."

"Sorry." But he was sure he'd been awake.

Raina sighed theatrically and rolled over to face him. He could see the whites of her eyes in the dim firelight. "Starting tomorrow there's going to be a man in my bed every single day for the rest of my life. Do you think it's selfish of me to want to spend one last night alone?"

Hell. He wasn't used to Raina making demands. Kind of rude ones at that. He slowly got to his feet, though. He didn't know much about brides. Maybe she was having jitters. Maybe she was pissed that she'd have to hobble down the aisle rather than walk it.

Maybe she was afraid she wouldn't get there at all.

"Not there, you idiot," Raina said, shaking him from his thoughts. He'd just been about to open the door to Blake and Byron's room.

"Then where?" He was losing patience, fast. He needed sleep, too.

"There!"

He could barely make out her arm in the gloom. Was she pointing to Hope's room?

"I don't think—"

"Oh my god, you are so dumb! You need a wife, Curtis. Like… in the next forty-eight hours. Am I right, or am I right?"

"You're right."

"And you're totally lusting after Hope."

Was it that obvious?

"You told her you were going to marry her," she pointed out.

"Wishful thinking, I guess."

"Wishful wussing out, you mean. I didn't think you were a quitter, Curtis Lloyd."

"I'm not, but—"

"Get in there and make a play for my friend. She likes you, too. That's obvious. And I don't want to wait ten years for her to be married. I'm going to have kids next year. I want to do mommy things together. I want our girls to be best friends, just like we were. So get in there and make it happen!"

"I'm not going to force my presence on someone who doesn't want me."

"Then go ask if she wants you."

"She said she doesn't want a relationship."

"Ask her to marry you."

Curtis winced. "What if she says no?"

"Then you'll sulk and moan and get over it. Get in there. Ask her. Make her love you, Curtis. Do it for me." She clasped her hands together like an old-fashioned heroine.

"I thought you're going to live in Bozeman—"

"We'll see about that. Besides, Bozeman isn't that far from Chance Creek."

That was true, and Curtis knew damn well that Hope and Raina were the kind of friends who shouldn't be separated. He changed direction and made for the door of Hope's smaller bedroom, telling himself he was doing it for Raina. It was a total lie. He wanted Hope badly, and he was running out of time. If he didn't make a play for her now, he wouldn't get another chance.

Daisy stood up, yawned and followed him.

Raina patted the couch cushion beside her. "Daisy? Stay." The dog looked from her to Curtis questioningly.

"Stay with Raina," he instructed.

He needed time alone with Hope.

"HOPE? YOU ASLEEP?" someone asked.

Hope turned quickly in bed and found her door open a crack. It unnerved her she hadn't heard the handle turn, but there was no mistaking that deep voice.

Curtis.

"I'm awake."

He slipped inside the room and shut the door behind him, then crossed to sit on the edge of her bed. She pushed herself to a sitting position.

"What's wrong? Is it Raina?"

"No—well, yes. She's fine, but she says I snore. She kicked me out. Told me to come sleep in here."

Hope was going to kill her. She'd almost been asleep, after struggling to clear her mind of a series of salacious images of herself and Curtis in intimate position after intimate position. Now all those images came raging back.

He was so close she could reach out and touch him.

"She's matchmaking," she said.

"Blatantly matchmaking," he agreed with a chuckle.

"It's the marriage thing. She wants everyone around

her coupled up."

"Is that so bad?"

"I guess not."

"So, do you mind if I sleep in here? Contrary to your friend's assertion, I don't snore."

"I don't mind." Although she wouldn't sleep a wink if he did.

He began to lay blankets on the floor, and Hope curled up her knees and rested her chin on them. It was going to be cold down there. The floor was hard. There was no reason they couldn't share a bed for one night.

"Curtis—" She didn't know how to go on. Would he think she was coming on to him? "I'm not going to have sex with you."

"Glad we cleared that up," he said dryly.

"I mean—you can sleep up here. With me. If you don't touch me." She patted the bed.

In the dim light she saw the glint of his eyes as he turned to her. "You and me in a twin bed are going to touch, no matter what I do. You sure you want me in there?"

"Yes. We're both adults. It doesn't have to mean anything—if we do touch."

He sighed, but he stopped messing around with the blankets on the floor. Instead, he peeled off the T-shirt he still wore, which left him in his boxers, she realized, and he lifted the blankets to climb in.

"You need to sleep by the wall," she told him, clambering out. "I get claustrophobic."

"Okay." He got in, slid over and stretched out full

length, then held up the bedclothes for her to climb in, too.

Hope did, and he tucked the blankets around them both, brushing her arm as he did so.

"Sorry. See? Touched you already," he said.

"You know what I mean."

"It was a pretty clear message."

Curtis took up most of the bed, and Hope found herself clinging to the edge of the mattress to stay on it. When he turned on his side behind her, she could feel the heat of him all along her body, even if he did try to keep a few inches' distance between them.

He was being silly. If he put his arm over her waist, they'd both fit so much better.

She was the one who'd forbidden any touching, though.

She let out a gusty breath and wriggled backward until she pressed along the length of him. That was better.

"Hey, you're breaking the rules," he said, his voice tickling her ear.

Now that they were this close, she wanted more. She reached back, grabbed his wrist and circled his arm around her waist. There, that was much better.

"Lady, you are on very thin ice," he warned.

"Am I going to get a citation?" Somehow that sounded sexy. Why did that sound sexy?

"You better believe it." He pulled her in closer and kissed her neck. Hope closed her eyes. The touch of him was heavenly. Her entire body was drinking in his proximity, energized by it.

God, she wanted him.

Would that be wrong? she wondered. To touch him? To turn over and kiss him? To invite him to—

"Hope Martin, I want you," Curtis breathed. "I want you so bad."

Her pulse leaped.

This wasn't in her plans.

This wasn't sensible—or correct—or anything. But she wanted him, too.

Hope turned over, wrapped a leg around his waist, twisted her fingers in his short, dark hair and kissed him like she meant it.

"I want you, too."

CHAPTER EIGHT

C URTIS STIFLED A groan. Hope was going to kill him if she kept up like this. He'd climbed into her bed telling himself he'd be a gentleman and appreciate being close to her, but that was all. Hadn't he just wrestled his conscience to the ground out in the living room and told himself to let her go?

He couldn't be a gentleman when she was wrapped around him, her curvy, wonderful body warm from the heavy covers on the bed.

"Hope," he groaned.

"Don't think. Make your mind a blank," she told him. "That's what I'm doing."

He couldn't argue with that, even when a sensible voice in his head told him he was sure to regret it in the morning—when he had to deliver Hope and Raina to Bozeman and walk away.

He'd regret it more if he didn't have this one night with her, he told that voice. Something to cling to when he went and married whoever Boone had chosen for him. He pushed all thought of Boone and backup brides out of his mind, focused on Hope—and the way she was making him feel.

"You're wearing too many clothes," he growled into her neck. He slid his hands toward the hem of her tank top but got distracted when he palmed her breasts through the thin fabric of her top, and she moaned again, arching back, the better to give him access.

Curtis tugged the garment up and over her head, ripping the neckline a little.

"Sorry."

"Not sorry," she breathed back and let out a shaky breath when he covered her breasts with his hands again. "Curtis—that feels so good."

Up on one elbow, Hope on her back, he leaned over her, dipped his head and took one of her hard nipples into his mouth, circling it with his tongue, teasing the nub until her she arched again.

He could play with her breasts all day. Soft handfuls of loveliness that revved him up and made his body come alive when he touched them. Curtis couldn't get enough—

But he wanted to explore every part of her.

Hope shimmied out of her panties, and he shucked off his boxers. "Should we slow down?" he asked. "Check your planner to make sure sex is on the schedule for tonight?"

"Hell, no. I want this. I want to feel you—"

He knew what she meant. He couldn't stop skimming his hands over her curves, loving the dip between her breasts and hips, the feel of her ass.

Curtis rolled over onto his back and brought her with him to straddle him. The heat of her perched over his erection made him throb with want, but before they went further, he wanted to look at her.

In the low light she was a goddess, her heavy breasts and wide hips a wonder of nature. Curtis settled her firmly on him. "Do you have any idea how beautiful you are?" he asked her, somehow knowing she didn't. Most women didn't.

That was a crime.

Hope shrugged.

That wasn't good enough for Curtis. "Say it," he commanded her, rocking his hips a little, just to feel her on top of him.

"Say what?"

"Say you're beautiful."

"Curtis—"

"Do it."

"I'm beautiful." She leaned forward and shook her head. "Do you know how stupid that sounds?"

"It isn't stupid. It's true, and you should know it down to the very heart of you. Hope, you are something special." He skimmed his hands up her body. The flare of her hips gave way to the curve of her waist and then the exquisite bloom of her breasts. Why didn't women play with themselves all day? There was so much to appreciate.

"I'm beautiful," she said again, leaning farther forward to tempt him with her nipples.

It worked. Curtis gave them their due, nuzzling

them and teasing them until he knew Hope was as desperate as he was to get even closer.

"Protection?" he asked, hoping against hope they were good. It wasn't like he was carrying a condom.

"I'm on the Pill," she affirmed. "I'm good."

"Me, too."

He couldn't wait anymore. Seizing her hips, he lifted her and positioned himself beneath her. As he nudged against her, the warmth of her inner folds caressing the tip of him required him to exert every ounce of control he had. She slid down around him effortlessly, wet enough to welcome him inside in one slick swoop. Curtis's breath went ragged.

This was heaven.

This was everything he wanted.

He began to move.

HOPE CLUNG TO Curtis's shoulders, allowing him to set the pace, loving every sensation he was creating inside her, acknowledging how right it felt to take him inside.

She'd never known this kind of desire. Had never found it this easy to become this intimate with a man. It was as if her body had always known his, that it was welcoming him home, not inviting him in for the first time.

She loved this. Loved connecting with Curtis, feeling him, encircling him, taking him in.

She loved feeling this womanly, knowing her breasts made his heart beat harder, knowing that every way they touched was driving him closer to losing control.

Hope didn't want to stop. She didn't want this to ever end.

This room. This night—were everything.

She closed her eyes and rocked with him, and as he sped up inside her, she opened to him, allowing him deep, giving up control, letting him move her, position her, make love to her.

He imprisoned her wrists behind her, and the angle increased her pleasure even more. She arched her back, spread her thighs and settled more firmly on his hips.

A sound escaped him, and she knew Curtis was close. Hope tilted back her head, sent her consciousness deep inside, wanting to feel every last sensation.

She came with a cry that tore from her throat as if it had a life of its own, and pleasure pulsed along with every thrust Curtis made inside her. He followed suit, grunting with the energy of his thrusts, his orgasm taking her into another wave of release. Sensation crashed through her, shaking her body, wringing her dry of feeling until she collapsed on top of him, breathing as hard as if she'd run a race.

Curtis gathered her to him, whispered something into her hair and kissed her forehead. Hope listened to the strong, regular beat of his heart. This was a man to reckon with. A man who made her feel things no one else ever had.

Could she really walk away from him tomorrow?

Hope didn't know.

It was a long time before Curtis spoke, and she didn't want to break the spell, either. His body pressed against hers still felt wonderful, as did the lazy strokes of his hand over her skin.

The real world was already intruding, though. Hope wondered if everyone in the cabin had heard her cry and known what she and Curtis were doing. She wondered what it would be like tomorrow morning when it was time to get up.

What it would be like to leave him behind?

"Tell me about Yellowstone," Curtis said.

"It's been my dream to work there all my life." She stroked her hand over his hard chest, feeling his heartbeat. What an amazing thing the human body was. "I went with my folks when I was little. They're back in Ohio where I grew up. We spent a week there. I was enchanted. The wide open spaces, the campgrounds, the geysers. The bison. The wolves."

"Wolves?"

"There was all this information about re-introducing wolves into the park to restore the top predator to the food chain. I was fascinated by it—by the idea that even if humans made mistakes, they could reverse them, and by the idea that we could decide to allow things—or even to reinstate them—even if we didn't like them much. I mean, wolves are scary. They eat livestock. I know why ranchers don't want them around. I understand why we just about wiped them out. Then we made discoveries about why it might be a good thing to have them around—at least in some places. And even though they still scare us, we helped them return. Human beings can be wonderful like that." She traced a finger over his bicep. "So often all we hear about is the bad or the cowardly things we do. I love it when we're brave."

He nodded. "I get that."

"Our third night there I woke up when everyone else was sleeping. I snuck out of our tent to use the bathroom, and once I was out there, I couldn't believe how beautiful the night was. There were so many stars. The night was thrumming with energy. I could feel all the different critters around me in the darkness even if I couldn't see them, and Curtis—I wasn't scared. I was... alive. Then the wolves began to howl." She didn't know how to describe that, but she had a feeling Curtis was a man who could understand it anyway. "In that moment, I knew what braveness meant. It meant that you know all the possibilities—everything that can go wrong—and you go ahead and follow your lights anyway."

His arms tightened around her.

"I want to be brave like that again." Her voice wobbled, and she got control of it again. "I want to live like that. In nature. Outside. Striving toward an ideal. Do you understand that?"

"Yeah." Curtis chuckled. "I absolutely understand that."

THE DESIRE TO live outside in nature—to strive toward an ideal—was exactly what had propelled him to join Base Camp and move to Montana. He wasn't really being brave, though, right now, was he? He'd told her wanted her. Told her he'd marry her.

He hadn't told her why, though.

"I understand because that's the way I feel about Base Camp. I know you don't watch the show." At the moment he was glad she didn't. "Do you know what we're trying to do there?"

"Sort of."

He settled in, drawing the covers more firmly around them, loving the soft weight of Hope covering his torso like a human blanket.

"Boone, Clay, Jericho and Walker had the idea first. They wanted to find a parcel of land to develop sustainably, figure out the best way to build housing, grow food, make use of green energy and so on. They wanted to do it in such a way that other people could learn from them. They partnered with Martin Fulsom."

"Isn't he a millionaire?"

"Billionaire. Crazy as a loon. Great at getting publicity. He came up with the reality television show idea. He's the one who made everything possible—but also set it up so we could lose everything."

"Lose it? How?"

"If we don't meet his criteria. We have to build ten tiny houses to certain specifications. Get the energy grid up and functional. Grow food through the winter. Things like that."

"Sounds complicated."

"It is. You know I help with the tiny houses. I'm a carpenter."

"I liked the one you showed me, but are tiny houses practical?"

"A single tiny house on its own plot of land might

not be. But a whole bunch of them sharing a plot of land, with community gardens and a shared community space for larger gatherings, is."

"Yeah, I see that."

"Our gardens are great, and we're working on growing food throughout the winter. The best part is the bison herd. Bison graze differently than cattle do. They're part of Montana's ecology, so like the wolves in Yellowstone, they help balance things out."

"They certainly looked like they belonged at Base Camp." She sounded wistful.

"They make me happy every time I see them," he admitted. "I guess I feel like the life I'm building there is brave. People think we're crazy for worrying about where our energy comes from and how we grow our food and live, but I don't care, because when I die I want to know that I tried the best I could to do what's right. I'd rather give it my all and fail than give up before I even start."

"I can understand that." But she clammed up after that, and Curtis knew better than to push her. Maybe he'd made her think a bit, though.

In fact, maybe he needed to give her more to think about.

He turned over and spilled her onto her back, quickly fitting himself between her thighs, lifting her wrists above her head. He shifted his hips to see her reaction. When she lifted hers to meet his, he knew they were on the same page.

Still, he wanted to hear her say it.

"I want to make love to you again, Hope. What do you think about that?"

"I want you to make love to me."

"Yeah?" He was hard again. Aching to be inside her.

"Yeah. Please, Curtis. Hurry."

As he buried himself inside her, Curtis knew Hope had hold of his heart for good. It was too late to second guess the wisdom of getting this close to her.

She'd either reel him in or toss him back out to sea.

His fate was in her hands now.

WHEN HOPE WOKE up the following morning, she made love to Curtis a third time, neither of them saying a word, their bodies working together as if they'd known each other for years rather than days. She tried to stay in the moment, pushing the knowledge that soon they'd part ways from her mind.

She couldn't remember the last time she'd felt so good. Curtis's hands moved over her body as if memorizing her curves, and she found herself doing the same to his, wanting to be able to remember every inch of him when he was no longer close.

She felt ravenous for him and as awake as if she'd just drunk her very first cup of coffee. Her veins thrummed with longing for him, even as he was filling her, moving with her, bringing her once more to the kind of earth-shattering orgasm that only he could elicit from her.

Afterward, she had to blink back the tears that collected in her eyes, and she was grateful Curtis didn't seem to notice them as she disengaged from him and climbed out of bed.

Brave, indeed. Was she being brave running away from him?

Would she find another man someday who could make her feel what she was feeling now?

Or was she making a mistake—?

Blake and Byron's bickering out in the main room brought Hope back to the present. There was no more time to think of herself.

"We need to get Raina to her wedding," she said.

Curtis just nodded, bundled a blanket around himself and slipped out to the bathroom. A half hour later they were too busy packing and prepping for the next stage of their journey for her to give her feelings for him any more thought. Raina could barely walk, which meant they were going to be hard-pressed to continue.

"Raina will ride on the sled, holding the basket of kittens," Curtis decided. "We'll store everything we can around her. Blake and Byron, you'll take turns skiing. I'll pull Raina. You two will take turns helping me. All of us will have to carry some gear."

"Are we close to the highway?" Raina asked.

"I hope so," Curtis said. "It snowed all night, and it's still coming down, so it's going to be rough going out there, but we'll stick together and make as much progress as we can."

Hope noticed Curtis left some bills tucked under the sugar canister in the kitchen and made sure to replenish the wood they'd used from the large stack on the front porch and that the door was shut tight when they left.

As it turned out, their progress was faster, even though the snow had gotten deeper overnight, because Raina was no longer slowing them down. She was quiet today, and Hope knew she had to be despairing that they'd ever make it to Bozeman. Hope had quietly applied bandages to her own toes and was grateful to be back in her own boots today since they'd dried overnight by the fire.

"I haven't given up yet," Curtis remarked about a half an hour into their excursion. Byron had forged ahead on the skis. Blake was slogging along behind them. Raina was absorbed in her own thoughts. Daisy trailed behind them, keeping close but sticking to the trail they'd tamped down in the snow.

"On what?" She thought she knew, though.

"On being with you."

She wanted that, too, but being with Curtis meant giving up Yellowstone.

"It would never work," she declared, aiming for a bit of levity. It was Raina's wedding day, after all. "The commute from Chance Creek to Yellowstone is too damn long. Who'd cook dinner?"

"You'd have to do that when you got home," Curtis said swiftly. "I'll be too busy running my tiny house building company."

Hope snorted. "I'm not cooking at midnight, which is when I'd get home."

"You'd have to feed the dog, too. Daisy will be hungry by then."

"What about the cats?" She looked over her shoulder.

"Oh, no. I'm not falling for the basket of kittens trick. Those are going with Raina."

"You'd have to do all the vacuuming," Hope told him. "I don't hold with cleaning."

"At all?"

"Too busy restocking the country with wolves."

"I'll vacuum, if you take out the trash. I don't hold with trash."

Hope smiled despite herself. "What kind of a Navy SEAL are you?"

"The kind who gets women to take out his trash."

She rolled her eyes. "What else would I have to do?"

"Library books. Return them. Can't seem to manage that."

"If you'll de-scale the fish. I hate de-scaling fish."

"You do a lot of fishing?" he asked.

"None." She grinned.

"Guess I can manage that. But you'll need to pop all the bubble wrap. Just in case."

"In case of what?"

"In case it doesn't come popped. That stuff is a menace."

"You're lucky Byron isn't filming this," Raina put in. "Both of you would lose all your street cred."

"I'm not sure I ever had any street cred," Hope said.

"Mine's impenetrable," Curtis said.

"Like your thick skull?" Blake asked, picking up his pace and trudging past them. "Hurry up, or we'll never get there."

CHAPTER NINE

CURTIS IGNORED BLAKE and slowed a little, letting the other man get ahead of them. "What made you such a planner?" he asked when Blake was out of hearing range. The question had been bothering him because Hope had proved last night she could be every bit as much the "leap-before-you-look" type as well as a buttoned-up schedule type.

At first he thought Hope might not answer. She took her time, trudging along beside him.

"It was prom. Junior year," Raina prompted softly from behind them.

Hope cast a look back at her Curtis couldn't decipher but then nodded. "She's right," she said reluctantly. "It was prom. Junior year. I was going with Liam North."

"The boy she'd had a crush on for years."

"That's not important."

"Yes, it is," Raina said.

Hope's lips thinned. "It was just prom," she said firmly. "I got the dress—"

"It was stunning," Raina put in.

"I got the dress," Hope repeated caustically, and Raina finally subsided. "Got my hair done. Nails. Everything. It was a huge fuss. You know the way prom is. My parents were over the moon about it all—my mom especially. I didn't date much in high school. No one wanted to be connected with a freakishly tall geek."

"She was beautiful even back then," Raina asserted. "She just didn't know it. Guys liked her, but she intimated them. Her mom wanted her to go to prom so she would finally realize how wonderful she is."

"Are you going to let me tell it or not? Raina's wrong, you know," Hope told Curtis. "She always thought I was beautiful because she's so damn loyal, but boys back then didn't even see me. Their eyes just skipped past me on their way to her."

"That's not true," Raina said softly. Hope ignored her.

"Anyway, Mom kept going on about the photos. Liam had to come early so we could get lots of photos. She'd been waiting for years to get photos of me with a boyfriend." She swallowed hard. "She was always proud of me for my academic record and the sports and everything else I did, too, but Raina's right: she worried about me. The week before prom was this frantic last-minute craziness," she went on. "Appointments. Homework. Plans. I didn't see Liam much."

"Where were you in all this?" Curtis asked Raina when Hope stopped. "Didn't you go to school together?"

Raina busied herself with re-tying her scarf. "I went to prom with Teddy Johnson," she said softly.

"A football player," Hope said.

"A football player," Raina echoed. "Teddy's parents rented a limo for him and all his friends. Liam and Teddy didn't get along…"

She trailed off, and Curtis began to understand. They hadn't gone to prom together, and something had happened to Hope. Something Raina at least partially blamed herself for.

"We planned to meet at the dance and spend as much time together there as we could," Hope said matter-of-factly. "I was fine with that. Prom night came. Liam was supposed to pick me up at six to go to dinner first," she went on. "We had reservations with a few friends at this fancy place in town. Not football players, of course. Normal kids. People like me."

Curtis noticed the way Raina's shoulders were drooping. Her normally cheerful countenance was grave.

"What happened?" he asked. This was important—Hope needed to talk about it.

Six o'clock came. Liam didn't show up. Six fifteen. My mom was beside herself. We wouldn't have time for photos before the reservations."

Curtis's heart squeezed at the thought of Hope all dressed up with nowhere to go as the clock ticked on. He'd experienced it, and that was fine. It might have annihilated him in the moment, but he was strong. A SEAL. He'd made it out the other side. Someone as beautiful and wonderful and honorable as Hope should never have to—

"Six thirty rolled around. Liam wasn't answering his phone. Finally, my mom called his mom. They'd served on the PTA together in the past. As far as Liam's mom knew, he was supposed to be with me, but finally she tracked down a friend of his who admitted Liam had hooked up with someone else that week. Another girl at school, Brynn, who'd broken up with her boyfriend last minute and needed a date to prom, and figured she'd steal mine. What can I say? Brynn was fun and pretty and all the things I wasn't."

Curtis's throat ached with sympathy for Hope. He knew how old hurts lingered on, even when they shouldn't. Had Hope asked herself what she'd done wrong? How she'd fallen short of the mark? It was hard to get past that kind of question when you got left behind.

He'd asked himself those questions for years.

Hope's face was a stony mask as she related the story. "My mom couldn't fathom it. 'What about the photos?' she kept asking. My dad offered to take me. Or get someone else to take me, but of course I didn't go. I cried for hours. It was so stupid. It was just a dance."

"That kid made a big mistake," Curtis told her, his voice thick with sympathetic pain. He knew the hurt she was describing, the agony of wondering... why?

"Yeah." Hope's voice wobbled, and she struggled to get it under control, blinking back tears that were collecting in her eyes. Curtis moved to touch her but held back, surprised at the rawness of her grief. Getting stood up sucked, but her junior prom must have been eight or so years ago.

"Hey, are you all right?"

She swallowed. Shook her head and held out a hand to stop him when he moved nearer. "Liam did make a mistake. A really big one. Liam died—" She broke off and turned away, burying her face in both hands.

Curtis stiffened. Died?

"He was in an accident," Raina supplied quietly. "Brynn was driving. She'd had too much to drink. Four of our classmates, including Liam, never made it home that night."

"Jesus." This was the kind of pain Curtis couldn't stand. The pain that came out of nowhere. The deaths that were senseless. The ones that struck people down who had no reason to die. He'd seen too many of those during his time in the Navy. He should have been hardened to them.

He wasn't.

He moved toward Hope again, but she waved him off, scraping away the tears that were spilling over her cheeks with the back of her hand. He wanted to gather her into his arms and hold her there until those tears were spent, but he recognized that need for control, too. She was holding it all in—holding herself together.

"He didn't deserve that. Liam was a jerk to me, but he didn't deserve to die."

"No, he didn't. You didn't deserve your prom night to end like that, either," he said.

"If we'd stuck to the plan, none of it would have happened," she burst out, and understanding crashed over Curtis. That damned planner. The way she clung to it like a lifeline.

"You had no control over—"

"He wouldn't have chosen Brynn if I was prettier, or more interesting—more like Raina. He'd be alive today, and I wouldn't be like this. I wish I'd been someone different back then. I wish he'd never asked me at all!"

Raina made a choked sound, and when Curtis looked her way, she'd covered her mouth with her hand. Tears were bright in her eyes, too. "I'm sorry," she cried, as if the words were torn from her throat. "Hope, I'm sorry. I wanted you to be happy, that's all! I wanted you to go to prom! I never meant for any of that to happen—"

Hope stared at her. "None of it is your fault—"

"Yes, it is!" Raina began to cry, and Curtis's heart sank. The way Hope was watching her friend told him she was beginning to figure it out, too.

"What did you do?" Hope asked finally, her voice flat and raw.

"I just... I just told him... to ask you," Raina sobbed. "I said... I said I'd get him tickets to the *Damned if You Do* tour."

"You... bribed him?" Hope laughed, but it didn't come out right, and Curtis's heart ached for her.

"I just knew that if you spent time together, he'd like you. You never gave anyone a chance—"

"Raina!"

"Prom wouldn't have been any fun without you. You're what makes things fun," Raina cried. "I didn't want to go without you. You're my friend, Hope."

"Am I?" Hope was as white as if Raina had slapped her. "Do you bribe people to date your friends?"

"It wasn't like that—"

"What was it like?"

"You weren't happy. You know you weren't. All you did was work and hang out with me, and you wanted more. You wanted a boyfriend. You wanted to go to that dance!" Raina's voice rose, her face flushing. "I made it happen. That's all I did—"

"But it didn't happen. I didn't go to the prom, and Liam's dead!"

"I know!" Raina wailed. "I know, I know, I know!" She faced off with Hope, breathing hard, tears streaming. "What I don't know is why you're still friends with me, because I don't deserve you. I don't deserve Ben. I don't deserve anyone!"

Tell her she's wrong, Curtis urged Hope in his head, but he could see Raina's revelation had struck her to the core. Was she wondering why Raina needed to bribe a boy to take her to the prom? Was she questioning every relationship she'd had since?

"I can't... I can't do this." Hope turned on her heel and headed off the road into the woods.

"Hope!" Raina struggled to her feet, limped a few paces after her, gave a cry, spun around and ran clumsily in the other direction.

Not good, Curtis thought. They were splitting up, spreading out in conditions that were still deadly. Worse than that, they were destroying a friendship that was crucial to them both.

"Hope! Raina!" He didn't know how to get them back there—

Blake, who'd watched the entire thing like a tennis match, flipped open the lid of the picnic basket and tossed it lightly into the snow. "Oh, hell," he cried loudly. "I dropped the kittens—and they're getting away!"

RAINA STOPPED INSTANTLY. Stood still. Turned, and came rushing back. "Feldspar!" she shrieked. "Minna, Louise—where's Reggie?"

The panic in Raina's voice stopped Hope in her tracks, too, and in spite of her fury, she half turned to look back the way she'd come.

Raina was floundering in the snow this way and that. So was Blake. Curtis was backing away.

"They're sinking in the snow," he shouted. "They could be anywhere! I don't want to step on one!"

She huffed out a sigh. Fine. She'd help with the kittens, and then she'd… what? What exactly was her plan? Her throat ached with Raina's betrayal and the knowledge that Liam hadn't ever wanted to go to prom with her. If Raina hadn't meddled, would he be alive today?

Or was it her fault for being so boring he'd taken the first chance to go with someone else?

She'd thought she'd moved on from these old wounds, but somehow, with Curtis making her rethink her plans to put off marriage, they'd all bubbled up as fresh and new as they'd been back in high school.

"I can't find Edgar!" Raina cried.

Edgar? Hope picked up her pace, then broke into a run. She found pandemonium where she'd left the others.

"Damn it," Blake said, bending down and dropping one of the kittens into the snow. "The thing bit me."

"Don't let it get away! What's happening? It's like they've gone crazy!" Raina scooped up the one Blake dropped and handed it to Curtis, who swore a minute later and set it down in the snow again. Every time Raina corralled a kitten, the men were managing to lose one of the others.

It was as if—

"There's Edgar!" Blake pointed, and Hope lunged for the kitten, losing her train of thought. Once she had Edgar safely in her arms, she held out a hand to Blake. "Give them to me, before you lose them again. They won't bite me."

She snagged the overturned picnic basket out of the snow, set the three kittens into it, took Feldspar from Curtis and turned to find Raina hugging Reggie under her chin.

"I'm sorry," Raina said again. "Hope, I am so sorry. About everything. All I've ever wanted was for you to be happy."

Hope closed her eyes, defeat overtaking her. She

knew that. Throughout her life when she felt at odds with everyone else, Raina had always been there. It was her own damn fault she was so bad at love.

"Why?" she asked. "Why do you want to be friends with someone as messed up as me?"

"Because I can depend on you," Raina said. "You don't make the kind of mistakes I do."

"You don't need me to keep you from making mistakes."

"Don't I?" Raina gave a sad laugh. "It's like Blake said. Everyone knows I need a babysitter. I always do the wrong thing, and then I have to pretend to be cute and sweet and happy so everyone forgives me again."

Hope's breath caught in her throat. "Do you really feel like that?"

"Sometimes."

"This is all very after-school-special," Blake broke in, "but don't you have a wedding to get to?"

Raina's eyes widened. She looked up at the sky as if it could tell her the time and let her shoulders drop. "I'm not going to make it, am I?"

Hope didn't think she'd ever seen Raina give up before. It was like watching an eclipse block out the sun. She made a decision. "We can't stay together," she said. "Curtis, this isn't working. You have to take Raina. You'll be faster on your own."

"I'M NOT LEAVING anyone behind," Curtis began, but Hope shook her head.

"Yes, you are. You and Raina go on. Get to the

highway. Get to Bozeman. Send someone back for us. We'll be fine."

Curtis took a deep breath. Hope was right; it was the only way. He was going to have to trust that it would work out. After Blake's trick with the basket of kittens, he was beginning to think he'd underestimated the man.

"You two stick with Hope. Get her to the road. I'll send someone back to pick you up."

"Fine," Blake growled. "But we'd better reach that highway soon."

"Not fine," Byron said, lowering the video camera he'd been filming with all this time. "You're still on the show," he told Curtis. "That means I have to stay with you. I need to document what's happening. You don't want to lose, do you?"

Curtis wanted to tell him to hell with the show, but he knew Byron was right, and in the end he nodded, sick to his stomach at the thought of leaving Hope alone with Blake. "We're going to move fast," he warned Byron. "As soon as we hit the highway, we'll find someone to send back to you. I promise," he told Hope.

"Of course. Don't worrry about us," she said again.

"You don't let her out of your sight. You hear me?" he said to Blake, who gave him a lazy salute. "Daisy? Stay with Hope," Curtis commanded.

Daisy whined, but she did what she was told, and Hope was right: they made much faster time once he and Byron had forged on ahead. Byron went first and set a trail on his skis. Curtis followed, pulling Raina. Two hours later, he could have cursed himself when they reached the highway. He couldn't believe they'd been this close.

"We should have stayed together," he said.

"Look!" Byron surged forward and waved his hands above his head as a grader approached, a large piece of machinery that made short work of the snow piled on the road.

"You folks in trouble?" a man called out of the vehicle when he spotted them.

"You bet we are," Raina said, hopping up, cursing and hopping in a circle, cradling her ankle. "I'm late to my wedding!"

"Wedding? Where is it?"

"Bozeman. Can you get me there?"

"That's where I'm headed," the man said. "Jump in. All of you."

Curtis breathed a sigh of relief. In a vehicle like that, Raina would make her wedding easily.

She turned to face him. Put her hands on her hips. "Curtis Lloyd, I'm not getting married without my maid of honor. You go back and get Hope."

Curtis grinned, feeling lighter than he had in days. "Yes, ma'am," he said and helped her climb into the truck. Byron got up after her.

"There's more of you? How far back are the others?" the grader driver asked, looking back up the pass from where they'd come.

"About an hour, maybe less," Curtis told him.

"They're on foot, not skis."

"Let me make a call."

"I THINK I kind of like Montana," Blake mused. "Maybe I'll get myself a hunting cabin here one of these days."

"Really?" Hope was cold. Hungry. Tired. And still somewhat stunned.

She'd thought she'd known the worst of her history, and she didn't know what to think of the fact that Raina had practically forced Liam to ask her to the prom. She expected that to hurt more than it did. The thing was, now that she was over her shock—it didn't.

It wasn't anyone's fault that Liam hadn't really liked her, just like it wasn't anyone's fault that given the chance to go with Brynn, he'd taken it. Brynn's drinking and driving was the real tragedy, and that had nothing to do with her.

The deaths of Liam and his friends had devastated her—and had affected the rest of her class, too. It had brought them all closer together in a way, which made senior year different for her than the previous years had been. She and her classmates had stuck together in a way they never had before, far more solicitous of each other. Almost like a family.

She'd participated in more school activities and had been asked to the senior prom. She'd gone with a boy from her chemistry class. Her mom had gotten those photos, and while it had been sad to think of Liam, and by then she'd already been carrying the kind of planner that had become an obsession over the years, she'd had a good time.

She'd had other relationships in the intervening years. Relationships Raina had nothing to do with, which meant men could find her attractive, even if she'd always held them at arm's length. It was her choice to focus more and more on her career. Her choice to create a life plan that put off love for years.

Hope realized her real mistake was that she'd never come to grips with the lesson junior prom night should have taught her: she couldn't control anything. Couldn't predict when something would go wrong. Couldn't know if someone she cared about would live or die.

She'd tried to protect her heart from ever being hurt again by pulling back from other people and focusing on work instead of relationships.

That had to stop.

Once again that magical night in Yellowstone came back to her. The stars twinkling overhead. The wolves howling. Hadn't she promised herself then she'd be brave?

Things didn't always go according to plan. Sometimes people didn't show up, or they let you down, or even died.

That didn't mean she should give up on love—and men—forever.

Surely there was a way to be with Curtis and have her dream, too.

She tried to picture Base Camp in the summer. The tiny houses, gardens... bison. Spending time there with Curtis wouldn't be a hardship. He'd sounded interested in Yellowstone, too. The two places weren't that far apart—when it wasn't snowing.

They could travel back and forth. Visit each other. Go on dates.

Would that really be so bad?

"What's that?" Blake asked.

Hope woke up from her reverie and peered ahead at the source of the noise that had started as a low hum and was increasing to a low roar. "I don't know."

But suddenly she did know. She'd heard that sound before.

"It's a snowplow!"

The large vehicle revved around a curve in the road and stopped several yards away. The passenger side door opened, and a man climbed down.

"Curtis!" Hope ran toward him as fast as she could, and he caught her in an embrace.

"Hop in. We've got a wedding to get to. Come on, Daisy," he added. "Jump up, girl."

Daisy did eagerly, giving Curtis a face wash with her tongue.

"Where's Raina?"

Curtis filled her in as she wrestled her skis off and watched him stow them away. She climbed into the back seat of the extended cab, Blake taking a seat beside her. "She's already on her way to Bozeman with a plow operator. He called Mike here to come pick me up and help reach you. Now he's going to drive us to Bozeman, too."

"Thank you so much," Hope cried.

Mike waved off her gratitude. "Happy to help. Quite a storm we've had."

"Isn't that the truth."

An hour and a half later, Hope stumbled into the vestry of the small church in the city where Raina's family, her groom, his family and all their guests were already gathered. The closer they'd gotten to Bozeman, the less snow there'd been piled up on the highway. By the time they reached the church where Raina's wedding was to be held, the sun was coming out.

Its light transformed the landscape, and Hope's heart expanded. They were going to make it. Raina would marry the love of her life, and she'd be there to see it.

They were going to have to talk more later, and she hoped she could help Raina let go of the pain that had made her feel less than everyone else. Raina deserved to be happy—and to know she had what it took to do whatever she wanted.

"Hope! I'm so glad to see you," Raina's mother, Diana, said when she climbed out of the snowplow truck. "Come on inside—"

"Is that my maid of honor?" Raina cried, coming to the door.

"Raina, get back in there and get ready," her mother said but watched with a patient smile as Raina ran to give Hope a hug.

"I was afraid you wouldn't make it."

"I wouldn't miss your wedding for the world."

"Come on. You'll need to change quickly. The ceremony is supposed to start in five minutes," Diana said.

"Five minutes?" Hope rustled through her things to find her planner as they walked indoors, into a small room at the back of the church set aside for the bridal party to prepare. Surely there were a million things to be done.

"Hope, take a breath. It's all okay."

"But, I—" Hope spotted the picnic basket of kittens and broke off.

"Mom got everything done," Raina said. "And a vet is on the way to pick up the kittens and check them out. She'll bring them back after the wedding. As for you, all you have to do is walk down the aisle ahead of me."

"Okay. Oh my god." Hope stared at her in horror. "What about my dress? My makeup? What am I going to—"

"I've got your dress," Raina said triumphantly. She pointed to the hook on the back of the door where Hope's bridesmaid gown hung. "I packed it with my wedding dress when we had to leave the rest of our things behind and walk. You were too busy flirting with Curtis to notice."

"You are so smart!" Hope took the dress and began to peel off her clothes. "We've got to hurry. I promised Ben I'd get Raina to the altar on time," she told Diana.

"You got me to my wedding through the blizzard of the century," Raina said. "Ben can wait for a few more minutes. Come here, let's make you presentable."

Hope admired her calmness, and she realized Raina looked different. More... confident. Maybe she was already on her way to getting out from under the baggage of her past.

Raina's mother worked miracles, taming Hope's wild hair into an updo that looked as sleek as if she'd come straight from a salon. Raina worked on her makeup while Hope stepped into her dress. With earrings and a matching necklace, her outfit was complete.

"You clean up nice," Raina said.

"I haven't even had a shower. Do I smell?"

Raina's mother squirted her with perfume. "Not anymore. You're perfect, just like my daughter."

"Are you ready for this?" Hope asked Raina. "It's all happening so fast."

"I'm ready. Where's Curtis?"

"I don't know. He was right behind me."

"I'm sure the men are seated already," Raina's mother said. "Come now, girls. Let's get in place."

And there wasn't time to think of anything else before Hope was walking down the aisle.

CHAPTER TEN

URTIS MET UP with Raina's fiancé as the man was making his way to the front of the church to take his place. When Curtis introduced himself, Ben said, "You're the one who got my bride here safely. I owe you a lot."

Curtis shook his proffered hand. "You don't owe me anything, but there's a favor you could do for me."

"Oh yeah? Does it have to do with Hope?" When he took in Curtis's surprised expression, Ben grinned. "Raina told me what she planned to do before she lost cell phone service."

"She told you she planned to crash her car in front of Base Camp?"

Ben shrugged. "That she planned to throw you and Hope together and keep you together until you realized you were right for each other." His smile grew wider as he watched Curtis take that in. "People underestimate Raina. I don't. That's why I'm with her. What?" he asked when Curtis guffawed.

"Guess I don't have to ask for that favor after all. I

was going to say you need to take Raina seriously. To listen to her. She's a smart lady."

"I already know that," Ben affirmed. "I think this move is going to be good for her. Back in Illinois everyone has her pegged as being a certain kind of woman. Here she can start over. She's going to miss Hope, though."

"Hope says you're going to get her a job."

"Maybe." Ben looked over his shoulder to where the officiant was taking his place at the altar. "I'd better get going. Having a husband in Chance Creek would keep Hope close to Raina, too."

"I like the way you're thinking," Curtis told him. "Good luck."

"Good luck to you, too."

HOPE THOUGHT IF her heart swelled any more her chest wouldn't be able to hold it in. Raina was beaming as she spoke her vows and listened to Ben speak his. The ceremony seemed to pass in seconds, but she thought its beauty and sweetness would change her forever.

Her friendship with Raina had gone through the wringer and come out stronger than ever in the past twenty-four hours. All this time she'd thought she carried the burden of the past alone, and now she knew that just like in all other things, Raina had been there beside her, carrying her own burden.

Raina's marriage wouldn't change that, but it would add more dimensions to her friend's life. She knew Raina was ready to start her family and settle down in

Montana where Ben's work was. She knew, too, that Raina would throw her heart and soul into making a home for Ben and her children.

Where did that leave her?

She couldn't pretend she wanted to stay single for another decade anymore. She wanted to marry Curtis, and she wanted children, too. She wanted something more, though. A chance to create something bigger than her family. Something that would leave a legacy.

That's what working in Yellowstone was all about.

Could she have both? There were practical reasons against it, but... wasn't it worth a try?

She caught sight of Curtis in the audience sitting with Byron and Blake. All three were toward the back, trying to be inconspicuous. When Curtis raised his gaze to meet hers, her heart skipped a beat at the way he focused on her, like he could pick her out of any crowd.

Did he feel like she did? Did he want more, too?

Did he wonder if he could have it with her?

He'd told her he meant to marry her—in a few days. They'd never gotten to talk about it further, and Hope wondered now if he was... serious.

Could he be? Had he seen something in her he wanted so badly?

As she held his gaze, she trembled a little, remembering what it felt like to be with Curtis—to have him filling her. Moving inside her.

She wanted him again. Didn't think she'd ever get enough of him.

Was it time to take a chance?

To take an unscheduled detour that could change everything?

A smile tugged the corner of her mouth.

Or had she already done that?

Maybe there was no turning back.

CURTIS DIDN'T GET the chance to speak with Hope until the reception, after Raina and Ben had taken their first dance. Hope had sat with Raina, Ben and the other members of the wedding party at dinner. She'd met his gaze a half dozen times, and Curtis wondered at the shine in her eyes and the color in her cheeks. She was happy for Raina, of course, but there was something else going on. When she looked at him—

He found it hard to breathe. She was trying to tell him something. He wished he knew what.

"Dance with her," Byron said finally. "Look, you can cut in." He had his video camera out, filming everything, as usual.

Hope was dancing with Ben while Raina danced with another man he didn't recognize. All around them conversation flowed, champagne glasses clinked and a happy buzz filled the room.

"Good idea." Curtis wished he was more properly dressed, but he knew Hope wouldn't mind. He eased his way through the couples on the dance floor and tapped Ben's shoulder.

"Take care of her," Ben said as he backed off. "Where did my wife get to? Raina?"

"Here," she sang out, and her partner passed her to

Ben.

"He's over the moon," Hope said to Curtis as they watched him sweep Raina into his arms again. Byron had come closer and was filming them. "So's she."

"I'm glad we got here on time."

"Me, too." She fit in his arms like they were made for each other, and Curtis began to sway to the music. It was now or never. He had to tell Hope everything and ask her if she could find her way to making a life with him. He knew he wanted one with her.

"Hope—"

"Curtis—"

They laughed, and each broke off, waiting for the other to go on.

"You go first," Hope said.

"I don't want to let you go," he said simply. "I feel like we're just getting started."

"I feel that, too."

His heart rose, but Curtis knew there were lots of obstacles in their way. "Do you think—could we try to be together?" He caught sight of Byron pointing the video camera their way and waved him off, but Byron didn't budge.

"I'd like that. I know it'll be hard, with us so far apart, but—"

This was the difficult part. They couldn't be far apart—not yet. Not until the show was over.

"Look," Curtis said, drawing her closer. "There's a lot you don't know about Base Camp. Like Raina keeps saying, you really should watch the show."

"I will just as soon as I can. I never thought I'd be interested, but I was wrong."

"I'm just not sure you understand how much I'm bound by my contract."

"I know we won't have a lot of time for each other at first," she rushed to say. "I understand we'll only see each other every few weeks. I don't even know when I'll start work—or if they'll hire me—but if they do I figure it'll be a month or two before I'm settled in. Once I have my schedule we can figure out times to meet up."

A month or two? That wasn't going to work.

"Hope—there are… rules. More than I told you about before." Would she understand?

"What kind of rules?"

They couldn't do this here. Curtis took her hand and led her away from the dance floor to a quiet table in one corner of the room. He swore softly when he realized Byron was following them, then remembered that Fulsom was getting bored of the show. Time to bare his innermost feelings on national television.

"The easiest way is to show you," Byron broke in, coming closer. He took out his cell phone, tapped on it a few times and held it out to them. "All you need to see is the introduction. Right, Curtis?"

"Right." No more time for beating around the bush—it was now or never.

"Okay." Hope dutifully sat in a seat, her head tilted to see the screen better. Curtis took the phone and held it while Byron got back into position to film them.

"Ready?" Curtis asked. She nodded.

He took a deep breath and pressed play.

HOPE DIDN'T UNDERSTAND why Curtis seemed so worried. She was the one asking him to put up with delays and uncertainty about how or when they might be together. She'd thought he might balk at the idea of a long-distance relationship, but instead he was acting like he was asking her to do something difficult.

She might not watch television a lot, but it wasn't any big deal to watch a video clip. The introduction started with a panoramic view of a ranch that took Hope a moment to recognize as the location of Base Camp. This was the settlement in summertime, though, with bright blue skies overhead, green pastures, and hardworking men building the tiny houses she'd seen, working in gardens or with the bison.

She loved those bison.

Hope leaned closer. The ranch looked like… paradise.

"Welcome to Base Camp," a female narrator intoned with a plummy British accent.

"That's Renata Ludlow. She's the show's director. Byron's boss."

"Got it."

"…where ten men must pit themselves against time and technology to build a model sustainable community before time runs out," Renata went on.

"Runs out? You have a deadline?" Hope asked Curtis. She hadn't known that.

"Just listen."

"They must build ten houses that consume a tenth of the power of a normal North American home. They must create a renewable power grid from which to run all their appliances, lights and machines. They must grow all the food they'll need to last through the winter," Renata said. Hope was still entranced by all the footage of life on the ranch. She liked how everyone worked together, and she was fascinated with the huge wind turbines they'd erected, the solar system on the bunkhouse roof, the lush gardens they'd grown in summer.

And the herd of bison. That was Walker and Avery tending them, she realized, her heart leaping. And there was Curtis carrying a stack of lumber toward a half-built tiny house. He wasn't wearing a shirt in the footage, and his muscled chest and shoulders were a sight to behold.

But she'd seen that firsthand.

She was so busy identifying all the people she'd met at Base Camp, she nearly missed what Renata said next.

"…every 40 days without fail, and there must be three babies on the way—"

"Wait, what was that?" Babies? Where did babies come in?

Curtis shook his head but rewound the footage.

"…all the food they'll need to last through the winter," Renata said again. "They must each marry before the year is up, one wedding every 40 days without fail, and there must be three babies on the way, or risk losing everything."

Curtis stopped the video and met her gaze. Hope

stared at him.

"That's the part I needed you to see. Kai and Addison married thirty-nine days ago. It's my turn next," he said quietly.

"Your turn."

He nodded, and her breath caught as she finally understood.

"Your turn to marry—tomorrow?"

"That's right."

"But—who?" Suddenly cold, even though the room was quite warm, she looked around as if he might have had a woman with him this entire time. "Is she back at Base Camp?"

"No. At least, she won't be unless things don't work out—"

"What does that mean?" Had he been seeing someone else this whole time? While flirting with her? Sleeping with her? "Wait—you said you tried to marry someone right before I arrived. Michele. You said it was a business arrangement."

"That's right, because the deadline was so close, but we broke it off and I kept looking. I don't have much time, so Boone's supposed to find me a backup bride, just in case."

"Backup?" She still didn't understand. "You... made love to me, knowing you were going to marry another woman!"

"You're not listening." He took a breath and got control of himself. "Hope, I slept with you because I want you to be the woman I marry! I told you that."

"I... thought you were joking!"

"Guys... incoming," Byron hissed suddenly.

Hope swung around just as someone said, "Excuse me. Hope? Is that you?"

Hope stared up at the newcomer, finally realizing who it had to be. She opened her mouth but didn't know what to say. "Scott?" she managed weakly. Byron was still filming them, and she wished he would stop. She needed all of this to stop until she could catch up with what was happening.

Curtis had to marry tomorrow. Boone had found him a bride.

A backup bride. In case—

What? In case she didn't agree to marry a man she'd just met?

"That's right." He held out his hand, and she forced herself to shake it, aware of Curtis's gaze on her the whole time. "Is this a good time to talk?" Scott asked.

"No—"

"Yes," Hope cut Curtis off. "This is the perfect time, Scott." She stood up quickly, ignoring Curtis's thunderous expression. She needed to get away from him. Needed to process everything he'd just said. How could he know after a day or two that he wanted to marry her? Or was that not important? After all, he had to marry someone. "Let's find somewhere quiet."

Scott hesitated, then crooked his elbow, and she linked her arm with his, allowing him to lead her through the crowd. Byron trailed after her.

"Hope—" Curtis called out, but she kept going,

grateful when Scott pushed open the door and they emerged into a corridor.

"Are you sure this is a good time? Sounds like that guy had something he wanted to say to you." Scott was a stocky, athletic-looking man, an inch or two taller than her, with the weathered features of someone who spent all his time outside.

"You didn't interrupt anything," she assured him. Just the shocker of a lifetime. The end to all her dreams. No one who needed to find a bride in a couple of days could be serious about her—or about marriage.

Another thought overtook her, and she swallowed against the pressure building in her throat. Was his need for a wife the reason why Curtis agreed to help Raina get to her wedding? Had he thought Hope would be so grateful she'd throw herself into his arms—and marry him? Tomorrow?

Byron was still filming, and she tried to swat him away, but he ducked.

"Hope?" Scott repeated. "Ben said you had something you wanted to ask me?"

"What? Oh." She tried to corral her racing thoughts, but the truth of her situation was sinking in. She'd allowed herself to feel something for Curtis. She'd opened her heart a crack and let him in. She'd speculated there was a way for them to run a long-distance relationship.

What a crock of shit.

He'd been using her this whole time. All he cared about was Base Camp—

"Hope?" Scott prompted her.

"I… I want a job. Need a job," she corrected herself. "In Yellowstone. It's what I've always wanted." Except for the past forty-eight hours she'd found herself wanting something more. A life that included a partner—now, not in ten years.

A man like Curtis.

"A ranger job?" Scott guessed.

Hope nodded, blinking back the tears that threatened to fall. Curtis wasn't anything like she'd thought he was.

"Do you have any qualifications?" Scott asked.

This is what happened when you deviated from your plans, Hope thought. You lost your way. Havoc broke out. Things went wrong.

Very wrong.

And you were left with a heart split in two, the pain of it crumpling you to the floor—

Except you couldn't crumple to the floor. You had to go on. You had to smile. Nod. Answer questions.

Especially when the questions were coming from a man who held the key to your future.

A future that now felt more like a consolation prize than a long-held dream.

She forced herself to tell Scott all about her qualifications, wondering how she was managing it. Who was this Hope who went on when everything inside her wanted to die? She'd trusted Curtis. Opened her heart to him. Why on earth had he held back such an important piece of information?

And Raina... Had Raina known perfectly well what was going on?

Why hadn't she said anything?

She remembered eleventh grade. Her joy when Liam had asked her to the prom out of the blue.

Her pain when he didn't show up.

Raina had orchestrated all of that.

Hope went cold. Was Raina behind this, too?

"You sound like the perfect candidate to be a park ranger," Scott said heartily.

"That's great," Hope said. She'd been right all along. She needed to stick to the plan. Someday—maybe— she'd find love, but it wouldn't be today.

It wouldn't be with Curtis.

And maybe it was time to walk away from Raina, too.

HE HAD TO leave. Now. Before he ruined Raina's reception. Before Raina even realized anything had happened, because for all her pretended flightiness, Raina cared for Hope deeply enough to derail the entire event to comfort her friend.

Curtis knew without a doubt Hope would keep up appearances despite what had happened. She'd never breathe a word of her anger to her friend on her wedding day. Raina would be disappointed her match- making hadn't taken hold, but she'd sail off on her honeymoon none the wiser about their disastrous conversation.

What had he thought would happen when he confessed about his deadline? Had he thought Hope would jump into his arms, delighted at the opportunity to marry a stranger under duress?

What woman would act like that?

He had to let her go.

Had to go home, suck it up and marry the woman Boone had chosen for him. Make sure his friends got their community.

That was what was really important, wasn't it? Giving back to the community? That's why he'd joined Base Camp to begin with. He'd known when he pledged to marry that he was rolling the dice and that he'd have to confront his biggest fears to step up to the altar when the time came.

He remembered what Hope had said only a night ago: he wanted to be brave, too. In this instance, that meant giving Hope the space she needed to live the life she'd always dreamed of.

He'd had a dream, too, though. One he rarely told to anyone. A dream of creating a home. Having a family to serve and protect. Creating a place that was special.

Base Camp was that place. He knew it in his bones, just as Hope knew Yellowstone was the place for her.

This was one of those moments that hurt—

But there were always moments that hurt.

Part of being brave was knowing they would come, standing strong in the face of them, allowing them to happen—

A vibration in his pocket jolted him out of his train of thought.

His phone.

It was Boone, and Curtis stepped away from the reception to answer it. His future was calling.

His commitments were calling.

His dreams and plans.

He could stay here and mourn for the woman he was losing and by doing so destroy the dreams of all the men he'd sworn to build a new community with.

Or he could answer the phone. Listen to Boone. Head home.

And get married—

To someone else.

"MAYBE YOU SHOULD apply to a place in our first aid group," Scott was saying when Hope focused on him again. "With your medical knowledge you'd be a big help. You wouldn't believe how many people manage to injure themselves in the park. Not just climbers, either. People walk down paths and manage to trip and break their own legs. On solid ground. It's astounding."

"I was just a receptionist, and I don't want to work in medicine. I want to make a change. To work with the animals. To help keep Yellowstone's ecology in balance. To further research in—"

Scott frowned. "Yeah, most people say that."

"Like I said, I've been taking classes in natural resources management…"

"Let me stop you right there. Hope, you're Raina's friend, so I'm going to be frank with you. People have really romantic notions about this job, but the reality is, when you're a park ranger, most of what you do is be a babysitter. A babysitter whose job it is to keep track of a bunch of overgrown toddlers in adult bodies. Toddlers who drink too much, who start fights, who trash campsites, who miss the toilets when they puke. Adult toddlers who take selfies with bears and bison—as if they were behind a six-inch reinforced Plexiglas barrier rather than five feet away with no fence between them. People with no self-control, no appreciation for nature and beauty. No common sense." Scott visibly pulled himself together. "Sometimes we get to work with animals. Sometimes we get to make plans to make the park a better place. That's high-level stuff. With your drive, if you stuck with the job for years, you'd get there, I don't doubt it. Just don't go into it with rose-colored glasses, okay? Yellowstone doesn't need help with its bison. It needs help keeping all those damn toddlers from breaking their own necks."

Hope drew in a ragged breath. She had to admit this wasn't the first time she'd heard something like this. Online forums for rangers and applicants had held similar messages.

She hadn't wanted to believe them. Scott worked at Yellowstone, though, and there wasn't any good reason for him to lie.

"I know I could do a really good job," she began.

Scott nodded. "I know you could, too, Hope. Don't let me dissuade you. It's just—been a rough year. I want Yellowstone to stay natural. We all do. Most people would be great with that, too. Then there's always that one person who messes it up for everyone else. We have to make more rules. More barriers. Make it safer. Keep people away from the very things they came to see. I just—I don't know. I guess I'm burning out. I'm thinking of changing careers," he admitted. "I'm done with people. I want to get to the real work, you know? That Base Camp guy is so lucky."

"Base Camp guy?" Hope repeated.

"The one you were sitting with. Curtis. I watch that show every week. Those people have it made." He shook his head. "They think up something to do, and they do it. At Yellowstone we have to create proposals, write them up, do studies, discuss it some more..." He threw up his hands. "It takes ages to get any new ideas adopted. I need more leeway than that." He focused on Hope. "That's what you should do, you know. That Curtis guy? He needs a wife—fast. It's all over the internet that his fiancée married someone else. You should make him fall in love with you, marry him, join Base Camp and help expand their bison program. Do something hands-on and immediate. Hell, maybe I should marry him." He gave a laugh that had little humor and a lot of bitterness in it, fished his wallet out of his pocket and drew out a business card. "But if you want to go ahead with Yellowstone, email me. I'll get you in, no problem."

"Thanks."

"I can't believe it's going to be the end of Base Camp. It'll make me sick if they let that developer bulldoze the whole thing," he confessed.

It made her sick to think about it, too. "Boone's got a backup bride lined up for him, I think."

"Curtis isn't going to marry a backup bride. You could see on his face he never wanted to marry that woman in the first place. Now he's got another chance. He'll hold out for love—mark my words. Guy like that deserves it." He chuckled. "Heck, I'm not usually this sentimental. Guess it's the wedding doing it to me."

"I guess." She was feeling sentimental, too, despite her anger at everything that had happened. It was hard not to believe in love when Raina and Ben were doing such a good job at displaying it inside, and it was hard to stay angry with Raina when she knew her friend had only been trying to help. Again.

Hope was beginning to think she was beyond help.

"Well, let me know what you decide. And good luck, whatever you do," Scott said.

"Thanks."

"He's right."

She realized Byron had shut off the camera. He indicated a chair and sat down next to her. "That guy's right. Curtis will try to marry whatever woman Boone puts in front of him, but he's not going to be able to do it. Not now. He wants to find true love."

She shook her head. "He doesn't have time to find true love."

"He already did." Byron sighed when she didn't answer. "Hope, he loves you."

"How can you say that? You don't know anything—"

"I spend all my time looking through this camera.

Filming everything. Watching everything. I know how he looks at you. I know he hardly looks at anything else when you're around. I know he did everything he could to get Raina to her wedding—to make you happy. If you turn your back on him, you're going to regret it, and so is he."

"But—"

"Isn't happiness worth a risk?"

For the first time Hope looked at Byron. Really looked at him. He was a slim, young, studious-looking man with clear eyes and an engaging smile. He was also quiet, probably shy. He probably knew a thing or two about waiting for love.

"Maybe," she heard herself say. "But how can I be sure Curtis really loves me? Raina was the one who set this all up—"

"Raina got you here. She bought you time. You and Curtis did the rest. Be honest—do you love him or not?"

Hope took a breath. "Yes," she said. "I do love him."

"Then go find him. Tell him that—before it's too late."

CHAPTER ELEVEN

"**Y**OU CAN'T GET through. The avalanche still hasn't been cleared from the road. They're getting close, but it's not done yet," Boone was saying. "You've got Byron there, right? Is he filming the wedding?"

"He's trying to. Boone, I need a bride. What am I supposed to do?" Was the Universe really going to fuck with him—again—after denying him the woman he wanted more than anyone else?

"If you can't get through, you'll have to find one there. I can put a call out on the website. Find someone local for you."

"Overnight?"

This was worse than marrying one of Boone's back-up brides. This was rolling the dice with the rest of his life in the worst way.

"You're at a wedding. Aren't there any single girls there?"

Curtis paced in a circle. There was only one single girl who mattered to him. The one who'd just walked away from him.

"What's my pickup line? Hi, I'm Curtis, will you marry me?"

"I'm on it. I'll figure this out—somehow," Boone said. "Keep it together. Remember what's on the line. Curtis, this sucks. I know it. But we're counting on you—"

"Just tell me where to go, and I'll do what it takes." He jabbed at the phone until he cut the call, furious at himself—at Fate—at life for putting him in this position.

Hell, this was a mess. A complete and utter mess.

He just wished he understood why this was happening to him. He had a whole heart to give, but no one seemed to want to take it.

"Curtis!"

Hope slammed into him, a cloud of peach-colored chiffon that nearly knocked him to the earth. Curtis caught her reflexively and set her on her feet as Daisy danced around them, barking. "Hope—"

She dropped to her knees in the snow. Took Curtis's hand. Daisy got very still, standing like a hunting dog beside her, nose pointed at Curtis.

"Hope, what are you—?"

"Curtis Lloyd, will you marry me?"

SHE DIDN'T WANT to babysit adult toddlers. Hell, that described half of the clients who came to the physical therapist's office. Adult toddlers who got drunk and climbed behind the wheel. Adult toddlers who thought they could skateboard at sixty-three. Adult toddlers who got into fights at birthday parties they threw for their real toddlers.

She didn't want to keep cleaning up other people's messes. She wanted to get things done. Wanted to be a steward of the earth.

She didn't want to exchange one bureaucracy for another, either. When Scott had talked about how long it took to implement a new idea at Yellowstone, she'd known exactly what he meant. The same thing was true at the clinic where she worked. In that moment, something had clarified in her mind: she wanted to act. Not think, not talk, not plan.

To act.

Today.

And every day.

Even if that meant sometimes she made mistakes or had to change course now and then.

Scott was right; she could do that at Base Camp.

More importantly, she didn't want to give up on love—or wait for another ten years for it to show up.

She wanted Curtis.

She wanted to give him a chance. He was a man who cared for others. He'd shown that by the tender care he'd offered a sack of kittens found on the side of a road. He'd shown that by risking his life to get Raina to her wedding on time.

He'd shown that by opening his heart to her.

She wanted a man with an open heart.

Now. Today.

Not in ten years.

Curtis stared down at her, his face a mask of confusion.

"Well?" she asked. Byron had caught up with them. He was filming the scene.

She didn't care.

"Will you marry me? Please? I... I don't have a ring. I'm sorry—I didn't have time to plan—but will you spend the rest of your life with me—at Base Camp— together? Raina's going to stay in Bozeman so there'll probably be kittens and all kinds of trouble, but—"

"Hope—are you...? I don't understand—"

He wasn't answering the question. Why wasn't he answering the question?

Hope suddenly realized they were surrounded by onlookers, everyone in the crowd holding up phones and filming.

Curtis was standing perfectly still, watching her, too, the look on his face so blank it dawned on her he was going to say no.

He didn't want her after all.

Icy cold fingers of shame traced down her spine. She'd bared her heart—let the world know how she felt about him.

Once again, she'd misjudged—

"Yes." Curtis took her hand, tugged her to her feet and into his arms. "I will definitely marry you. And even if you didn't let me be the one to propose, I've got a ring. Now stand there so I can kneel down and do this right."

Hope gasped out a sound of relief, as her heart filled to the brim. He'd said—

Curtis pulled out a little velvet box and got to his knees. "All my life I've had trouble making big decisions. Making commitments when I knew the decision was going to change my life. I agonized for months before I popped the question to my high school sweetheart." He waved a hand. "Forget that. I agonized about joining the Navy, and making the call to come join Base Camp nearly killed me, but the second I laid eyes on you—the second, Hope—I knew I had to spend my life with you. You are everything I ever dreamed of in a woman. Being around you is heaven, and leaving you behind this morning—even for an hour or two—was my idea of hell. I'm your man. I hope you get that—" He cleared the emotion from his throat. "I hope you get how real this is to me. I'm your forever—if you'll have me."

"Of course I'll have you—I just proposed to you—" Hope squeaked when Curtis surged to his feet, wrapped her in his arms and kissed her, long and hard.

They were both short of breath when they came up for air again. Curtis held up the little velvet box. "You know, it's funny, when I bought this ring, Rose Johnson—the woman who sold it to me—told me whoever would wear it was going to lead me on a merry chase."

Raina, standing close by, sucked in a breath and clapped both hands over her mouth. She dropped them to her sides again and nearly bounced in her excitement. "Oh my god, oh my god, oh my god, I'd forgotten all about that." She turned to Hope. "Rose gets hunches about couples when they buy their ring. I thought she was talking about Michele."

"That's what I thought, too—except Michele never wore this ring," Curtis agreed. "I didn't know I'd be walking halfway across Montana to get the chance to woo you."

"Was that why you did it? To woo me?" Hope asked.

"Damn right that's why." Curtis kissed her again. "Worth every step, too. Hope, like I said, Michele never wore this ring, but if you want a new one, I'll get it for you. Just know that when I bought this—I was looking for you."

Hope held up her hand. "Put it on."

Curtis took out the ring and carefully slid it on her finger. He grinned. "It fits."

"It's perfect."

"Are you sure about this?" Curtis demanded, taking both her hands in his and searching her gaze. "Are you positive marrying me is the right choice for you? What about your life plan?"

"My planner!" Hope looked around, but Raina held it up as if she'd known Hope would need it.

"I already updated your itinerary for tonight and tomorrow." She turned to the right page and tilted it so Hope could see. Everything Hope had listed for Raina's wedding day was crossed out, and HOT SEX WITH CURTIS was written in the evening hours.

"I'm down for that." Curtis chuckled, reading over

her shoulder.

"Better check out tomorrow, too," Raina said.

Hope turned the page, and her heart swelled. There was only one to-do left on her list.

MARRY CURTIS.

"Ben's already changed our flight until late tomorrow night," Raina said.

"But—your honeymoon," Hope said.

"We'll still have ten days to lie around in the sun. This is more important. You're only going to get married once, and I'm going to be here when you do."

Hope threw her arms around Raina's neck. "You are the best friend ever."

"You have no idea."

"YOU'RE DOING IT, huh?" Anders said on the phone that evening. Curtis had reported to Boone there was no need to find a backup bride, and Boone had fallen all over himself to congratulate him.

"You really want to marry her?" he kept asking. "It's been killing me thinking that someone was actually going to have to marry a backup bride."

"I thought you were dead set on me doing that."

"I'm dead set on Base Camp surviving," Boone said. "That doesn't mean I want anyone to be unhappy."

"I really want to marry her," Curtis had assured him. "I've wanted it for… days," he ended lamely.

Boone laughed. "Sorry. That was funny, though. I'm glad you want to marry her. Glad it's working out."

"Don't put the cart before the horse," Curtis told him. "She hasn't arrived at the altar yet."

Boone paused. "Are you worried about that?"

He wanted to say no, but the truth was he couldn't shake the fear that this time wouldn't be any different than the others.

"She'll be there," Boone assured him.

"I sure hope so."

"How do you feel?" Anders asked him now. "Getting married is a pretty big step."

"I feel... good. I'll feel better when it's over," he admitted, petting Daisy, who lay on the rug beside him. "There's still time for Hope to run away."

"She proposed to you," Anders pointed out.

"Not sure how I feel about that."

"You said you told her you were going to marry her first."

"Yeah, I did. It all happened kind of backward, though."

"That's life, isn't it? I wish I was there, man. I'd like to see you finally get to say your vows."

Curtis shifted. He wished he was getting married in front of the people who mattered. Wished his parents would be able to be here, too.

He hadn't realized he'd said that out loud until Anders grunted. "Yeah. I can imagine. Give me a minute, okay?"

"What are you doing?"

"Making one quick phone call. Be back in a flash."

"THERE HAS TO be a drugstore near here," Hope said late that night, digging into Raina's little poof of a purse to find her cell phone. She'd left hers with Diana earlier and hadn't gone back to retrieve it, but Raina never went anywhere without a phone. "I need makeup, hairspray, deodorant—"

Raina tried to hand her another glass of champagne. "Enjoy the reception first. Time enough for all of that later."

"I'm sorry. I'm ruining your night," Hope said, looking up.

"Not at all. People are starting to leave anyway, and I don't think I can dance anymore. My ankle hurts."

"I just need one quick trip to a store, and then I'll make do for everything else," Hope lied. She needed a ton of things for her wedding, and she didn't know how she'd locate them all on a Sunday evening. Luckily, Raina's phone was already in a map app. She must have been looking for an address the last time she used it before they'd both lost reception.

Looking for…

"Base Camp?" Hope said. She looked up. Met Raina's guilty stare.

Raina grabbed for the phone, but Hope pulled it back. "This is where we ended up turning off the highway. Where we went off the road. You were looking for Base Camp? I thought it was just a coincidence." She'd known Raina had worked to throw her and Curtis together, but this took the cake.

"No," Raina said. "I looked to see where it was—

just to see if it was close. It's not like I drove us there on purpose."

She dropped her gaze, flicked it up again and looked away.

She was lying. She always did that when she was lying. Hope couldn't believe it.

"You *did* drive us there on purpose. In the middle of a snowstorm. When we had to get to your wedding."

"I thought we had plenty of time," Raina said. "I was curious. Sue me."

"What would you have done if we hadn't spun out into that ditch?"

"I would have driven right on past and gone straight back to the highway."

She dropped her gaze again.

"No, you wouldn't. Oh my god. It *was* a setup. You did it all on purpose."

"Not *all*." Raina got out of her seat, but Hope followed her.

"I already knew you threw Curtis and me together. You made sure he had to drive us to your wedding. I just didn't realize you went to Base Camp deliberately. What else did you make happen?"

"I didn't take that detour, and I didn't run us off the road. That was all Byron," Raina said defensively.

"How did you get those kittens in that snowbank?" Hope demanded.

"I didn't!"

She didn't drop her gaze. Okay, that was fate, Hope decided.

"Did you damage the gas tank?"

"No."

"What about your wedding dress? Did you knock that duffel bag off the sled so it got left behind?"

"Maybe," Raina said in a small voice.

"Unbelievable! And Curtis doesn't snore, by the way."

Raina grinned. "Nope. But you two had fun, didn't you?"

"You are sick."

"I'm your friend. I saw the way you lit up when you met him. If you hadn't, I wouldn't have done any of this. I had to try, though. I had to give you enough time to fall in love. It's not every day you come across someone like Curtis."

That was true, Hope thought.

"Are you mad?" Raina asked.

"What do you think?"

"Do I still get to be your maid of honor?"

"No, I'm going to ask Blake instead."

Raina gasped. "Fine, just for that, I'm not going to lend you my wedding dress."

"You'd do that?" Hope softened. It was hard to stay mad at Raina, even if there was no way in heck she'd fit into her wedding gown.

"Of course. I'd look silly wearing it to be your maid of honor."

"It won't fit, you know. I'll have to find something tomorrow morning, I guess."

Raina studied her. "Hope, are you sad you're not

having a real wedding?"

Was she sad?

She had to admit she was. Even if she shouldn't be. After all, she was getting to marry Curtis, and he was handsome and exciting and funny and wonderful... "A little," she admitted.

The phone in her hand buzzed. Hope glanced down. "Why is Curtis calling you?" She handed it to Raina, who read the message and started to smile.

"What is it?" Hope asked.

"The wedding's off."

"What?" Hope grabbed the phone from her hand. As she read the text, a smile tugged the corners of her mouth. "The governor of Montana called out the National Guard to clear the avalanche?"

"Guess marrying a Navy SEAL brings some perks. You can get married back at Base Camp instead of here, which means you'll get a real party!" Raina said.

"That sounds good," Hope admitted. "Let's go enjoy the rest of your reception. You're coming, right?" she added.

"To Base Camp for your wedding? Hell, yeah. I wouldn't miss it for the world!"

CHAPTER TWELVE

A S THE SNOW-COVERED landscape slipped past them the following morning, Curtis held Hope's hand. Ben was driving. Raina sat beside him. Curtis, Hope and Byron sat in back.

"I can't believe how long it took us to travel to Bozeman and how short a trip it is home," Hope said.

"The kittens are sick of baskets," Raina said, reaching in to pet them. Beside her, Ben watched her fondly. Byron was filming everything. They'd left Blake behind in Bozeman, but he'd promised to be there for the wedding later.

"Just need to take care of my Jaguar first," he'd said.

"Soon they'll all be free to roam around Base Camp. They won't ever have to travel again," Curtis told her.

"I thought you said I had to take them all with me."

"Not all. Kind of gotten attached to one or two," he said.

Hope gave his hand a squeeze, and he squeezed hers back. He couldn't wait to marry her and start their new life, but first there were several errands they needed to run.

When Ben pulled to a stop in front of Ellie's Bridals, Hope said, "This isn't Base Camp."

"Nope."

"What's going on?" Hope asked.

"If we're having a real wedding, you need a real wedding dress. And flowers. And whatever else you want." He opened the door and ushered her inside.

"But—"

"No buts, Hope." He turned her to face him. "This is fast. You just met me. But when I make my vows to you later today, I'm going to mean it. I want forever with you. Got it?"

When she tried to answer, no words came out.

"Curtis and I will take care of the flowers," Ben said. "You ladies get the dress. Meet back in half an hour?" he said to Raina.

"Sounds good. Come on." She pushed Hope toward the door. "We've got to get you to the altar on time, after all."

"YOU'RE SHAKING," RAINA said. "You won't faint, will you?"

"I don't think so." They stood in one of the large, beautifully appointed guest bedrooms at the manor, up the hill from Base Camp. The other women who lived there kept bustling in and out in their beautiful gowns.

"I love their dresses," Hope whispered to Raina.

"Good thing, seeing as how you're going to have to wear Jane Austen gowns, too."

"What?"

"Don't worry about it," Raina said. "You're getting married today. Concentrate."

Hope decided to simply roll with the punches and figure out Base Camp's dress code later.

Raina had recovered herself, and the two had taken a quick tour of the large, beautiful home with Samantha—the woman who was supposed to have married Curtis but had married Harris instead. Talking to her wasn't as awkward as it could have been, Hope reflected, mostly because Sam was so obviously overjoyed that Curtis had found the right woman.

It was moments before they'd be called to the wedding. Hope had been thrilled to find her parents ensconced in one of the other guest rooms when they arrived. Curtis's folks were here, too. Blake had arrived a short time ago, dapper in a nice suit. "Maybe I'll meet someone at the reception," he'd told her. Boone and the others had been very busy making a lot of last-minute arrangements. Luckily the day had dawned clear, and the avalanche had been cleared away in plenty of time.

"How did you know everything I wanted?" Hope asked Riley, one of the women who'd been at Base Camp since the start, who'd just come in to show her the bouquet she'd be carrying.

"Your notes. They were so thorough it was easy." She waved a sheaf of papers, and Hope realized they were copies of the wedding section of her planner.

"Where did you get those?"

Raina looked sheepish. "I slipped Avery your planner the morning we set out for Base Camp. She photographed the section on wedding plans, just in case. She thought you were a good match for Curtis, too."

"You are completely bonkers. You know that, right?"

"But I'm also your best friend, so you'll forgive me. You look stunning, by the way," Raina said, pulling back from where she'd been fussing with Hope's makeup. "Oh, Hope—that dress. It's amazing."

Hope knew what she meant. It was as if Ellie, the owner of Ellie's Bridals, had read her mind. She and her niece had both waited on Hope, with several dresses picked out before she even walked in the door. Hope had despaired of finding the perfect thing, always imagining it would take days or weeks of shopping to find something that would make her feel like she wanted to feel when she said her vows.

Instead, she'd turned down two dresses, slipped on a third and known she'd found the one for her. Its beautiful, fitted bodice hugged her curves, and its trailing skirts made her look like royalty. Ellie had handed her a tiara, and Hope had laughed, but when Raina fitted it into place, Hope had found herself blinking back tears.

She hadn't felt this beautiful since the prom night she hadn't attended—since before the first time she'd decided she had to control everything in her life if she wanted to stay safe.

"Curtis will be blown away," Raina said, giving her cheeks one last dusting with the blush brush.

"Who's ready for photographs?" her mother said, bustling through the door. "Hope, honey? All set? I need a picture of you at the mirror, just like that."

Hope nodded, afraid to speak, her heart so full she found she could let go of the past. She sent a message of forgiveness into the universe to the teenager who'd broken her heart. Liam had just been a boy who'd followed an impulse. And Brynn had just been a girl hurting so badly she'd turned to alcohol to dull the pain. They'd both died far too soon, and everyone who'd survived them had suffered long enough, including her.

It was time to let go of that old pain. Time to recognize all the good that had happened since then. Today she would stay in the present. With the people who loved her.

With Curtis, the man willing to take a chance on her for the rest of his life.

You never knew what would happen next. All you could do was reach out for a connection, hold on when you found one and hope for the best.

"I'm ready," she said. She stood straight and tall as her mother got all the photographs she wanted.

Then she took her father's arm and walked to the head of the aisle.

"YOU KNOW WHAT time it is!" Boone announced as he strode into the guest room where Curtis was finishing getting into his Revolutionary War uniform.

When he'd told Hope about the tradition, she'd simply smiled. "Sounds good to me," she'd said. Curtis had struggled not to pull her close and kiss her for that. She was going to fit right in here.

Boone stretched out his arm. In his fist, he clutched four straws. "Let's see who's up next! Anders, Walker, Angus, Greg, come on down."

All the men gathered around, the married men laughing and teasing the holdouts.

"It's got to be Walker's turn," Clay said.

"I bet it's Greg. It's the quiet ones who surprise you," Kai put in.

"All right, Walker, you pick first. You always hang back, and you always get away with waiting another month."

The big man shrugged, considered the straws in Boone's fist and picked. Held up a long one. "Not me."

Groans came from all around.

"Greg, you're up," Boone said.

Greg drew, too, and got another of the long ones.

Clay drummed a beat on his thighs. "It's down to Anders and Angus."

"Hell, I'll go next." Angus grabbed a straw testily and breathed out a gusty sigh when it, too, was long. "Thank you!" he called up to the ceiling.

"Anders! Good luck, man. I've got a passel of back-up brides—" Boone began.

"Don't even start!" Anders said. "Not until tomorrow, anyway." He held the short straw Boone passed to him. Met Curtis's gaze. "Guess I'm next."

"Guess you are."

"Time to get you hitched." Boone clapped Curtis on

the back. "Let's get out there. Make us proud."

"Will do, Chief." Curtis found himself grinning as he headed for the door with the others.

Still, he held his breath when he stood at the make-shift altar someone had set up at the end of the aisle between the folding chairs in the manor's great room. Guests filled the seats, many of them community members from Chance Creek, and all of them turned as the bridal march swelled and filled the air.

With a short bark, Daisy broke free from where Greg had been sitting with her in one of the rows of seats. She loped up to Curtis's side and sat down.

"Good dog." Daisy wouldn't leave him alone at the altar. Curtis braced himself. What if Hope didn't come? What if she'd changed her mind?

He swallowed past a sudden lump in his throat as the moment stretched out. His palms were damp, his heart picking up its pace. If Hope changed her mind, he couldn't stand it. Not only would Base Camp run out of time—he'd run out of Hope. She was the one for him. The only one he wanted to spend his life with.

"Wow," Anders said softly by his side.

Curtis looked up. Raina had started down the aisle in a pale blue bridesmaid gown. Hope entered the room after her, and as he met her gaze across the rows of seats, his heart swelled to fill his chest. For the first time in months, Curtis knew he wasn't going to let down his friends. Wasn't going to lose Base Camp.

Wasn't going to be left at the altar ever again. He took a deep breath, promised himself he'd spend the rest of his life making Hope happy—

And watched the most beautiful woman in the world walk down the aisle to take her place by his side.

"DEARLY BELOVED," REVEREND Halpern began. Curtis found Hope's hand. Her fingers curved around his, and she clung to him, needing his strength in this moment when she was about to step into her future—

Without a single plan.

She didn't know all the people at Base Camp.

She didn't know what she'd do here after she married.

She didn't know what role she could play, or where she'd live, or who she'd be friends with, or—

Anything.

All she knew was that she'd come to love the man standing beside her with a fierce love that burned bright inside her. A love she somehow knew would never dim, no matter what they faced together.

That was all the plan she needed—to hold Curtis's hand. To stay with him. To trust him—

And to trust the future to unfold however it wanted to, in its own sweet time.

That was enough.

"Do you, Hope Martin, take this man, Curtis Lloyd, to be your lawfully wedded husband, to have and to hold, for better or worse, in sickness and in health, to death do you part?"

"I do," Hope said. She could barely contain the emotion expanding her chest.

"Do you, Curtis Lloyd, take this woman, Hope Martin, to be your lawfully wedded wife, to have and to hold, for better or worse, in sickness and in health, to death do you part?"

"I do."

She read the truth of it in his eyes.

The rest of their vows passed in a blur. All Hope could do was watch the man who was becoming her husband, cling to his hands, and know that this was right.

"You may now kiss the bride."

Hope waited for Curtis to draw her close.

"I love you," he said huskily when she tilted her chin up to meet him.

"I love y—" Her words were buried in his kiss, a kiss that told her everything she needed to know about her future with Curtis. That he loved her. Cherished her. Would do anything for her.

That she was home.

Right where she was meant to be.

"SO, YOU SAW this place once before," Curtis said many hours later when he led Hope into the tiny house he'd helped to build. Back then, it hadn't had any special meaning for her, and he wondered what she thought now that she knew it would be her home. There were still some finishing touches left to be made. If only Hope could see the final product as he pictured it in his mind, she'd know it would be—

"It's beautiful," she told him, kissing him again. "I

love it."

"It's not too small for you?"

"I was planning to be a park ranger. My needs as far as housing are concerned are modest."

"You never told me why you changed your mind about becoming a ranger."

"It was talking to Scott. He pointed out I'd get much more hands-on experience here than working in a national park."

"So that's why you married me!" He pulled her close and nuzzled her neck until Hope shrieked, squirming in his arms.

"Partly," she told him. "But mostly because you're awesome in bed."

"Oh, yeah?"

"Yeah."

"We could try that again. Since it's why you married me."

"I was hoping you'd say that." She pulled him to the ladder that led to the loft bed. Climbing up in her trailing skirts was a bit of a challenge, but Curtis followed, lifting them for her, fighting up the ladder lost in the voluminous fabric.

By the time they both made it into the loft, they were laughing, and Curtis wondered if it would always be like this.

He hoped so.

He joined her on his back on the mattress, the wood paneled ceiling several feet above them making a cozy space. Hope twined her hand in his, and he turned on his side and gathered her into his arms. She felt right there, and he felt strong and proud to hold her. He wanted to be all he could as her husband. A helper. A protector. A confidant and friend.

When Hope moved close, pressing herself along the length of him, his hunger for his wife grew, and his hands found the back of her dress. He groaned at the line of tiny buttons.

"What is this?"

"A test of your determination," she told him and kissed the underside of his chin.

"Let me see those." He rolled her over onto her stomach and got to work undoing them one at a time, stifling the urge to rip the dress off her. He had a feeling Hope wouldn't like that—although maybe they could try it later, with a rag from a thrift store.

The image revving him up even more, he worked his way methodically down the row of buttons, turned her over again and peeled off the gown. She took it from him and carefully laid it on the floor beside their bed. She wore a pretty satin pushup bra and a tiny thong.

Curtis hooked his thumbs through it.

"Don't you dare!" Hope warned him and wiggled out of it.

"Don't I get to rip anything off you?" he grumbled.

"Another night. Tonight is for unwrapping."

"I'll unwrap these next." He made short work of the fastening of her bra and let free her beautiful breasts. "Better make sure they didn't get damaged in transit."

He nuzzled first one, then the other, cupped their lushness in his palms and groaned. "You are spectacular."

"You're not so bad yourself. Let's see what you look like out of uniform."

Curtis was only too happy to comply, and when they were naked together, he let out a satisfied sigh. "My wife," he said, settling between her thighs and boxing her in with his arms. "Finally. What took you so long?"

"If I'd known you were waiting for me, I would have put you in my planner sooner."

"We're going to have to rewrite that thing," he said, pushing into her slowly. "I've got some ideas what to schedule in it."

"Sex," Hope said, arching her back and closing her eyes as he slid inside her. "For the next month, I say all we plan is sex."

"Sounds good to me."

"Then some food and some more sex."

Curtis laughed and kissed her. "I'm not sure I can go for a month without food."

"I don't think I can go for a minute without you inside me." She moaned as he began to move, a rhythmic stroking that soon had him struggling to hold back.

"I know what you mean."

"It's never been like this for me. Not this good."

"Me, neither," Curtis admitted. Something was right about Hope. They fit together in a way that made it even more special.

"I love all of you."

Curtis murmured against her skin, lost in the feel of her, saying what he needed to say with his body, not his words. She was soft and smooth, pliant in his hands, molding against him, accepting him, taking him in with a delicious sense of coming home.

As Curtis sped up he knew Hope was feeling the same way. Her small sounds urged him on; her touches enflamed his desire to get closer to her.

Hope was everything he'd ever wanted. She was his wife.

His world.

When he bucked against her, she followed with a cry that shredded any defense he had left, and Curtis came with such force he thought the waves of ecstasy that traveled through him wouldn't stop. Hope called out again and again, shuddering with the strength of her release.

When it was over, she clung to him. "More," she said. "More and more and more."

"You got it." Curtis rolled her over, perched her on top of him—

And started all over again.

"Yes!"

To find out more about Harris, Samantha, Boone, Riley, Clay, Jericho, Walker and the other inhabitants of Westfield, look for *A SEAL's Devotion*, Volume 7 in the *SEALs of Chance Creek* series.

Be the first to know about Cora Seton's new releases! Sign up for her newsletter here!

www.coraseton.com/sign-up-for-my-newsletter

Other books in the SEALs of Chance Creek Series:

A SEAL's Oath

A SEAL's Vow

A SEAL's Pledge

A SEAL's Consent

A SEAL's Purpose

A SEAL's Devotion

A SEAL's Desire

A SEAL's Struggle

A SEAL's Triumph

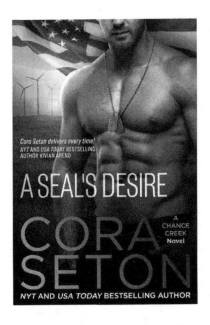

Read on for an excerpt of
A SEAL's Desire.

"**M**AYBE YOUR WIFE will show up like mine did," Curtis Lloyd said as he pushed open the door to the bunkhouse and led the way inside. He pulled off his woolen cap and unzipped the heavy jacket he wore.

Anders Olsen doubted it. Not many women crashed their cars in the ditch at the end of the lane that led to Base Camp, the sustainable community they were helping to build. It was mid-December, and fierce winds had blown the heavy snowfall they'd received in the past week into deep drifts. The road between here and Chance Creek had become became impassible once or twice.

Which made it hard to go searching for a wife.

"You've got thirty-five days."

"I know." Anders had made a calendar on one page in the small notebook where he jotted ideas and pertinent facts. It was in his pocket right now. Every night when he crossed off another square, his concern grew. He'd known he'd need to find a wife when he joined Base Camp—it was one of the requirements of participation.

Somehow he'd thought it would be easier than this.

Curtis didn't have to worry about the marriage requirement anymore. He'd married Hope Martin, a pretty brunette, just days ago, after a whirlwind courtship during Curtis's struggle to deliver Hope and her friend, Raina, to Bozeman in time for Raina's wedding. A blizzard had made that journey quite an adventure. He couldn't help envying his friend, though. The adventure was over and now he had a wife.

Anders had no idea where he would find one for himself. So far he'd struck out at the local bars and he'd never made new acquaintances easily. He wasn't as outgoing as Curtis was, and—

He nearly bumped into Curtis when the tall, burly, dark haired man stopped abruptly.

"What the hell is Fulsom doing here—again?"

Anders leaned sideways to get a look into the large

room. Curtis was right; Martin Fulsom, the billionaire funding this whole operation was deep in conversation with Renata Ludlow, who produced *Base Camp*, the television show that was documenting their progress in building their community. Fulsom was a fit, energetic, silver haired man in his late sixties, whose outsized personality filled any room he entered. Renata was a trim woman in her thirties, her raven-black hair tucked into a bun, her professional clothing finally modified from her usual pencil skirts and aggressive white blouses to slacks and sweaters, because of the cold weather. She was even wearing winter boots instead of the stiletto heels she had favored well into November.

Beside them stood a man Anders didn't recognize, but immediately disliked. A rangy, sandy-haired, smug faced man who was watching Renata in a way that spelled trouble.

"Who's he?" Anders asked Curtis.

"I don't know."

Greg Devon, another member of Base Camp, a serious man with a shock of black hair, edged closer. "His name is Clem," he said in an undertone. "Fulsom's siccing him on Renata."

"What do you mean?" Anders asked.

There wasn't time for Greg to answer before Boone Rudman, the de facto leader of their community, called out, "Everyone sit down. Mr. Fulsom's got something to say."

Anders took a seat on one of the folding chairs that had been strewn around the room. Meetings were always like this—a scrape of chairs and muted conversations dying down to silence as Boone waited for their attention.

"Fulsom?" Boone gave up the room and the older man stepped forward.

As always, the billionaire struck a pose before he began. Anders was getting tired of his lectures. Fulsom seemed to require attention at all times. If things got too quiet in California he came looking for trouble here.

"I am sick of your bullshit!" Fulsom boomed suddenly.

Anders looked around at the other men and women in the room. All of them were long past responding to the billionaire's histrionics, except maybe Hope, who had only been at Base Camp for a handful of days. This was the way Fulsom began most of his speeches. There was always a complaint, followed by a demand. An outrageous demand.

"I told you I wanted action," Fulsom went on. "Adventure. Controversy. SEX! And what happens?" He turned on Renata dramatically. "You and nearly the entire film crew abandon your posts because of a little snow, and you—" He pointed at Curtis, "try to leave the one remaining crew member home when you embark on the adventure of the century. Which means Byron here," he pointed to a young cameraman, "had to chase after you and managed to total a very expensive 4x4 in the process. Now this week's episode is entirely filmed on outdated, insufficient camera equipment, and it very nearly wasn't filmed at all. What is this? Amateur hour?"

Anders settled in. This could take a while.

He was right. Fulsom droned on in a similar vein while Renata glared at Byron, and Byron did his best to fade into the woodwork. All the while Clem's smug smile grew wider.

When Fulsom finally calmed down, he gestured the newcomer forward. "This is Clem Saunders. He's come to lend a hand to this production. Clem knows all about injecting much-needed life into a sorry excuse for a television show. This isn't the first production he's had to bail out. He's got ideas, and he's got the balls to see them through. And he knows how to keep a bunch of puissant, know-nothing, self-absorbed actors in line!"

Actors? Anders straightened. So did the other men in the room.

None of them were actors.

They'd all fought for their country as Navy SEALs. Survived situations Fulsom could only dream of—

"Yeah, now I've got your attention," Fulsom said. "You're supposed to be men of action, so get out there and do something worth filming, for God's sake. And you!"

Anders recoiled when Fulsom pointed at him, caught himself and straightened again. "It's your turn to marry, so do it—spectacularly. Got it?"

"Got it." Anders bit back a curse. How the hell did you spectacularly marry a woman? More to the point: how did you find a woman to marry, period?

"Good. Clem, got a few words you want to say?"

Fulsom stepped back and waved the man forward.

"You heard Fulsom." Clem stood before them with his legs spread, his hands behind his back. Did he think he could fool them into thinking he was their superior officer?

This guy took the cake.

"We're going to shake things up around here. Starting tomorrow morning. Expect the unexpected from here on in. We're going to base everything we do on ratings. We'll communicate with our audience. Listen to what they have to say. Give them what they want. That's all. Dismissed."

Everyone exchanged puzzled glances before standing up and putting away their chairs.

"Fuck," Curtis said under his breath. "They could cut us a little slack once in a while." He put an arm around Hope and kissed the top of her head. "Bet you're glad you joined Base Camp."

"I'm glad," she said with a grin.

"Renata looks pissed," Greg murmured. "If I was Clem, I'd sleep with one eye open tonight."

"Do you think Clem's here to replace her?" Renata was a ball-buster, but Anders was used to her, at least. They had enough problems here at Base Camp without infighting among the crew.

"Maybe." Curtis nodded toward the door. "You and me had better do one last plow of the lane. It's snowing again."

"Sure thing." He stood up and got his outer gear back on while Curtis gave Hope another kiss.

"...back at the house in a minute," Anders heard him say as Curtis turned toward the door. Still newlyweds, those two seemed joined at the hip.

Would he feel like that about the woman he married?

"Boone pestering you about backup brides yet?" Curtis asked as he opened the door.

"We talked about them." Outside, the cold air made plumes of their breath. Snow was falling softly, a slow accumulation rather than the crazy amount they'd gotten just days ago. They'd made a habit of keeping the lane as clear as possible, though, in case of an emergency. The state plows had a way of blocking the end of the lane as they passed. That took the most time to clear.

"I told Boone I'd set up my own ad," he continued. "I don't need him finding me a woman. I can do it myself." What he didn't way was that he'd already had profiles on some of the more popular dating apps, but he'd cancelled them all after the show got popular. He'd been overwhelmed by the kind of response he'd received, women far more interested in his notoriety, and getting on television, than on settling down in a real way.

He wanted a real connection, but how did you find that on a ranch in Montana, when you were a reality television star?

If only fate would deliver him a wife—like it had delivered one for Curtis. A wife he could marry in a spectacular way, to appease Fulsom.

Plowing the lane was easy, but as he'd predicted, the

drift at the end of it was harder going. In the end, they had to park the truck, get out and shovel it by hand as Fulsom, Renata and the rest of the crew members not spending the night here waited impatiently in their trucks.

The stillness of the night and the hard work gave him a reprieve from his racing thoughts. Out here, the world was large, and he was only a bit actor, one of billions of people getting through another day. When they'd cleared half of the pile, they stepped aside to let the waiting trucks past. Once they were gone, real quiet descended.

"That's that," Curtis said fifteen minutes later, throwing one more shovelful of snow onto the banks. "Let's call it a night. God knows we'll be back out here in the morning, doing it all over again."

"Sure thing."

Anders hesitated, looking down the road in both directions. Not a car in sight. They were alone out here, and he savored the peace. In a minute he'd be back in the bunkhouse, settling down for the night on the floor with the other single members of Base Camp. There was always someone around back there. Always talk and jokes. Just for a moment it was nice to be—

Anders squinted, peering through the dark. "What's that?" He pointed to a shape making its way slowly toward them.

"I don't see anything." Curtis moved to his side.

"There." The shape had stopped. Wavered. Was coming at them again. "Is that—?"

Curtis swore and began to run. A second later, Anders sprinted past him. He covered the hundred and fifty yards in record time, lunged forward—

Just in time to catch the woman who fainted into his arms.

"...IN SHOCK. WE'VE got to get her warm."

"...no shoes, no jacket—how'd she make it this far?"

"...come on, come on, wake up..."

Evelyn Wright tried to focus on the voices, but they slipped away and came back, slipped away and came back again with no rhyme or reason, evading her grasp.

She was warm, at least.

Warm after so much cold.

She knew she should be concerned. Male voices.

Men.

Like the ones who'd—

She didn't want to think about that.

"... losing her..."

"...Miss? Can you say something? Do you know where you are?"

Evelyn struggled to open her eyes. To make sense of things. Where was she?

A hospital?

No. Not with that wooden ceiling. The rough floor. Her fingers slid over wide planks, quarter-inch gaps between their up-curled edges.

Where was she?

And why was Anders Olsen bending over her?

Evelyn blinked. Shut her eyes and opened them again. She was dreaming. That was it. She'd climbed right into a television show. Into the show with all the Navy SEALs.

Smart.

They'd protect her from—

"…coming around again."

"… accident in town. A bad one. Ambulances all taken. Maybe we should drive her—"

"Look. She's awake!"

Evelyn opened her eyes. Tried to sit up. Groaned when the room spun and allowed soft hands to lay her back down again.

"What's… going on?" she managed to murmur.

"Miss, we found you walking up the road. You had no jacket, no gloves or hat. Your boots are wrecked. It looks like you were walking a long time. Do you know what happened?" a man asked. Curtis. Curtis Lloyd. From the television show.

Was she still sleeping?

"Start with something simpler," another man said. Anders Olsen. "Miss, can you tell us your name?"

"Evelyn. Eve," she managed. "Eve—" She shut her mouth, self-preservation instincts suddenly snapping into place, as images crowded her mind. The men. The metal pipe. The truck—

No one could know who she was. Or where she was. She had to get out of—

"Woah, woah!" Anders held her shoulders and gently lowered her down again. "It's all right. Whatever happened out there, you're safe here. You got that? You're safe."

She read true concern in his startlingly blue eyes. A fierce protectiveness in the lines of his muscular body. He was a Navy SEAL, after all, she told herself. They all were. And from what she'd seen of the show, they were good men who wanted to do right in the world.

She could be hallucinating, though.

She could be still out there. Still walking. Trying to get away—

"Eve," Anders said. "We're going to transport you to the hospital—"

"No!" This time she surged to a sitting position, braced her hands on the floor and waited for the room to stop spinning. "No, I can't go to the hospital."

Anders searched her face with his gaze. "Who did this to you?"

It took a moment to realize what he meant, until an image slid back into her brain. A man coming after her, a length of metal pipe in his hand. Another behind him.

"I don't know," she said truthfully. "Never saw them before." Could she trust these people? Or should she stay quiet until she could get away?

"We should call the sheriff," a woman said.

Eve turned. Avery Lightfoot. One of the last of the original women on the show who was still single. Where was Walker, the man she so obviously loved?

There. In the corner of the room, sitting on the edge of a large wooden desk.

Boone's desk.

Eve bit back a wild laugh. If she was dreaming, her brain had conjured an incredibly accurate vision. Everything was just like the TV show.

Then Avery's words penetrated her brain. Eve spoke up.

"No! No sheriff! You can't call the sheriff!" She had to leave here, dream or no dream. She struggled up again. Anders caught her and urged her to stay seated.

"We won't call anyone," he said. "Not until you decide you want us to. Take a deep breath. One thing at a time. Can you tell us what happened?"

What happened?

What happened was this was supposed to be a routine trip. A visit to some clients. A courtesy. A way of showing that Altavista Imaging cared for the people who used its satellite imaging technology. A chance to find out if there were concerns. Things the company could do better. Eve had made these trips before, although never alone. Usually as a secondary. She was head of quality control and spent most of her time supervising operations. She enjoyed these little jaunts away from company headquarters in Virginia.

Used to enjoy them.

If she made it back to Virginia, she'd never leave again.

"I saw—" Was it safe to even say it out loud? "I saw someone... do something."

Anders nodded. "How many men?"

Eve flashed back to the gas station, even as she wondered how he knew to ask the question.

Military training, she realized. He'd have been in plenty of difficult situations. Must be used to analyzing them and gathering facts.

In her mind she saw the three men who'd climbed out of a blue truck to confront a fourth as he'd exited the gas station. She saw him knocked to the ground. The men's flailing legs. The dull thuds of their boots against the man's flesh. Their animal grunts as they kept at their deadly game.

The one who'd turned her way.

"Three," she managed to say.

"What happened?" Anders pressed.

"They came after me."

She couldn't remember them speaking a word. It was as if they'd communicated with each other telepathically. They'd moved as one, leaving the man on the ground, chasing her.

Catching her.

The pipe coming down.

"I passed out. I woke up in the back of their truck. They were driving fast."

"On the highway?"

She shrugged. "I guess."

"How'd you get away?" Curtis asked.

"Jumped."

Someone swore.

"I ran."

"They didn't see you?"

She shrugged again. "There was an off ramp. I took it. Stayed in the woods as long as I could, followed the road. Got back onto it when I couldn't make it through the brush anymore."

"Where's your coat. Your gloves?" Anders asked.

"I… took them off in my car before I stopped at the station. Had the heat on high. Just ran in to get a soda." She hadn't bothered to suit up for the cold weather again.

"Where's your purse?" That was Avery. A woman would think of that.

Her purse.

Horror bloomed in Eve's chest. She looked up, met Anders' gaze. Saw her own understanding reflected there.

"They have it."

End of Excerpt

The Cowboys of Chance Creek Series:

The Cowboy Inherits a Bride (Volume 0)
The Cowboy's E-Mail Order Bride (Volume 1)
The Cowboy Wins a Bride (Volume 2)
The Cowboy Imports a Bride (Volume 3)
The Cowgirl Ropes a Billionaire (Volume 4)
The Sheriff Catches a Bride (Volume 5)
The Cowboy Lassos a Bride (Volume 6)
The Cowboy Rescues a Bride (Volume 7)
The Cowboy Earns a Bride (Volume 8)
The Cowboy's Christmas Bride (Volume 9)

The Heroes of Chance Creek Series:

The Navy SEAL's E-Mail Order Bride (Volume 1)

The Soldier's E-Mail Order Bride (Volume 2)
The Marine's E-Mail Order Bride (Volume 3)
The Navy SEAL's Christmas Bride (Volume 4)
The Airman's E-Mail Order Bride (Volume 5)

The SEALs of Chance Creek Series:

A SEAL's Oath
A SEAL's Vow
A SEAL's Pledge
A SEAL's Consent
A SEAL's Purpose
A SEAL's Resolve
A SEAL's Devotion
A SEAL's Desire
A SEAL's Struggle
A SEAL's Triumph

The Brides of Chance Creek Series:

Issued to the Bride One Navy SEAL
Issued to the Bride One Airman
Issued to the Bride One Sniper
Issued to the Bride One Marine
Issued to the Bride One Soldier

The Turners v. Coopers Series:

The Cowboy's Secret Bride (Volume 1)
The Cowboy's Outlaw Bride (Volume 2)
The Cowboy's Hidden Bride (Volume 3)
The Cowboy's Stolen Bride (Volume 4)
The Cowboy's Forbidden Bride (Volume 5)

About the Author

With over one million books sold, NYT and USA Today bestselling author Cora Seton has created a world readers love in Chance Creek, Montana. She has twenty-eight novels and novellas currently set in her fictional town, with many more in the works. Like her characters, Cora loves cowboys, military heroes, country life, gardening, bike-riding, binge-watching Jane Austen movies, keeping up with the latest technology and indulging in old-fashioned pursuits. Visit **www. coraseton.com** to read about new releases, contests and other cool events!

Blog:

www.coraseton.com

Facebook:

facebook.com/coraseton

Twitter:

twitter.com/coraseton

Newsletter:

www.coraseton.com/sign-up-for-my-newsletter

90193057R00178

Made in the USA
San Bernardino, CA
07 October 2018